The kidnapper ⟨...⟩ swinging his coach left towards the shore.

I tugged on the reins. As my horse banked sharply, the wheels of the cab gripped and we set off after the hearse. Seconds later we thundered up a stone slipway. But if racing across the ice was hair-raising, it was nothing to the labyrinth of alleyways I was now confronted with.

Still I pushed my horse on, desperately calling out warnings to everyone in my path. The area I was now entering was different from anywhere I'd seen in the city so far. It was darker and more medieval-looking, full of tortuous back alleys, crumbling archways and rickety wooden bridges.

At a fork in the lane up ahead, the Undertaker's hearse veered unexpectedly to the left, plunging through a gulley of frozen mud. A street vendor carrying a box of salted sardines was forced to dive out of the way. His fish went skidding across the ice into the hungry chops of a stray dog.

Just as the bewildered man picked himself up, I came hurtling towards him.

'Out of the way!' I screamed.

Also by Cameron McAllister:

The Tin Snail

THE DEMON UNDERTAKER

CAMERON McALLISTER

CORGI BOOKS

CORGI BOOKS

UK | USA | Canada | Ireland | Australia
India | New Zealand | South Africa

Corgi Books is part of the Penguin Random House group of companies
whose addresses can be found at global.penguinrandomhouse.com.

www.penguin.co.uk
www.puffin.co.uk
www.ladybird.co.uk

First published 2016

001

Text copyright © Cameron McAllister, 2016
Cover artwork copyright © Jeff Nentrup, 2016

The moral right of the author has been asserted

Set in 12/16.5pt Adobe Garamond by Falcon Oast Graphic Art Ltd.
Printed in Great Britain by Clays Ltd, St Ives plc

A CIP catalogue record for this book is available from the British Library

ISBN: 978–0–552–57404–4

All correspondence to:
Corgi Books
Penguin Random House Children's
80 Strand, London WC2R 0RL

For Katie and the boys,
and for my parents, Bruce and Lola

Prologue

In the fall of 1749, a few minutes after three o'clock on a humid Saturday afternoon, my father's heart abruptly stopped beating.

The ball that burst from Clay Snipeman's flintlock didn't kill him – not directly, anyhow. Instead it whistled straight past his shoulder and punched a hole clean through the window of Mr Driscoll's mercantile store behind. But as the gunman fled from the store, Papa's knees gave way and he crumpled to the floor like a sack of wheat . . .

That afternoon had started out much like any other. The sky had been indigo with unshed rain, making the air feel heavy and muggy as my father and I took our horse and trap into town. Once little more than a swamp, Williamsburg was by then a prospering, bustling place in the British colony of Virginia.

'May I call by Silas's before we head back, Papa?' I asked as our gig turned into the high street. Silas was a friend I'd met at church whose family owned the local gunsmith's. His father would let us try out the muskets in his store for size, pretending to be local militia.

'Don't be long, mind,' my father grunted. 'We don't want to get caught in the downpour coming back.' It was pretty much the last thing he said to me as we pulled up outside the mercantile store.

We hadn't always lived in Virginia. I – Thomas – had been born in England, in a rural hamlet called Isleworth, just west of London. My mother's family mostly came from Ireland, but Papa had a distant cousin they used to refer to as 'Uncle' who had moved back to London from somewhere abroad. Apparently his name was Henry and he had become quite a distinguished playwright. More than that I couldn't tell you because shortly after my second birthday we emigrated to Virginia.

By trade, Papa was a blacksmith, but I liked to think of him as an inventor. He was always hammering away into the night creating new contraptions of some sort or other. Recently he'd been working on a machine that he was convinced would revolutionize the way wheat was threshed. Until then it took an age to separate the grain from the stalks. But Papa's invention was fearsomely clever: it would utilize a steam piston to do the work of twenty men in a fraction of the time. *If* it worked.

Trouble was, it didn't . . . well, not yet, anyhow. The

answer lay in a small zinc pipe, my father insisted. He had ordered it in specially from Mr Driscoll's store, and we were heading there to pick it up.

After the misfortune with my hand a few years earlier, Mr Driscoll had taken pity on me and liked to slip me candies when his wife wasn't looking. Truth be told, she was a shrew of a woman, with a pinched face and a beaky nose. (They say you get the face you deserve, but even she didn't deserve that one.) But even now, just after my fourteenth birthday, Mr Driscoll would still throw me something from the jar on the counter when she wasn't looking. I think it gave him a thrill – it was his one secret act of subversion.

It also helped that Papa was well respected in the area. Though a man of few words – some people even called him *dour* – he was never mean and never once raised his hand, or even his voice, to me or my mother.

But what had really made my father's reputation was my left hand. I didn't really have one . . . well, not in the ordinary sense. Instead I had what can only be described as an iron fist.

A few years earlier I had mangled my real one in an accident. I say 'accident' – my father had warned me often enough not to play in his workshop, especially when he was working on one of his inventions. But as usual I'd paid no heed: my curiosity had got the better of me and I'd tried to fashion my own toy sword when my father was out of town shoeing horses.

Papa had forbidden me to go near the huge metal press he used to flatten molten steel. Sure enough, as I slid the blade of my sword underneath it, my cuff got caught in the crank wheel. Panicking, I struggled to tug it free, inadvertently knocking the safety catch. The vast metal plate crunched down and . . . Well, you can imagine the rest.

For weeks after, Papa worked into the night fashioning a sort of crude metal glove that slipped over what remained of my left hand. Rather than forge a metal hook, much favoured by smugglers and pirates of the time, he created something more like the gauntlet of a suit of armour. Inside, I still had the use of a few stumps – all that I had left of my crushed fingers. Using these, I was able to operate an ingenious system of wires that enabled me to clench and unclench two of my iron fingers. It was crude at best, but it allowed me to clasp a cup or a hammer; which, since I was unlucky enough to be left-handed, proved a godsend.

It was a very basic affair, but it was soon so much a part of me I couldn't imagine ever living without it.

Meanwhile, on this particular afternoon Clay Snipeman had been drinking his wages in a local saloon bar across the way from the mercantile store. The owner of the bar testified that Snipeman's mood had turned even uglier than usual after he'd come home to find that his wife had upped and left him for a travelling salesman from Charleston.

A little after three o'clock – a matter of minutes after my father and I entered the store – Snipeman suddenly appeared in the doorway, swaying and unshaven.

I knew something was wrong the moment I saw his hand: his fingers were twitching nervously near the butt of a pistol tucked inside his overcoat.

Weird how you recall tiny details: to this day I remember how a piece of the cherry wood that formed the butt had broken away. Cherry was unusual in those parts – perhaps he'd brought the pistol with him when he emigrated, or won it in a bet.

Anyway, as I watched him toying with the gun, Snipeman's fingers suddenly clenched around the handle. The next thing I knew he was waving it at a terrified Mrs Driscoll, demanding cash from her till.

I don't know what made me take that fateful step towards him – no doubt the same rashness my father often warned me against. He was always telling me to think before I opened my mouth, a skill I had yet to master. All I know is that, before I fully realized what I was doing, my foot had pressed on an uneven floorboard. The wood creaked, and suddenly Snipeman's pistol swung round so that I was staring straight down the barrel.

It must have been instinct or nerves that made his finger jerk on the trigger, because when the explosion came, Snipeman looked as shocked as anyone. Either way, within a matter of seconds my father lay in a heap beside me.

Wide-eyed with panic, Snipeman staggered backwards and fled from the store. As the bell on the back of the door gave a cheery little trill, Mrs Driscoll whimpered and fell to the floor in a dead faint.

For a moment I stood rooted to the spot, too stunned to move. My ears were ringing from the blast of the ball that had whistled past my ear, tattooing my cheeks with tiny scorch marks.

Finally, as Mr Driscoll rushed forward to tend to my father, I came to my senses and began frantically searching through Papa's waistcoat for any sign of an entry wound.

When I couldn't find one, I felt a little surge of hope that maybe he'd fainted like Mr Driscoll's wife. '*Papa, Papa*,' I said, gently shaking him.

I kept trying to rouse him, stifling the panic that was rising in my chest, until Mr Driscoll gently laid his hand on mine and shook his head. My heart clenching, I looked back at my father, lying still on the hardwood floor.

It was already too late. His soft grey eyes had clouded like frosted glass and his lips had turned lilac. I can't have been breathing, because all at once a great sob escaped from my throat and I slumped back in disbelief.

My father was dead. Not from Snipeman's lead shot, it turned out, but from shock. The doctor told us later that he must have had a weak heart.

Everyone blamed Clay Snipeman for Papa's death, of course. Everyone, that is, except me. Sure, Snipeman had fired the bullet that had made his heart stop. But if I hadn't rushed forward so rashly, he would never have pulled the trigger and my father would still have been alive.

1

Three months later . . .

I tried to work the metal fingers of my hand as I gripped the ship's rail. The freezing sea was muddy and marbled with foam as we lurched sickeningly over the waves. Another curtain of biting spray was suddenly thrown up, drenching me. But I was more concerned about the condition of my left hand. No matter how hard I tried to keep it clean and oiled, the salt had worked its way into the mechanism and was making it rusty.

My chapped lips weren't faring much better as I squinted through my father's old spyglass to see a thin smudge of grey on the horizon. It was very nearly a month since I had set sail from my home in Williamsburg, aboard a ship infested with lice, scurvy and the flux. My destination: Portsmouth, and from there on to London.

Why was I travelling back to England? The answer lay in the letter my mother had received shortly after Papa's death.

She had stolen up to me breathlessly as I stood outside his old forge, clutching the letter in her hand. Papa's distant cousin, 'Uncle' Henry, the playwright, had written to pass on his condolences. But in the course of his letter he let slip that his own fortunes had abruptly changed for the better. He had now been made a magistrate . . . the chief magistrate, no less, for London.

Despite being a sprawling metropolis of over half a million souls, London, it turned out, still had no police force. Instead it had a ramshackle system of doddery night watchmen and parish constables dating back to medieval times. Overseeing all of them now was my uncle. In other words, he was judge, jury and executioner rolled into one.

Before my father died, there had been talk of me taking up an apprenticeship and following him into the blacksmith trade. But my mother had always fiercely opposed this: she was adamant that she wanted more for me. Suddenly here was a chance.

'Just think, Thomas,' she'd said. 'With his help, you could train to become a lawyer.'

It was the first time I'd seen her eyes sparkle since my father had died – in fact, in as long as I could remember.

The years seemed to fall away as her face blossomed into a smile.

I tried to argue that I couldn't leave her – not now. How would she survive by herself? But there was no telling her. She had a stubborn streak that went with her copper-coloured hair, and she was digging her heels in. My father had put by more than enough savings for her to live comfortably, she said. The rest I could use for my passage.

'It's what your father would have wanted for you. It's what *I* want.' Her mind was set, she said, and there would be no argument.

A month later everything had been arranged . . .

Now, less than an hour after I'd glimpsed land, my ship finally docked in Portsmouth.

As I clambered down the gangplank, my head was still reeling from the motion of the waves. A grizzled man in an oversized greatcoat stood waiting at the bottom clutching a ledger. As I held out my sodden ticket, he reached for it without lifting his eyes from his paperwork. By now, the salt and damp had made the metal fingers of my left hand seize up entirely. As the official tugged the ticket out of my grip, his fingers came away with only a soggy stub – the rest was clamped firmly between my finger and thumb. He glanced up and his eyes boggled in disbelief as I prised the rest of the slip from my fingers and handed it to him.

Leaving him gawping, I boarded a coach bound for London. Two more days of travelling, this time by a series of stagecoaches, eventually brought me to the outskirts of the teeming city.

Nothing had prepared me for its vastness – or its temperature! Squalls of freezing snow whistled through the streets, seeking out every tiny crack in the window frame of my carriage to freeze me to the marrow. On every corner, down every pitch-dark alleyway, I glimpsed gaunt, sunken faces lit up by the flames of burning braziers as the homeless and destitute huddled for warmth. I shuddered just thinking how frozen they must be, safe in the knowledge that I would soon be nestling by my uncle's open fire, my belly warmed by the fine food that would surely be waiting for me.

Finally I alighted at a coaching inn called The George, and was immediately struck by the overwhelming volume of people and noise. I'd thought Williamsburg was heaving – but this was mayhem.

I'd barely had time to splutter the address of my uncle's rooms before my trunk was thrown into a horse-drawn cab called a hansom and I was being whisked across London Bridge at breakneck speed. The front of the cab was open – which meant that there was only the horse's backside between me and the onslaught of traffic thundering towards us. I was also completely unprotected from the biting wind.

The fingers of my left hand dug into the rim of the cab door as we swerved and careered across the bridge. It was a miracle how we managed to avoid the stream of pedestrians, carts, carriages and livestock pouring out of the city the other way.

Perched high above me, the cabbie shouted down, telling me that when he first started taxiing passengers across the bridge there had been no system for which side you should drive on: the traffic had just been a scrum. Then, in 1722, the Lord Mayor had decreed that all vehicles heading north over the bridge must keep to the left. The rest, coming the opposite way, had to keep to the other side.

You'd think this might have eased the chaos. Instead, as I squinted out of the front of the cab, my fringe plastered across my eyes, I felt like I had stumbled into the middle of a battlefield.

If I'd been hoping for a glimpse of the vast, snaking river, I was to be disappointed – for the moment at least. It was only a little before four o'clock on an achingly cold afternoon in December, but already the city was cloaked in darkness. To make matters worse, the bridge was flanked on both sides by a vast wall of crooked dwellings that reached haphazardly into the sky.

As we rattled our way over the icy cobbles, I peered into the windows to see a multitude of tradesmen and labourers. Never before had I witnessed so much humanity squeezed into so confined a space.

Inside one workshop I saw the huge glass vats of a perfumer, distilling his oils and essences, surrounded by a forest of dried herbs. In another a cooper was hammering deafeningly at a wooden barrel. Above him, a violin maker was delicately varnishing an instrument before hanging it up to dry with a dozen others. Through yet another casement, a wig maker was puffing powder over a gentleman as he protected his face with a large paper cone.

At every available window, grimy sheets and under-wear were hanging out to air, giving the street the look of a vast battleship with its sails billowing in the wind.

Soon an extraordinary sight met my eyes. On the pavement, a small olive-skinned boy was playing a penny whistle while a monkey performed a little jig in time to the music. A collection of ragged-looking children with filthy faces and gaps in their teeth had gathered round to clap. They watched, spellbound, as the animal grinned and pirouetted, then held out its tiny hand for money.

After growing up in a small Virginian backwater, the sights and sounds of all these people (and animals) almost took my breath away. But this might also have had something to do with the eye-watering smell. From the moment my stagecoach had passed through the turnpike at the edge of the city, my nose had been assaulted by a foul, reeking stench.

At first I'd put this down to the large tannery we'd passed. This was where the hides of animals were stripped and turned into leather. I knew from back home that these grim warehouses were notorious for the smell of putrefying animal carcasses being pickled in urine. But as I leaned out of the carriage to retch, I saw it wasn't just muddy sleet that our wheels were splashing through. The gutter running down the middle of the road was clogged with a veritable armada of turds!

By now we were approaching the northern end of the bridge and I realized that the pedestrians had been replaced by something else: a steaming mass of cattle was being driven to market. Men clad in heavy oilskins, their heads hidden by wide-brimmed hats, lashed and swore at the poor beasts to drive them through the mud.

Before we reached the market the cab plunged left, past the vast new dome of St Paul's cathedral, down a hill and over a stagnant ditch into Fleet Street. At the end of this thriving thoroughfare we passed under a huge gateway. To my horror, stuck on a spike above it was a severed head, gaping slack-jawed.

'Good riddance to him,' my driver shouted before spitting onto the street.

'What did he do?' I enquired, shuddering.

'He was a thieftaker. One of the most notorious villains the city's ever seen.'

I frowned. 'But aren't thieftakers supposed to arrest criminals?'

My question was met with a throaty rasp of derision, but before I could ask why, the cab swung right and we cut up a dark and forbidding lane. Here the houses teetered so precariously they looked as if they would topple over at any moment. All along the pavement, clusters of street children stood shivering in bare feet, staring suspiciously at me as I passed.

'Where are we now?' I called up to the driver.

'Wych Street. Trust me, you don't want to hang around here after dark. Or of a day, for that matter.'

As I peered ahead, I began to make out what looked like a large child huddled on a sledge. But as we got closer, I saw that it wasn't a child at all, but the crumpled figure of an old man, bent almost double. He had a long matted beard and a filthy, dented top hat. Closer inspection revealed that he wasn't on a sledge either: it was a sort of boat, complete with a sail and tiny mast.

'The surgeons over at St Bartholomew's sawed his legs off after he came back from the war,' my cabbie informed me, nodding at the old man. 'He used to be in the navy so they made him a little boat to wheel round in.'

As I watched, astonished, the old man trundled his cart into a tavern. The doors swung inwards with a crash, and a cloud of warm air reeking of gin belched out.

No sooner had he disappeared than a panic-stricken shout ripped through the darkness – from whom or where I didn't yet know.

'Call the constable! The Undertaker's stolen another girl!'

At the same moment I was nearly flung out of the cab as the horse reared up in terror. A jet-black coach, its windows blacked out by heavy crimson drapes, had burst out of a courtyard ahead, narrowly avoiding a head-on collision. The sinister driver – perched high up at the front – was wearing a long black overcoat and a tall, crooked top hat as he lashed his two steeds on.

The alarm had been raised, I now discovered, by a young black man – more of a boy – who suddenly sprinted out of the courtyard in hot pursuit. Dressed in what looked like the finery of a wealthy man's footman, he hurriedly raised an old blunderbuss to his cheek. This was a short flintlock musket with a trumpet-like barrel. There was a blinding flash before an explosion of gunshot spewed out of its muzzle.

In his haste, however, the footman had failed to see

that my own cab now stood between him and his intended target.

For a second I was convinced that I was about to be blasted to shreds. Miraculously, however, not one of the sizzling pellets struck me. I hastily patted myself down, feeling all over to see if there were any perforations, but I had escaped completely unscathed.

I spun round to see if any of the pellets had hit the fleeing coach driver. At the same time I reached into my breast pocket for my father's spyglass to get a clearer look at his face.

Before my metal fingers could reach it, the driver of the black coach had turned round and was pointing his gun into the air – perhaps to fire a warning shot. But as his coach lurched round the corner, the barrel was suddenly jolted.

Yet again – just as I had been in Mr Driscoll's store – I found myself staring down the barrel of a gun. This time, however, the lead ball *did* hit me. In fact, it would have torn a hole the size of a gold ducat through my heart. But by a stroke of good fortune it ricocheted with a loud clang off my iron hand. Suddenly re-routed, the missile then continued its journey upwards through the ceiling of the cab.

Immediately I heard a groan from my driver, and his body slumped forward and landed with a hefty thump at my feet. As his eyes stared lifelessly at me, a neat hole in his forehead began to ooze blood onto my boots.

Barely able to take in what was happening, I fumbled to press the spyglass to my eye, bringing the fleeing gunman sharply into focus.

As the smoke drifted from the barrel of his gun, I saw that he was dressed as some kind of sinister undertaker. The coach he was driving had four plumes of feathers, one at each corner, just like a funeral hearse.

More chilling still, though, was his face – or lack of it. Instead he wore a white mask shaped like the skull of some sinister bird . . .

2

For a moment the gunman and I were staring directly at each other – only this time it was the poor cabbie, not my father, who lay dead at my feet. The Undertaker's mask made my flesh crawl: it had a large, hooked beak, but it was the eyes that were most unnerving – deep, hollow sockets that seemed to have nothing behind them.

As I stood transfixed, the demonic figure spun back round, lashing his horses, and the hearse clattered down the road.

'Who was that?' I gasped, turning to the young black footman who had fired the blunderbuss.

'It's the Undertaker, sir. A murderer to be sure! He's kidnapped my master's daughter while we were at church.'

'*Kidnapped* her?'

'Stole her while no one was looking. He's hidden her inside the coffin in the back of his hearse . . .'

I could barely comprehend what I was hearing. 'Well, isn't there a constable . . . ?' I demanded.

'There's the high constable of Holborn. But my master – that's Lord Davenport – said the last he saw of him was in Spitalfields, which is miles away.'

I looked around helplessly. People were either standing round in shock, or beginning to slip back into darkened doorways. Surely someone would go after this fiend . . .

As my stomach knotted, I realized there was no alternative. Either I stayed rooted to the spot, as I had done when my father died, or I would have to go after the perpetrator myself.

But how could I? I had been in the city for less than an hour. I didn't even know where I was! Yet if I did nothing, the girl was sure to meet whatever grisly fate awaited her . . .

'Fetch the high constable and all the reinforcements you can!' I shouted at the terrified footman. I reached down for the reins, but the lifeless body of the cabbie was sprawled on top of them. This was no time for ceremony, so I shoved his body out onto the street then clambered up into his seat.

With a loud 'Hah!' I snapped the reins sharply. I was accustomed to driving my father's gig, so I fancied this would pose no problems. But to my embarrassment, the horse refused to budge an inch.

'It's no use,' one of the local tradesmen shouted. 'She only knows her master's voice.'

At that, an old scavenger – a street cleaner – stepped forward. 'This should get her going,' he drawled in a thick Irish accent. He belted the horse's backside with a brush made from a large bunch of tied twigs, and the startled animal burst into a gallop.

Whether I liked it or not, the chase was well and truly on. The only trouble was, I didn't have the slightest clue where I was going. Or, for that matter, how to get back again.

As we burst out of Wych Street, scattering passers-by in every direction, my eyes scanned the streets for any sign of my quarry. Suddenly I caught a glimpse of his coach disappearing down an alleyway to my right and urged my steed on.

Giving chase, I realized I was now thundering down-hill towards the docks. With the only road ahead leading directly to the river, surely I had the kidnapper trapped . . . Yet to my astonishment the villain showed no sign of slowing. Instead he kept thrashing at his horses, pushing them still faster.

This had to be suicide! Any moment he would plunge over the wharf, no doubt drowning Lord Davenport's daughter in the process. As his horses leaped over the edge, I held my breath, waiting for the moment when they hit the water.

Instead, with a resounding *boom*, the coach landed on firm ground.

How was this possible?

The reason hit me in an instant. The river was frozen!

Suddenly my own horse saw the edge of the wharf looming and made a last-ditch effort to refuse. Its front legs locked and its hooves skidded across the cobbles. But by now our momentum was too much and we sailed clean over, landing so heavily that I was convinced we would crash through the ice.

Luckily it held. But now there was another problem: how on earth would my horse stay upright on the frozen surface?

Fortunately its hooves had been fitted with frost nails. I'd seen my father hammer the same metal pegs into horseshoes back home when the roads turned icy.

As soon as I could gather my wits, I looked up to see that, on either side of the river, huge cargo ships were tied up to wooden jetties. But they need hardly have bothered: their hulls were frozen into the ice. More astonishing still, a circus troupe had set up camp in the middle of the ice and was performing to a large crowd. This, I later learned, was the Frost Fair, an exotic pageant that took place whenever the river froze over. As my cab careered across the ice, I saw that several horse-drawn wagons had formed a circle round a brazier full of burning coals. By the firelight I could see posters advertising a flesh-eating savage and a deformed woman with what looked like a tree of warts growing out of her head. Next to the fire basket, several midgets were juggling a spiky football that I soon found out was a pineapple.

Suddenly the spectators were sent scattering in all directions as the Undertaker's hearse plunged through the middle of them. One of its wheels crashed into the brazier, spilling the burning coals onto the ice and sending up a vast firework display of embers. A quick-witted dwarf began frantically picking up the coals with a spade before they could melt the ice.

I tugged hard on my reins to avoid him, but my iron hand must have clenched too tightly. Whinnying, my horse jerked its head up and the cab lurched onto one wheel.

By some miracle we didn't topple over, but when the wheel hit the ground again, I realized we had lost all traction. As we slid out of control, I saw two burly men carrying a large wooden box supported between them on a pair of poles. This was a sedan chair – the most common form of taxi service for the upper classes. Inside, the unsuspecting nobleman was reclining, oblivious to his imminent fate.

Almost too late, the two chair carriers looked up and saw my cab careering towards them. For a moment their eyes bulged in horror, before they dropped the box and dived clear. The startled passenger, unceremoniously dumped onto the ice, peered out and saw the danger. Scurrying to free himself, he clambered out, seconds before I smashed through the box, reducing it to splinters.

As my horse's hooves finally regained some grip, we surged forward again, galloping through the middle of the circus, earning shouts of protest and very nearly a pineapple in the head.

Soon I realized that my smaller, lighter cab was gaining on the more cumbersome hearse ahead. Before long we would be neck and neck.

Exactly what I was hoping to achieve hadn't occurred to me till now. The kidnapper, I knew, had a flintlock. I, on the other hand, had only my iron fist, and even this was dented from where the kidnapper's bullet had ricocheted off it. It was hardly much competition. But if I could draw alongside, maybe there was a chance I could leap across and brain him with one solid blow. It was madness, of course, and yet . . .

I urged my horse closer until the metal rims of our wheels began to spark against each other. But just as I prepared to leap across, my cab hit a piece of driftwood frozen in the ice and I was nearly flung over the side. If I fell, I would surely be crushed under the wheels – if the hooves didn't kill me first, of course! Luckily my hand caught the rim of the cab and I was able to haul myself back into the driving seat.

Finally – my eyes almost encrusted shut with frost – I readied myself once more. It was now or never . . .

But before I could throw myself across, the kidnapper abruptly changed course, swinging his coach left towards the shore. Meanwhile I was left teetering as my horse charged onwards, now in entirely the wrong direction.

I tugged on the reins – more gingerly this time for fear of throwing the cab into a pirouette again. By now, my ears and right hand were completely numb from the cold. Fortunately there was no such problem with my iron fist!

As my horse banked sharply, the wheels of the cab gripped and we set off after the hearse. Seconds later we thundered up a stone slipway and onto dry – or at least not frozen – land. But if racing across the ice was hair-raising, it was nothing to the labyrinth of alleyways I was now confronted with.

Still I pushed my horse on, desperately calling out warnings to everyone in my path. The area I was now entering was different from anywhere I'd seen in the city so far. It was darker and more medieval-looking, full of tortuous back alleys, crumbling archways and rickety wooden bridges.

At a fork in the lane up ahead, the Undertaker's hearse

veered unexpectedly to the left, plunging through a gulley of frozen mud. A street vendor carrying a box of salted sardines was forced to dive out of the way. His fish went skidding across the ice into the hungry chops of a stray dog.

Just as the bewildered man picked himself up, I came hurtling towards him.

'Out of the way!' I screamed, sending him diving for cover again. Another poor wretch playing an accordion was splattered from head to toe with filth thrown up from my wheels.

Soon I drew level with the kidnapper again, but on opposite sides of what seemed to be an open sewer. Our horses' hooves echoed deafeningly off the brick walls of warehouses. High above, wooden beams jutted out into the sky with pulleys that had long since fallen into disuse.

Suddenly, through the gloom, I saw that the road ahead didn't just twist: it didn't exist at all! Instead there was a sharp turn to the left leading to a tumble-down bridge. My hands shaking with panic, I threw my bodyweight as far to the side as I could, sending the cab slewing across the road and straight towards a fruit stall. A heartbeat later there was an explosion of wood, and my cab crashed into it, bringing an avalanche of mouldy apples raining down on my head.

Dodging the missiles, I glanced around to see if my

vehicle was still in one piece. Incredibly, it was. But as I geed my horse on again, something underneath began to groan. Looking down, I saw that one of the wheels was badly buckled. Suddenly one and then another of the spokes splintered and sheered clean off. Surely it would only be a matter of minutes before the whole wheel worked its way off the axle and the chase would be over?

Deciding simply to ignore it, I turned sharply into an old medieval alleyway. But my eyes immediately bulged with alarm: the way ahead was only a hair's breadth wider than my carriage.

There was *one* unexpected advantage. As my cab sparked and ricocheted off the walls, the broken wheel was unable to work itself off. It wobbled and groaned and continued to splinter, but for the moment it stayed on.

However, my luck was about to run out. As the alleyway began to wind its way uphill, I realized that it was also very gradually getting tighter. The Undertaker's hearse was longer and heavier than my carriage, but it must have also been a matter of inches narrower. It could squeeze through the passageway where I could not.

There was an ear-piercing squeal of metal against stone, and then my cab ground to a shuddering halt. I was well and truly stuck fast.

My mind racing, I thought about trying to unfasten my horse so that I could continue the chase bareback.

But from the way it was wheezing for breath, it was obvious that the poor creature was almost dead on its feet. Instead, I clambered over its back and leaped down, landing in a foot of icy mud. Spitting out straw and goodness knows what else that had splattered into my mouth, I staggered through the freezing puddles till I reached the end of the alleyway. Looking up, I saw a sign painted on the side of a crumbling old hovel: SHEEP'S HEAD ALLEY. Across from it was another, encouragingly called THIEVING LANE.

Suddenly I heard raised voices. Spinning round, I saw a crowd of locals heading directly towards me carrying sticks and burning torches. One of them was the man with the salted sardines. From the look on their faces, they weren't coming to help; they seemed more likely to break my neck for running riot through their street stalls.

I darted round another corner and found myself standing, panting, in the most forbidding alley yet . . . Bleeding Heart Lane. Here, the walls of the dwellings looked like they had been made out of nothing but straw and spittle. Rats were pouring out of one.

Squinting closer, I began to make out a writhing mass on the floor like a carpet of giant eels. But when one of them turned over, I realized they weren't eels at all – they were people. They were strewn across the ground in a drunken stupor, tankards and beer bottles discarded all around them.

'*There 'e is! Grab 'im!*' came a shout.

The mob was almost upon me, their burning torches casting ghoulish shadows across the sides of the houses.

Panicking, I threw myself down the tiny passageway opposite and stopped dead in my tracks. Straight ahead was the back of the hearse, wedged solid between the walls on either side. The two gleaming black horses were still harnessed to it, their breath making great clouds of steam.

Could it be that the kidnapper was still on board? More to the point, was Lord Davenport's daughter still inside the coffin?

With only seconds till the mob caught up with me, I pulled back the velvet curtains to find that the coffin lid was ajar. Holding my breath, I peered inside. As I'd feared, it was now empty. The kidnapper must have dragged the poor girl free.

With no room to squeeze past the hearse, there was only one way I could reach the other side: I would have to go underneath. I sank down onto my hands and knees and began to crawl through the disgusting slime. In between bouts of retching, I strained to hear signs of the Undertaker still lurking above. But when I finally clambered out the other side, he was nowhere to be seen.

To my right I saw that a tiny passageway – scarcely wider than my shoulders – led through to a sinister-looking courtyard. Even in the daylight hours I sensed that no natural light could ever reach into this forsaken place. As I peered through, it was clear that there was nowhere else the Undertaker could have hidden. I swallowed hard and began to edge my way closer.

On the far side of the courtyard stood a precarious hovel propped up on rotten timbers. It was held together by a lattice-work of wooden beams, the gaps filled in with what looked like a crumbling mixture of chalk, mud and dung. The weight of each overhanging floor made the walls below bulge and sag so that it looked as if the whole structure would collapse inwards at any moment.

Hanging above the door was a lopsided sign: THE FORTUNE OF WAR. Above that a golden cherub cast in bronze sat grinning indolently. I was clearly looking at some sort of Elizabethan inn, older even than the Great Fire of London. Had the kidnapper sought refuge inside?

I took a deep breath and summoned all my courage. But before I could reach the latch on the door, my head was filled with a sudden blinding flash. The next thing I knew I was face down on the ground, blood pouring from my chin where it had cracked on a frozen puddle.

Dazed and spluttering, I lifted my head to see which member of the mob had struck me. As my eyes slowly focused, I discovered that my assailant wasn't the sardine-seller, but a brute of a man with a wide, flattened nose like a street boxer's. His powerful shoulders were squeezed into an immaculate bottle-green coat. On his head he wore a majestic, wide-brimmed hat with gold braiding, not unlike something an admiral might wear. His huge clenched fist was gripping the source of my blinding headache – a staff that bore some kind of official-looking insignia. What it said I couldn't tell as my vision drifted in and out of focus.

'Who are you?' I moaned weakly.

The man stared down at me with an almost animal ferocity. 'Saunders Welch, High Constable of Holborn. And mark my words, you will swing for this when you come before the magistrate.'

3

It was no use. However hard I tried to force my foot out of my mud-encrusted boot, it wouldn't shift past the collar of iron clamped around my ankle. Still I kept trying, till I felt an agonizing pain shoot up my leg.

Several hours earlier, just after I'd been brained by the high constable, I'd been hauled to my feet and my ankles clamped in irons. I tried to protest my innocence, spluttering that I was a distant cousin several times removed of the magistrate and that I had been trying to rescue the kidnapped young lady.

Despite this, Saunders Welch told me in no uncertain terms to keep my mouth shut and save my lies for the dock.

I was then flung into a cage mounted on a horse-drawn trailer bound for the courthouse. Waiting for me inside was a collection of colourful suspects who eyed me warily.

A large, rotund baker with a rather cherubic face, still wearing the tall white hat of his trade, sat sweating nervously in the corner. Squeezed in beside him was a hollow-cheeked street urchin in filthy rags, sucking on a clay pipe. A large wicker basket was perched on his lap, stuffed to the brim with wigs of every description. As I glanced at him enquiringly, he blew a puff of smoke in my eye, making me cough.

In the other corner sat a very angry-looking red-haired dwarf in a leopard-skin leotard. Intriguingly, his right foot was manacled to a large set of dumbbells. I was about to ask him who he was, but before I could, the carriage lurched forward and I was thrown off balance.

The ride to the courthouse was short and uncomfortable, especially as the chains round my feet continued to bite through my boots. The courthouse itself was the fourth house in an elegant, flat-fronted terrace called Bow Street. On either side of the ground-floor window was a doorway. The one to the right was ornate, with a large imperious oak surround and a shiny brass plaque inscribed with the words: HENRY FIELDING, JUSTICE OF THE PEACE, CHIEF MAGISTRATE OF LONDON.

The other door was mean and squat, leading into a dingy unlit corridor. This was clearly the entrance for suspected felons and general lowlife, amongst whom I was now clearly counted.

Sure enough, I was hauled out of the cage and shoved roughly towards the small doorway. I was then marched down a corridor and thrown into a tiny windowless room. This was where I was now shackled to the floor.

Through the wall I could hear the muffled sounds of what I assumed was the court in session. My other companions – the boy with the basket of wigs, the weight-lifting dwarf and the cherubic baker – had been bundled straight inside.

I'd managed to capture only a fleeting glimpse inside the room, and was surprised to see what looked more like someone's front parlour. The shutters were closed to keep out the noise of the traffic and there was a fire crackling in the grate. But more than this I couldn't see because the door was promptly slammed in my face.

Now, more than an hour later, the pain of the shackles was beginning to make me feel faint. It had been more than twelve hours since I'd last eaten, and that was only a wedge of stale bread and a tankard of beer at a coaching inn. Since then I'd been mentally and physically assaulted in just about every way I could imagine.

I was also frozen through. My shivering was now so severe, it wasn't just my teeth that were chattering – the chains shackling my feet rattled against the wooden floorboards. I saw a grubby little mouse peer out of a crack in the wall, blink at me curiously, then scurry back inside.

Suddenly a much larger pair of eyes was watching me from round the door. Clearly deciding that I posed no immediate threat, a lad about the same age as me emerged and leaned casually against the doorframe. His more than ample belly strained against the buttons of an ill-fitting, tattered coat, the collars poking into his jowls.

Despite his ample girth, the lad's legs were surprisingly thin and knobbly. Under his coat he wore a stripy yellow waistcoat that looked ready to burst its seams. It was the sort of garish thing a dandy would wear to show off, but it looked strangely out of place on this plump, dishevelled creature.

Capping it all off was a shock of unruly blond hair plastered messily over his forehead like a damp floor mop.

As he stared inquisitively at me, he reached into the pocket of his waistcoat and retrieved a peanut in its shell. Tossing it into the air, he caught it in his mouth, crunched it between his teeth, then spat the shell out on the floor. Unfortunately the manoeuvre didn't go quite as suavely as he had hoped. As he tipped his head back to catch the next nut in his mouth, he banged it on the doorjamb.

Until that moment he'd been holding in his belly, but the shock of pain made him fart sharply, firing a button off the waistband of his breeches. It pinged off the wall behind me as the young fop was forced to clutch onto his trousers to stop them falling round his knees.

'Damned things,' he cursed, doing up another button. 'I must speak to my tailor.' The idea that he might actually *have* a tailor was so comical that for a moment it took my mind completely off my ankle.

'So,' the boy said, trying to recover his dignity. 'Are you the one who says he's Mr Fielding's nephew?'

'I *am* Mr Fielding's nephew – or at least his cousin,' I snapped, remembering my indignation again. 'My name is Thomas Fielding and I am most decidedly *not* a criminal. I was trying to stop whoever it was on the hearse from kidnapping that girl. What's her name?'

'Lady Grace Davenport,' the boy put in. 'The whole city's talking about it. Rumour has it, you're the one who made off with her,' he said, before sucking his teeth clean.

'I told you, I did not *make off* with her. I was the one trying to rescue her!'

'That's for the magistrate to decide.' He tried catching another nut in his mouth but missed it by an even greater margin. He eyed my metal fist suspiciously. 'What's with the fancy glove, then?'

I sighed, bored with having to repeat the same stock answer. 'My hand got mangled when I was little. My father designed this for me instead.'

The lad looked impressed. 'He was an inventor?'

'Of sorts.' I was getting tired of the idle chit-chat now. 'When can I see my uncle? As soon as he realizes who I am, that Saunders Welch oaf will have hell to pay!'

'Tricky,' the boy replied. 'Mr Fielding rushed out to interview the girl's father about her disappearance. After that he was going to brief the Home Secretary. That's the Duke of Newcastle to you,' he added, affecting an air of importance. 'All of which means that yours truly is in charge.'

'And who are you?' I asked dubiously.

'Persimmon Fleabane,' he said, sucking in his gut proudly. His trousers started to slide down again, revealing a pair of flowery long johns, but he hastily covered his modesty. 'Most people call me Percy. I'm what you might call the magistrate's right-hand man. Well, after Mr Welch of course. And once I've passed my clerk exams.' He coughed awkwardly, then added slightly less confidently, 'Which I will, obviously, seeing as the last few times they messed up the marking.'

I felt another smile creeping across my face. The more Persimmon Fleabane tried to make himself sound high up in the order of things, the more he came across as the exact opposite.

'Do you know when my uncle will be back?' I persisted.

'Hard to say. Normally Tuesdays is his night at the Anacreontic Society.'

'The *what*?'

'It's his gentleman's club. He goes there to sing. But I doubt he'll be going there tonight. Not with Lord Davenport's daughter missing.'

I slumped back in my seat and sighed. After weeks at sea, and then days being thrown around inside a stage-coach, not to mention a high-speed pursuit across the frozen Thames, I was cold, miserable and utterly exhausted. This was most decidedly *not* how I had pictured my arrival at my uncle's house: thrown into a damp, freezing prison cell, clamped in irons, talking to a buffoon.

Percy must have seen my dismay, because he seemed to soften towards me. 'So whereabouts is it you're from exactly? I can't exactly place your accent. Dorset perhaps?'

'Williamsburg.'

'Up Lincolnshire way?' He nodded knowingly.

'Williamsburg, *Virginia*,' I corrected.

'The *Colonies*?' He looked impressed. 'So what brings you over here? Apart from kidnapping?'

'When my father died, I decided to come and stay with my uncle.'

'And that's Mr Fielding?'

'As I keep trying to tell everyone, if they would only listen.'

'So how did your old man kick the bucket? If you don't mind me asking.'

'Look, as much as I'm enjoying our little discussion, I'd sooner continue it *after* my uncle has been told I'm here.'

'Of course,' Percy said, nodding sagely.

He stood watching me for a moment without saying anything. He seemed to be wrestling with some sort of dilemma. He glanced over his shoulder as if to check no one was listening, then stepped a little closer.

'Tell you what. Seeing as I'm the boss round here – and what a long journey you've had – I might be able to see my way to sneaking you up some bread and dripping. Might even throw in a beaker of beer,' he added with a wink.

'Thank you,' I said, returning his smile. It was the first act of kindness I'd received since I'd arrived in the country.

'Mind you, you've got to promise you won't try to escape. Wouldn't look good while I'm on watch. Might dent my prospects of promotion, if you catch my drift.'

'I think that's unlikely,' I said, nodding to the chain clamped around my ankle.

'And you're not to breathe a word of it to the others.

Especially not Mr Welch. Obviously I've got a pretty fearsome reputation to uphold. Wouldn't want any of them thinking I was a soft touch.'

'You have my word.' For a fleeting moment Percy dropped his facade and smiled warmly, revealing a jumble of crooked teeth like an old wooden picket fence. No sooner had he done so than he shrank back in terror as a booming voice rent the air.

'Fleabane! You snivelling wretch! Where is the prisoner?'

'Saints preserve us, it's Mr Welch,' Percy gulped, his face draining of colour. 'Please. You can't say I was nice to you.'

Suddenly the doorway was filled with the brutish figure of Saunders Welch.

Percy swallowed hard and cleared his throat. 'I – I was just telling the suspect he'd better cooperate, sir,' he stammered, trying but failing to sound professional.

Welch's flinty eyes slid sideways till they were boring into me. 'You must be quaking in your boots,' he drawled in a voice so low it almost made the manacles reverberate. But if he was amused, his stubbly jaw didn't betray even the ghost of a smile.

'Do you like your job, Mr Welch?' I asked, refusing to show how unnerved I felt.

'Why do you ask?'

'Because when my uncle finds out how you've treated me, you'll be looking for another.'

For a moment Welch fixed me with a terrifying stare. Then he slowly turned to Percy, who shuffled back until he was pressed against the door. 'Release him and show him up to Mr Fielding's study.'

It was hard to know who was more astonished, me or Percy.

'I – I don't understand,' he stuttered.

'You don't need to, you stupid hogweed. Just do it. And make sure you never take your eye off him.'

The boy immediately fumbled at a large set of keys attached to his waistband. He found the right one, and pounced on my manacles.

'Lord Davenport's servant, the footman who fired the blunderbuss, confirmed you are not the culprit,' Welch informed me grudgingly. 'I haven't had a chance to verify with Mr Fielding whether or not you are his nephew. But if you are who you say you are, it seems I will owe you an apology.'

'I *am* who I say I am. And you *will* owe me an apology,' I said hotly.

Welch took a step closer to me – so close I could feel his breath hot on my face. It stank of pickled onions. I tensed, certain he was about to strike me, but when he spoke his voice was icy calm.

'I admire your guts, young man. It's a pity a few others round here don't share them. But you would be wise not to make an enemy of me.'

I started to retort, but something made me tongue-tied. Probably the sight of his bulging biceps under his coat. Welch held my gaze, then turned to leave.

'Wait,' I blurted, finding my voice again. 'The girl who was abducted in the coffin. Lady Grace.'

Welch turned to regard me from under hooded eyebrows. 'What about her?'

'Did you find her?'

'Not yet. But be sure we will.' With that he prowled slowly out of the room.

Moments later the key clicked in the lock and my manacles dropped to the floor as Percy prised the padlock off. The pain seemed even more excruciating.

'Thank you,' I said, clutching my ankle.

'I'll tell you this,' Percy said, breathing freely now that Welch had gone. 'You'd better be who you say you are. Because not many people threaten Mr Welch and live to talk about it.'

4

The stairs up to my uncle's private chambers were so warped and distorted, I felt as if I was still aboard the ship from Virginia. In fact, it seemed that the whole building was lurching at an impossible angle, slowly sinking into the ground at one corner (which it probably was).

As I climbed the staircase behind Percy's ample backside, the black grime that coated all the surfaces of the courthouse gradually disappeared. The higher we went, so the rich turquoise colour of the wallpaper underneath began to show through. Soon the hallway took on a much more opulent feel. The skirting boards were still scuffed and grubby, and the wallpaper was beginning to peel, but the walls were now hung with gilt-framed oil paintings of what looked like classical gods and learned scholars.

Eventually we came to a large panelled door bearing a

plaque with the words, MR FIELDING'S STUDY. On either side of the door two large wooden pillars topped with ornately carved scrolls stood like sentries. Actually, only one of them was carved; the other appeared to have dropped off.

The door itself was made of darkly lacquered oak, apart from at the bottom. Here, years of boots kicking it open appeared to have worn the shine off. Because the whole house was on a tilt, there was a large gap in one corner where the door no longer met the floor. Through it I could see a warm glow flickering invitingly.

Suddenly a bushy ginger cat bolted past us. Almost wider than it was long, the enormous creature shoved past my leg and began to squeeze through the hole under the door. Eventually, however, the laws of physics got the better of it and it gave up, wedged tight.

'This is Titian,' Percy explained. 'As you can see, he eats even better than I do.' He gave the moggy an encouraging prod up the backside with his boot and the cat shot through the hole.

Fumbling for a key, Percy unlocked the door and it swung open with a creak to reveal a large, cluttered room. My cheeks immediately began to burn from the heat of a fire glowing in the grate. Before I could step inside, Percy put his hand across my chest to bar the way.

'*Uh-uh*,' he tutted, nodding at my muddy boots. 'Best

leave them out here. Miss Esther is most particular about keeping the study clean.'

'Miss Esther?' I asked, curious.

'You'll meet her soon enough.' Something about Percy's tone made me suspect that this might not be something to look forward to.

Tugging my boots off was no easy task, partly because they were caked in mud; partly because I had begun to outgrow them in the last few months. The expense of my passage here had meant I'd had to forgo a new pair.

In the end it took two of us to pull them off, with Percy tugging one of them so hard he toppled backwards, cracking his head against a heavy oil painting.

'Here,' he said, rubbing his head before putting an arm under mine.

He helped me to my feet, and I hobbled through the door. My eyes were watering with pain – until I took in my surroundings.

The room looked like it must belong to an extremely learned professor – or perhaps a mad sorcerer. Every surface was covered with scrolls of manuscript and parchment, empty wine bottles and discarded plates. Piles of papers were stacked in precarious towers, each topped with a chicken bone or brandy glass; while the tables and chairs were evenly coated in scribbled documents and bits of paperwork.

All around the walls, right up to the lavishly moulded ceiling, bookshelves were stacked with dusty, tattered tomes. Occupying most of the room was a huge oak desk. At least, I assumed it was a desk: there wasn't much of it to be seen under the manuscripts and books.

'I thought you said that this Miss Esther was most particular about keeping the room tidy?' I asked, confused.

'She is,' Percy replied, shooing Titian off a chair. 'Mr Fielding won't allow her in very often. Says he likes it the way it is.'

Next to the fireplace stood a tall, high-backed arm-chair, also covered in books. It could almost have passed for a throne, if it hadn't been for the spring poking out through the upholstery underneath.

'That's Mr Fielding's reading chair,' Percy explained. 'He spends most of his time perched in that – when he isn't in one of his drinking dens.'

I glared at him indignantly. 'Surely someone as important as my uncle would not frequent *drinking dens!*'

He raised a sceptical eyebrow. 'You've not seen your uncle for a while, I take it.' Something about his tone unsettled me but I overlooked it for the moment.

I glanced around the room and noticed that the wall behind me was covered with an assortment of display cases. Each one contained a different artefact – everything from exotic-looking butterflies to dried lizards to ancient astrological devices. Perched on a side table in the corner was a larger glass cabinet. Peeking out from inside with wide, staring eyes was a monkey.

'He won't bite,' Percy assured me. 'He's stuffed. Look . . .' Lifting the stuffed animal out, he popped it on his shoulder and grinned. 'Here you go, Artemis, my old chum,' he said, pretending to feed the monkey nuts from his pocket.

'Where did he come from?' I asked, astonished.

'Mr Fielding brought him back from his travels in the West Indies. Reckons it's a rare species the locals down there like to eat. Apparently they chop the top of the head off like an egg and boil the brains. Look,' he said, pinging open a little catch on the top of its skull with a flick of his thumb. 'Completely empty.'

Sure enough, the little cavity where its brains should have been was completely scooped out.

'Mr Fielding used it for an ashtray for a while,' Percy added, popping Artemis back in his cabinet. 'Then one day he set the fur on the top of its head alight. After that he thought it best to keep it in the cabinet.'

'Why does he give everything those weird names?' I asked.

'Titian and Artemis? Mr Fielding's very scholarly. Travelled all over the world. Mostly running away from people he owes money to.'

'Why do you say that?' I was beginning to feel distinctly uneasy about the image of my uncle that Percy was painting.

'Rumour has it he ran up quite a lot of debts in his youth,' he told me confidentially. 'Very partial to fine wines, you see. Not to mention cards. That's why he took up the law. You can earn quite a pretty penny from all the fines.'

'He just keeps them himself?' I asked, taken aback.

'How else is he supposed to make a living? This place costs a fortune. I should know – I do the accounts. Well, overseen by Mr Fielding's half-brother, of course. That's John. Blind since childhood. Has to wear a bandage to cover his eyes so people aren't terrified. You must have heard of him . . .' I was about to answer that I hadn't, but Percy continued without waiting. 'Anyway, the long and the short of it is that there's a lot more goes out than comes in. Expenditure-wise. Plenty of other magistrates like to dish out far more fines. But Mr Fielding . . .' Here Percy faltered. 'Pardon my saying, but he can be a bit of a soft touch. His brother – that'll be your half-uncle – is always complaining he's far too easy on all the lowlife that get dragged in here.'

Something else – apart from Percy's incessant rambling – was confusing me now.

'All these books and papers . . .' I said, marvelling at the chaos. 'Surely they aren't part of his work as a magistrate.'

'Goodness no,' Percy laughed. 'This is Mr Fielding's writing. He's more famous as a playwright. Or he was till that old walrus Sir Robert Walpole shut down all his plays.'

'Who's he?'

Percy stared at me in disbelief. 'Don't they tell you anything over in the Colonies? He's the Prime Minister. Or he was till he dropped dead a few years back. But by then he'd pretty much put paid to Mr Fielding's career as a writer.'

'Why?' I asked, more baffled than ever. It seemed my uncle was an even greater mystery than I'd imagined.

'Mr Fielding's plays were very' – he considered for a moment – '*scurrilous*. That's the word. Basically he poked fun at all the people in high-up places. Showed how useless they were at their jobs and what stuffed shirts they were. None more so than old Walpole himself. Well, you can imagine, Walpole didn't like the boss making him look like a fool. So he saw to it that they shut down all the theatres. Talk about abusing your power! Anyway, that was part of the reason Mr Fielding had to become a magistrate. He was that much in debt, he'd have ended up in the sponger's prison otherwise.'

My head was spinning from the barrage of information. But before I could ask another question, the door flew open and a girl not much older than myself walked in. She was proud-looking, with high, chiselled cheekbones and dark eyebrows. She wore a very plain, sober frock with a coarse grey apron over the top.

But it wasn't just her looks that caught my attention. It was the colour of her skin. It was a golden, dusky hue like honey. Her hair too was soft and tawny, a riot of curls tamed by a pretty green ribbon. A few unruly wisps curled over her eye.

Of course, black people were a common sight where I came from, on account of the long-standing trade in slaves. But children born of mixed race, as this girl clearly was – well, that was more of a rarity. Not in the Caribbean colonies, though, I'd heard. Rumour had it that a whole class of society called mulattos had grown up there. Their fathers were usually white settlers from Europe or North America, many of them overseeing sugar plantations where the mothers were forced to work as slaves.

'What are you doing in here?' she asked sharply, snapping me out of my trance. It struck me that she was unusually well-spoken – not to mention bossy – for a maid.

Percy had settled himself in my uncle's chair, but now he shot up as if his breeches were on fire. 'Come, come, Miss Esther,' he said, trying to regain his swagger. As he did so, he inadvertently stepped on Titian's tail. The cat hissed and spat at him before rushing out. Percy smiled sheepishly. 'This young gentleman here says he is Mr Fielding's nephew.'

Esther threw a fierce glance at me. 'How come I haven't heard anything about you?'

'I've got no idea,' I said evenly. 'But my ankle is killing me after Mr Welch clapped me in irons.'

'Why would he have done that?' she asked suspiciously.

'He mistook him for the kidnapper,' Percy explained.

'Someone *else* has been snatched?' Esther looked shocked.

'Lord Davenport's daughter. Abducted this very night from her father's chapel,' Percy informed her.

'Wait . . . this has happened before?' I asked, astonished.

'Three times in the last two months alone,' Percy said, rather too enthusiastically. 'It's always the same. He wears spooky undertaker clothes and hides his victims in his hearse. No one's ever seen them again.'

However, Esther clearly had no intention of entering into a discussion with me.

'Whoever you are, you can't go spreading your muddy feet around in here.'

'Are you sure you're in a position to decide that?' I snapped. I'd had about enough of her haughty airs and graces. On hearing my question, Percy gulped and shot a nervous glance at her.

'And what *position* is that?' she asked, narrowing her eyes scarily at me.

'As the maid, of course.' As the words came out of my mouth, Percy let out a snigger, then hastily clamped a hand over his mouth to stifle it. 'You *are* the maid, aren't you?' I asked, suddenly feeling the ground slipping from under me.

Esther looked like she was about to explode, but before she could, several sets of heavy footsteps could be heard tramping up the stairs, accompanied by a strange shuffling noise. Moments later a portly figure filled the doorway.

Henry Fielding cut an imposing figure in a long crimson coat with vast gold-braided collars and cuffs. Long, slightly dirty shirt sleeves trailed out beyond each cuff. On his head was a rather scruffy, frayed grey wig with a tight scroll of hair on each side. His breeches were made of fine cream silk and must once have been quite luxurious. Now, they were threadbare and stained. On one foot he wore a leather riding boot, while the other was swathed in a vast, scruffy bandage – the reason, I now realized, for the strange shuffling noise.

'You must be Thomas,' he lisped, holding a large, florid handkerchief to his jaw. 'Please excuse my speech. I have the most excruciating toothache. And apologies for not being here when you arrived. I must confess, the exact date of your arrival had escaped me. Then, of course, the tragic events surrounding Lady Grace's disappearance rather overtook matters. Well?' he boomed. 'Doesn't your uncle deserve an embrace?'

With that, he tugged off his wig to reveal a bird's nest of wispy grey hair. He then engulfed me in a huge bear hug that nearly broke my ribs. I couldn't help noticing, as my face was pressed against his unshaven jowls, a distinct aroma of alcohol.

'Father,' Esther admonished him. 'You reek of brandy!'

'Purely medicinal,' he told her. 'I swabbed my handkerchief in it to disinfect this infernal toothache. Perhaps you'd be kind enough to ask my dentist to visit me as soon as possible. In the meantime, we must celebrate young . . .' He looked at me uncertainly, clearly having forgotten my name.

'Thomas,' I prompted.

'Of course. Young Thomas's arrival.' He reached for a decanter on his desk, only to find it empty. 'Ah. Supplies seem to have dried up,' he lamented.

'I hardly think more alcohol will cure your toothache.' Esther sniffed disapprovingly.

'You'll have met my daughter,' my uncle said to me.

'Your *d-daughter*?' I stammered. I threw a shocked look at Esther, who was now smirking at me.

'Thomas mistook me for the maid,' she announced crisply.

'*Really?*' Henry chortled to himself. 'Well, that's a first. Normally people take her for my mother-in-law.'

Esther scowled at her father reproachfully. 'Perhaps if you behaved with a little more *sobriety* . . .'

'Esther sees herself as my moral guardian.'

'I'm simply trying to keep you alive,' she said.

'So,' my uncle continued, 'I gather you've met Saunders already.'

At this, Saunders Welch stepped forward and made a short, stiff bow. 'It seems I made a misjudgement of your character. I hope you can forgive me.' Something about his tone suggested he wasn't in the least bit sorry, but before I could take the matter any further, my uncle slapped him heartily on the shoulder.

'You'll have to excuse Saunders. He can be a little headstrong. Talking of which, how is the head?'

'I'll survive,' I murmured. In truth, my head was still pounding, but I didn't wish to make too much fuss.

'Excellent. In which case, we have urgent business to

attend to. The sooner you can give us a full account of what you witnessed this evening, the sooner we can go about finding that poor girl.' He gestured to a chair close to his. 'Please, sit down. The rest of you, leave us now.'

'I'd like to stay,' Esther said. 'I might be able to help.'

But my uncle shook his head. 'My dear, the best thing you can do is bring this poor fellow some victuals. He must be half starved.'

'How exactly?' Esther said sarcastically. 'The larder is bare. Your cards evening last night left nothing.'

'Then young Percy here can run along to the Four Keys. The landlady will be happy to provide a haunch of venison on credit.'

'Surely you'll want me here—?' Percy fell silent when he saw Welch glowering at him. 'I'll go straight away.' He backed out of the door, half bowing. Unable to see where he was going, he bumped into the doorjamb, causing his breeches to drop to half-mast again and scatter nut shells across the floor. He hastily gathered them up, blushing profusely, and darted out of the door. Welch rolled his eyes.

'Papa, please . . .' Esther implored. 'Let me stay. There might be something you miss.'

'With respect,' Welch interjected, 'this is official court business. No place for a child.'

'I'm fifteen,' Esther replied sharply. 'Well, almost . . .'

'Saunders is right,' Henry said firmly. 'Now go, child. Every second we waste puts that poor girl's life in further jeopardy.'

I saw Esther bite down on her frustration, then she swept out of the room without another word. Henry lifted his bandaged foot and rested it gingerly on a footstool.

'Did you hurt your foot as well as your tooth, Uncle?' I asked, concerned.

'Call me Henry,' he insisted, wincing as he tried to find a comfortable position. 'My good-for-nothing physician calls the condition *gout*. My darling daughter says I bring it upon myself by eating and drinking too much. I prefer to see it as an occupational hazard. Too many official dinners and late suppers.'

'Perhaps if we could start questioning your nephew . . .' Welch suggested.

'Of course,' Henry said, remembering the urgent business in hand. He took up his quill, then looked around the room, perplexed. 'Now where did I put it, I wonder . . . ?'

He began rifling through the papers on his desk, creating a cloud of dust. Rolling his eyes again, Welch lifted out a pot of ink from behind a huge book and handed it to him.

'Ah, there it is,' Henry said with a smile. '*Dimidium facti qui coepit habet.*' He saw me looking at him, bewildered. '"He who has begun has half the work done." It's Horace.'

'Who?' I asked.

'He was one of the greatest Roman poets of his time.'

'He does that,' Welch said to me with a sigh.

'What?' I asked, even more baffled.

'Talks in riddles.'

'It is not a *riddle*, Saunders,' Henry corrected him. 'It is Latin. The language of scholars, poets and lawyers. Now, let us not delay a moment longer.' He dipped his quill in the pot. As he did so, I noticed that his fingers and thumbs were stained blue, presumably from years of writing. 'Right, my dear fellow. You must tell us everything you saw tonight. Do not omit a single detail.'

5

For the next half an hour or more, I told my uncle and Welch everything I could remember of that evening: how I had been startled by the kidnapper bursting out of the side street; how the young black footman had raced after him and fired the blunderbuss; and how my poor cabbie had received a lead bullet clean through his skull . . .

At this, Henry frowned. 'Poor fellow. I will speak to the parish vestrymen and see if we can arrange some compensation for his family.'

But Welch was impatient to get to the facts. 'Did you see anything of the kidnapper's face?'

'What little I could see was covered by some sort of mask,' I said.

Henry and Welch exchanged a worried look before my uncle reached for a dusty old tome perched on the table next to him. He flicked through several thick pages to one that had been earmarked. 'Is this what you saw?'

I peered at the page. Staring back at me was an illustration of the exact skull I had seen. 'Yes,' I whispered breathlessly. 'What is it?'

'*Corvus corax.* Otherwise known as the common raven – part of the crow family.' He closed the book with a loud thump. 'Each time the Undertaker's struck, he's worn a mask shaped like this.'

'But why a crow skull?' I asked, trying not to sneeze from the dust that had gone up my nose.

'Maybe he has an obsession with birds. In mythology the crow has a strong connection to death. In Irish folklore, crows represent the goddess of death, and in some Norse myths they are supposed to be the spirits of murdered men.'

'The skull also looks uncannily like the mask that plague doctors wore,' Welch chipped in.

'*Plague doctors?*' I asked with a shiver.

'They treated the infected during the bubonic plague. The beak was filled with flowers to fend off the stench of rotting bodies.'

'But never before has the Undertaker resorted to shooting anyone,' Henry sighed. 'A most worrying development.'

'The other victims . . .' I said. 'May I ask how they were kidnapped?'

'Much in the same cunning way as he took Grace. All three times he struck after dark. He'd wait till his victims were alone, then fall upon them. He must have muffled their cries somehow, because no one heard a thing. By the time a passing member of the public spotted what was happening, he was already making good his escape.'

'Not one of the victims put up a fight?'

'That's why he picked women, children and old men,' Welch grunted. 'The coward knew they couldn't put up a struggle.'

At this point the door opened a crack to reveal Percy hovering with a tray of food and drink. To the obvious irritation of Welch, Henry beckoned him in and he placed a tray of sumptuous, steaming food on the desk: a whole side of venison and a large flagon of warm frothy beer.

Henry waved a hand eagerly towards the food. 'Eat. You must be starving.'

I didn't need telling twice. My uncle stuffed a large napkin under his neckerchief and joined me, only to wince with pain from his toothache. 'Damn this infernal thing!'

Welch took no interest in the food. 'What happened once you gave chase? Tell me everything you remember.' His stare was so penetrating, I felt as if I could keep nothing from him.

Henry gesticulated towards his quill. 'Percy – if you'd be so kind as to take over the notes while I eat.'

Percy did as he was told, perching on a tiny footstool and dutifully scratching down everything I said.

I told them how I had pursued the kidnapper onto the ice, and how he had turned into the warren of streets on the north shore.

'Jack Ketch's Warren.' Henry sighed, dribbling some beer down his napkin.

'His *what*?' I asked.

'Jack Ketch's Warren is one of the most festering, god-forsaken rat-holes in the whole city,' Welch explained darkly. 'It was named after an executioner from the last century. Most of his victims came from the area, so they named it after him.'

'You were lucky you ran into Saunders first,' Henry added. 'Any longer and you might not have escaped with your life.'

'Surely it can't be that bad?'

'My dear nephew, I'm afraid many parts of this city are completely beyond redemption. The people who live in these warrens are so desperate, they live like animals.'

'They're vermin,' Welch snarled. 'The only thing they're good for is extermination.'

Henry gave him a reproachful glare. 'Forgive the high constable. He tends to have a rather low opinion of the less fortunate in society. Now tell us what happened after you entered the rookery,' he said, turning back to me. *Rookery* was clearly another name for a slum.

'I kept after the hearse as fast as I could, but eventually the streets became too narrow. When I turned into the last street – Bleeding Heart Lane, I think – I found the hearse stuck solid. It was wedged between the walls.'

'You showed the most exemplary pluck, my dear boy,' Henry told me. 'Thanks to your bravery, we now have the hearse in custody. Not to mention the two horses.'

'What about the public tavern?' Welch asked. 'It's the only place the kidnapper could have taken her. Did you see him enter the building?'

'Not exactly. I was about to go inside, but then . . .' I trailed off, reluctant to mention Welch's blow again.

'Have you searched it?' Henry asked Welch.

'I'm trying. But finding a constable who isn't either asleep in his bed or half drunk is nigh on impossible.'

'Unfortunately the government doesn't see fit to actually pay the parish constables.' Henry sounded somewhat embarrassed. 'The post is a voluntary one decided by lots. Most of the poor wretches who end up taking the role have been paid by others to get out of it.'

'A more drunken, lazy set of mongrels it is hard to find,' Welch added bitterly.

'Do the best you can,' Henry urged him. 'I will ask the

Home Secretary if he will put a company of soldiers at our disposal. This is their highest priority.'

'If I may be so bold . . .' I ventured. 'It's just . . . I got the impression that the kidnapper didn't *mean* to head for the tavern.'

'Didn't *mean* to?' Welch said sceptically.

'What I mean is . . . when I was chasing him across the ice – I could be wrong, but I think he was planning to go straight on up the river. He only turned into the rookery because I panicked him.'

'A most interesting hypothesis,' Henry said, mulling the idea over.

Welch looked less impressed. 'The rookery is the obvious place to try and lose someone. If you ask me, this felon planned his escape very carefully. It's no secret that the Fortune of War is a refuge of criminals and smugglers. There are no end of secret hatches and passageways that lead into the sewers below. The kidnapper could have fled down any one of them.'

'A very good point.' Henry nodded. 'Have your men search the entire area. Someone must have seen something.'

'Plenty of people will have *seen* them,' Welch said cynically. 'Not one of them will admit to it.'

'In the meantime' – Henry turned to me – 'you should get some rest. You must be exhausted.'

It's true that I was. But I was far more concerned with trying to track down Lord Davenport's daughter.

'One thing I don't understand . . .' I said. 'Why would the kidnapper use a hearse?'

'Simple,' Henry replied. 'Posing as an undertaker is the perfect disguise. Lady Grace was attending a small family funeral service at her father's chapel. Everyone assumed that the kidnapper's hearse was there to take the coffin away. They had no idea of its real motive until Grace had been snatched.'

Henry began to rise from his chair, but my mind was still racing with questions.

'The Undertaker's other victims? Who were they?'

'That's the baffling thing,' Henry said. 'One was a small urchin snatched off the street. The month before that the villain took an old beggar from outside a mental asylum. Before that, a young charwoman on her way home from a tavern.'

'What's so baffling about that?'

'All three of them were either homeless, destitute or insane.'

'In other words, no one gave a damn about them,' Welch added. 'Not so Lady Grace.'

'You see, so long as the victims were all poor, the government was happy to turn a blind eye,' Henry explained. I could see that he was angry. 'Lady Grace, however, is a very different matter. For the first time a member of the upper class has been snatched. That is why I was summoned by the Home Secretary earlier this evening. Grace's father, Lord Davenport, is a close friend of his.'

'But why take her? Why take any of them?'

'That, my dear boy, is the conundrum. The kidnapper has never demanded a ransom.'

'Even if he did,' Welch said, 'Lord Davenport might pay, but no one would give two farthings for a homeless pauper.'

A grim thought popped into my head and made me shudder. My uncle must have read my mind.

'You think this *monster* might just be doing it out of some depraved appetite? Because he enjoys killing?' he said. 'But if that were the case, why no body? We've never found a trace of the victims.'

'So Lady Grace could still be alive?' I said cautiously.

'Let us sincerely hope so.' His face clouded a little and I sensed there was something else troubling him. 'There are rumours, however . . . idle gossip circulating in the vulgar newspapers.'

'What rumours?'

'People are talking about the *vampyre*,' Percy blurted. He'd been so silent in the corner, I'd almost forgotten he was there.

'Cock and bull!' Welch roared, making him shrink back. 'There's no such thing. And if I hear you say another word about it, you'll be stitching sacks in the workhouse for the rest of your pathetic, miserable existence.'

'I'm sorry, but what exactly is a vampyre?' I asked. I'd never even heard of the word.

Henry pulled off his napkin and threw it down. 'A travel writer of a rather *low* reputation wrote a piece for one of the less intellectually rigorous newspapers. He was describing a recent trip to the Balkan countries – Romania, I believe. Apparently the locals there tell a rather colourful story about some supernatural fiend who is neither dead nor alive. According to them, he roams the countryside feasting on people's flesh and drinking their blood.'

At this, Percy dropped his quill in horror. When he picked it up, I saw his hands were trembling.

'Obviously it's just a folk story,' Henry continued. 'But certain newspapers are panicking the public by suggesting that the Undertaker could be the same creature. That's why he only strikes after dark. According to the story, sunlight would make his flesh burn up.'

'Wait . . . You mean he's not *alive*?' I gasped, hardly believing what I was hearing.

'Naturally, it's complete balderdash. But whoever this villain is, he's clearly using the public's panic as a mask for his true identity.'

'But if he's not this vampyre, have you any idea who he could be?'

'I fear your guess is as good as ours,' he replied. 'Now, we have kept you for quite long enough. You must get some rest.'

'Please, Uncle,' I protested. 'I would rather stay and help. There must be something I can do.'

'You have already done more than enough, my dear boy. But there is one useful service you could do me in the morning. My horse, Archimedes, was stolen from outside the Home Secretary's office this very evening. I'm afraid this kind of crime is all too common. Tomorrow is the horse market at Smithfield. There is a chance that whichever brigand stole him may try to sell him. Perhaps you could look out for him and let young Percy know if you spot anything. He or Esther can provide you with a full description.'

'Of course . . . but what about Lady Grace?'

'As your uncle said,' Welch replied with a scowl, 'you have already done more than enough.' Something about his tone suggested he'd rather I kept my nose out of official business.

'You can sleep in the attic bedroom,' Henry said cheerfully. 'Percy will see that your things are taken up.'

Feeling disappointed not to be of more use, I turned to head out of the room before hesitating.

'Was there anything else?' my uncle enquired.

'It's just . . . well . . . normally people want to know about my iron hand. You didn't ask.'

'I rather assumed that was your concern,' he replied. I returned his smile, appreciating the courtesy. I was beginning to discover that my uncle was nothing if not surprising.

I followed the stairs up to the next landing and shivered. The air got chillier as I reached the top of the house. I was about to climb up the final set of stairs to the attic when I noticed a door ajar across the hallway. Curious, I craned round to look inside and saw that it was simply furnished. There was a pretty homespun quilt on the bed and some flowers in a jug beside it. On the other side of the bed lay a stack of clothes, neatly folded. Looking closer, I realized with a start that they were a mixture of frocks and undergarments. I had clearly stumbled across Esther's bedchamber.

I was about to hurry on my way when I spotted something on top of a chest of drawers. It was an old etching of a beautiful black woman in an elegant dress. The resemblance to Esther was striking.

'What are you doing?' came a sharp voice that I recognized at once.

I spun round guiltily. 'I'm sorry,' I spluttered. 'The door was open—'

'So you thought you'd snoop around my room?'

I had completely lost the power of speech, but Esther wasn't interested in hearing my excuses.

'I think you should go.'

'Yes. Absolutely,' I blustered, finding my voice again. 'Goodnight.'

With that I hurried on up the stairs, cursing my stupidity. My introduction to my cousin several times removed couldn't have got off to a worse start. First I had insulted her by calling her the maid. Now she would think I was a peeping Tom.

I slumped, shivering, on my bed in the tiny attic bedroom that was to be my new home. Beyond the crooked window, London was almost entirely pitch black, save for the occasional pinprick of light coming from someone's fireplace or a link-boy. These were street children employed by pedestrians to light the way with an oil lamp or burning rag. Snow was softly falling, covering the mud – and a rotting dog carcass – in the gutter below.

Beside me on the floor, my wooden trunk sat unopened. It had been retrieved from the hansom cab I had been forced to abandon in Bleeding Heart Lane and dragged by Percy up the three flights of crooked stairs. Carved into the wood were the initials of my father, *JF* – Jeremiah Fielding. It had belonged to him as a boy, then passed on to me.

I smiled sadly and traced the letters with my finger. To my surprise, when I lifted the lid I discovered a small note that I hadn't seen before, tucked amongst my things:

My dearest Thomas,

By the time you read this you will have arrived in your new home. I know that, whatever the circumstances in which you find yourself, you will make the best of it and be an asset to your uncle. Be sure to pass on to him my warmest gratitude for taking you in.

My darling boy, know how proud your father would have been to see what a fine young man you have become. I see so many of his admirable qualities in you.

Remember that I am praying for you every single night until your safe return to me.

Your ever loving
Mother

P.S. I have enclosed some extra oil from your father's workshop to keep your hand in good condition.

Whether it was because of the letter, the shock of Lady Grace's grisly disappearance or the death of the innocent cabbie, I must confess that I felt a sharp pang of homesickness as I folded the letter and placed it under my lumpy pillow.

I looked around at my meagre room. What would my mother think if she could see where my voyage had brought me?

As I sailed across the Atlantic, I had imagined my uncle to be a distinguished gentleman – *professional* at the very least. Someone I could look up to. Yet in the flesh he seemed little more than a kindly drunkard and wastrel, presiding over a courthouse staffed by an inane fool, a foul-mouthed thug and a stuffed monkey.

I removed my jacket and, as I did so, a small metal object rolled out onto my bedclothes. It was a little tin boy holding a drum. In his back was a miniature key. Once, a child would have wound it up to make the boy beat his drum, but the mechanism had long since seized up.

I rubbed my thumb gently over the little figure's face. Like my hand, it was crudely fashioned, the paint long since worn away.

Papa had made it for me before I could even walk. My mother had thrust it into my hand, her face wet with tears, as we parted on the harbour-side in Virginia.

I stared at the scuffed little drummer boy and suddenly felt overwhelmed with emptiness. Ever since my father died I'd existed in a state of numbness. His passing was so sudden . . . so ugly and final. Now, all at once, I felt his loss as if it was my own heart that had stopped beating. I'm not ashamed to say that I lay down on my bed and cried myself to sleep.

6

A loud crack of gunfire woke me abruptly. As I peered over my blanket, I could see my breath in the freezing air. It was still early; not much after dawn. An eerie grey light was struggling to find its way through the wooden shutters at my window.

Assuming that the noise had come from the street below, I shrugged off my bedcovers and pressed my face to the warped glass. Already scavengers were trying to sweep away some of the filth, now frozen solid, while night-soil men were emptying the stinking latrine pits of the more wealthy local tenants. Just across the road, a steady stream of colourfully attired young dandies shuffled across the snow into fashionable new establishments known as coffee houses.

Suddenly I heard raised voices coming from somewhere inside the house. My uncle was shouting obscenities at someone. I pulled on my jacket and breeches and dashed down the stairs. The commotion was coming from his study. Throwing the door open, I was confronted by the sight of my uncle plunging his head into a basin of water. An extremely fat man, whose tiny face was almost entirely lost in huge curtains of blubber, was fussing over him apologetically.

'Your honour, I'm so sorry. This has never happened before!'

My uncle raised his head, sending water everywhere, and glowered at him. 'What were you thinking of, you buffoon! You could have killed me!' As he spoke, I noticed a gaping hole in his teeth.

'I heard gunfire,' I said. 'Is everyone all right?'

'This scoundrel nearly blew my entire head off,' Henry answered, fuming.

'I did try to warn you, sir,' the beleaguered gentleman told him. 'It really isn't advisable to smoke after the treatment.'

'What in God's name did you put on my teeth?'

'Gunpowder, your honour,' the man – evidently his dentist – admitted sheepishly.

'Gunpowder! No wonder I exploded.'

'It was only a few grains, your honour. Just to clean the area of all infection.'

'It nearly cleaned the area of my head, you fool!' Henry roared.

Esther appeared at the door beside me, hastily pulling a dressing gown on over her night clothes.

'It's OK, my dear,' Henry reassured her. 'Despite Mr Tenderfoot's best efforts, my head is still attached to my body.'

'Whatever have you been doing?' she asked, startled.

'I prescribed a few grains of gunpowder to be rubbed onto Mr Fielding's teeth to clean the enamel before I removed the infected tooth. But while I was out of the room, he lit up a pipe and . . .' He trailed off gloomily.

'Luckily for you, Mr Tenderfoot, your prescription worked,' my uncle replied. 'Though not in the manner you intended.' He revealed a gaping hole in his gum where the offending tooth had until recently been throbbing. 'The explosion blew the tooth clean out of my gum. Had it not, you would be in one of the cells downstairs awaiting a charge of attempted murder. Now if I were you, I would pack up all your instruments of torture and leave this house forthwith!'

'But, sir,' the dentist squeaked, 'I still need to cauterize the exposed nerve.' He held up a length of wire. The end glowed red where it had been heated.

'You think I'd let you anywhere near my teeth again?' Henry barked at him. 'Now get out, before I have you thrown in the stocks!'

Almost melting into a puddle of nervous sweat, the

dentist threw his assortment of tools into a large leather bag and shuffled out of the room, trailing various charts and tubes behind him. As he passed me, he saw my iron hand and stopped, agog.

'By deuce, sir! What a remarkable invention. If I may be so bold as to enquire who patented it—?'

'Out, you infernal charlatan!' my uncle roared, throwing his pipe across the room. It narrowly missed the dentist's head, sending him scurrying on his way.

Henry slumped into his chair and poured himself a glass of port from a newly stocked decanter.

'Father!' Esther chided him.

'I need something for my nerves after that confounded man tried to kill me,' he said, trying to defend himself.

'Is there any more news on Lady Grace?' I asked, when the dust had finally settled.

'None, alas.' Henry nodded towards a folded note on his desk. 'I've already received an urgent message from the bishop, asking me if I believe London is in the grip of satanic witchcraft. Even the King is asking if this Undertaker has risen from the grave!'

'What did you tell him?'

'That it's absurd, of course!'

'What about local undertakers?' Esther suggested. 'If the kidnapper was driving a hearse, he must have acquired it from somewhere.'

'Capital point, my dear,' Henry replied. 'I'll get Percy straight onto it.'

'I could look into it,' she offered. 'I'm not busy.'

But her father shook his head. 'I want you to accompany young Thomas to Smithfield. He has an important errand to run for me.'

'But, Father—'

'No buts,' he insisted. 'Now go. I have a court full of felons to try before breakfast.'

I saw Esther's jaw tighten with frustration, and for a second I thought she was about to unleash her fiery temper. But instead she bit her tongue and swept out of the room.

A few minutes later I wandered down into the basement in search of some breakfast, before setting off for the market. As I descended the back stairs, the air became thick with a putrid stench. Percy appeared, chivvying along the corpulent baker and the angry dwarf I had met the night before. He was evidently taking them up to the courtroom to have their cases heard by my uncle.

'Morning! I hear I missed some fireworks earlier,' he said cheerily. 'Oh, and if you're wondering what the pong is, it's the cells. The cesspit is leaking through the wall.'

Hearing this, I thought I might actually retch. 'I was looking for some breakfast,' I said – though I was already having second thoughts.

'Esther's dishing it up in the kitchen. Good luck trying to get any. She seems to hate you even more than she does me.' With that, he prodded the baker in his ample behind and they trudged up the stairs.

The foul stink had put me clean off any idea of food, but I decided I should try and make my peace with Esther. I still hadn't apologized for taking her for the maid.

Continuing down the rickety stairs, I reached the coarse flagstones of the cellar and pushed open an old wooden door.

Stooping to enter, I found myself in a low-ceilinged kitchen directly underneath the courtroom. Against one wall was a grimy-looking cooking range with a cauldron of gruel bubbling away on top. The stove doors were wide open, filling the room with the glow of a wood fire.

Esther was busy ladling the sloppy liquid into pewter bowls. She then served it to an assortment of filthy wretches who sat at a large table in the middle. One of them was a child of no more than five or six; another was a woman dressed in what must once have been a fine gown, now reduced to rags. Her cheeks had some crude rouge rubbed on them, mixed in with dirt and soot. I suspected she must be a prostitute. The third 'guest' was a wizened old man whose face was ravaged by cold, starvation and, I suspected, far too much cheap gin.

'Close that door!' Esther barked. I did as I was told and the stench faded. I wandered over to the range and sniffed the gruel pot. To my surprise, it smelled quite appetizing. Closer inspection revealed some of the leftovers of my uncle's supper from the night before.

'It's for them,' Esther said gruffly. 'You can get something at the market.'

'Are they waiting to go before your father?' I whispered, nodding at the poor creatures at the table.

'Oh, they're not here because they've been arrested.'

'Then why *are* they here?'

'My father finds them on the street and brings them home. It might be the only hot food they get all week. Better that than the Undertaker takes them.' She grabbed her coat and a basket. 'Now, are you coming?'

Moments later we emerged into the icy street. London was now well and truly awake, with every manner of horse and cart weaving its way through, wheels crunching over the frozen puddles. The freezing air was thick with the cries of street sellers: everything from a scrawny young lad shouting '*Pies! Hot pies!*' to the squeal of a knife-sharpener at work.

A cruel breeze had picked up and I tugged my collar higher. A few yards up the road, I glanced over my shoulder. Henry was being helped into a waiting sedan chair – he was due to brief the Home Secretary on Lady Grace Davenport's disappearance.

When I turned back, Esther was gone. I scurried along the pavement, managing to leap between icy cracks and snow drifts, until I reached the corner. My eyes searched frantically until I saw her moss-green bonnet bobbing purposefully through the crowd. It was all I could do to stay on my feet as I slipped and skidded my way up the street until I caught up with her.

'I was surprised,' I said, keen to strike up a conversation. 'I thought the scullery maid would have been serving breakfast. What with your father being so important.'

'I thought *I* was the maid,' Esther said sarcastically.

I groaned inwardly. 'I was wrong to think that. It was because of—'

'My skin colour?' She shook her head in disbelief and headed off again.

'That wasn't what I meant.' I hurried to catch up with her again.

For a while neither of us said any more as we weaved our way through the labyrinth of back streets. Ahead of us the dome of St Paul's could just be seen poking out above the crooked rooftops. Suddenly a small girl in rags and bare feet thrust a newspaper into my hand. I was about to hand it back when the headline caught my eye:

NOBLEMAN'S DAUGHTER BECOMES DAEMON UNDERTAKER'S
FOURTH VICTIM! Underneath, a lurid illustration showed
the Undertaker fleeing the scene of the kidnapping on
his hearse. The illustrator had paid particular attention to
the skull-like mask with its chilling, hollow eyes. Looking
up, I was astonished to see that several of the shops and
stalls were selling wooden staves and garlic – everything a
would-be vampyre-killer might need, or so their ad-
vertisements claimed.

Soon we came to a bridge crossing the muddy channel
I had galloped across the night before.

'The Fleet Ditch,' Esther informed me, finally
breaking the silence between us. 'Basically a sewer carrying all the filth and dead dogs from the slums straight
into the river.' I peered over the rotten railing – all that
stood between me and the festering quagmire. 'A few
weeks ago they found a huge boar in it belonging to one
of the local butchers,' she continued. 'Apparently he'd
been fattening it up by letting it eat whatever it found.' I
shuddered at the thought of what that would have been.

'Look, I'm sorry about what I said,' I blurted, determined to clear the air between us. 'It was stupid of me.
Can't we just start again?'

She let out a sigh of frustration. 'It's not just that.' I
could see in her eyes that she wasn't annoyed any more
– she was hurt; humiliated even. 'I know what you must

think . . . about my father. How it *looks*. But he wasn't always this way. He's a good man,' she insisted. 'He's just . . . well, he's never really recovered.'

'Recovered from what?' I asked. 'Was he ill?'

She looked at me, incredulous. 'Even you must have heard the rumours.'

'Which rumours?'

'I might as well tell you,' she said with a groan, 'since you'll hear it from everyone else. My mother was Papa's house maid. When he lived in the Colonies. That's how they met and fell in love.'

'Where is she now?' I asked without thinking.

'She died giving birth to me.'

I stopped abruptly. 'I'm so sorry,' I mumbled, suddenly feeling like I'd intruded.

'It's fine. I just thought you should know.'

Suddenly I heard a horse whinnying somewhere close by, and then an angry rebuke. The horse market was only a few streets away.

'Come on,' Esther said, and set off up the hill at a brisk pace.

Soon we were making our way through a low medieval arch and found ourselves on the edge of a vast open field. At least, it must once have been a field.

'They used to call it Smooth Field,' Esther explained. 'That's where it got its name.' Now it was just a muddy wasteland overrun by an army of jostling horses. Clouds of steam rose from their sweaty flanks and hovered over the area like a mist. The stench was overwhelming: a mixture of dung, frothing urine, sweat and, coming from somewhere, rancid fat.

'How do you know all these facts?' I asked, impressed.

'Useless information, you mean? You can thank my father for that. He's determined to teach me everything he knows. Which is enough to fill about four lifetimes. Not to mention several libraries.'

'What will you do with it all? Become a teacher?'

She looked at me as if I was insane – or just a fool. 'The best I can hope for is to become a lady's companion.'

'What's that?'

'A hired friend for bored rich ladies who haven't got anyone else to be boring with. God, the thought of it fills me with dread,' she said, shuddering. 'Now, enough talking. You need to start looking for Archimedes.'

'*I* need to start looking? Surely you mean *we*?'

'I have other business to attend to,' she said slightly grandly. 'I want to take a look at the chapel where Grace was abducted.'

'By *yourself*?'

'You don't think I'm going to leave it to that thug

84

Welch, do you? Besides, everyone will assume I'm just a maid. You'd be surprised how useful it is as a cover,' she added with a mischievous glint in her eye.

'But where would I start looking?' I felt suddenly over-whelmed by the idea of trying to find my uncle's horse amongst the heaving crowd of livestock and dealers.

'Archimedes is as round as a barrel and has a white streak down his nose. But then, whoever stole him has probably painted over it,' she said, rather unhelpfully.

'So how will I recognize him?'

'Whistle like this.' She put her fingers between her lips and wolf-whistled so piercingly it left my ears ringing. Even over the riot of noise, several horses reared up, earning ugly scowls from their owners. 'When he hears it, he'll bow down on his front leg,' Esther continued. 'My father taught him to do it.'

'But wait a second. How am I supposed to whistle when I've only got—' I was about to say 'only one hand', but she had already disappeared into the throng.

In the little time that I'd known her, Esther had gone up immeasurably in my estimation. Sure, she was a bit bossy, but she could whistle louder than any boy I'd met. Certainly better than me.

I decided to make my own attempt at whistling one-handed, looking around sheepishly when I blew what sounded more like a raspberry. I noticed a couple of street urchins – *blackguards*, as I would discover they were called – eyeing my false hand suspiciously and whispering. Looking more closely, I noticed that they both had similar markings on their hands – a crudely tattooed number. They were watching me with open hostility now, so I decided to begin my search for Archimedes sooner rather than later.

I threw myself straight into the thick of things, pushing my way through the ranks of horses and riders. Every few yards one of the horse dealers would crack a huge whip to try and control a nervous animal, but this only served to make them more terrified.

As I looked around for any sign of a fat bay horse with a white streak down its nose, I found myself crushed between two startled animals, their eyes staring wildly. The owner of one cursed at it before bringing the butt of his whip down on its nose. The poor creature staggered away from the blow, nearly trampling me underfoot.

I barged my way free and stooped to catch my breath. It was then that a curious sight met my eyes. Until now I had assumed that the horses were being sold in order to be ridden. But some of the animals looked so weak and malnourished they could barely support themselves, let alone a rider. These animals were now being led away to private houses around the edge of the market. Seeing two wretched creatures being escorted through a gate into a yard, I decided to discover what fate awaited them.

As I reached the gate, I noticed a pool of dark, glistening blood seeping underneath. It began to work its way along the cracks between the cobblestones where the snow had melted, and trickled towards the marketplace to join the rest of the effluence.

I glanced around to check that I wasn't being watched, then pushed the door open an inch or two. My eyes immediately widened with horror. A man wearing a filthy leather apron and carrying a rusty cleaver stood ankle deep in gore and matted fur. As he raised the knife above his head to dispatch one poor, shivering beast, I quickly stumbled back out into the marketplace.

My stomach lurched and I thought I would retch, but suddenly my attention was distracted by the sight of a bay horse, far plumper than the rest. The well-fed creature was being led away towards the Fleet Ditch. Without my spyglass, my eyes struggled to focus. Could it be Archimedes?

If it was, I had to act quickly: within seconds he would be lost amongst the other horses. I pinched my right forefinger and thumb together and pressed it against my lips to whistle. Yet again the only thing I produced was a pathetic snort.

There wasn't a moment to lose. I set off through the crowd as fast as my legs would carry me.

This, it turned out, was not very fast. On more than one occasion I lost my footing, slipping in the soup of faeces and urine and landing flat on my backside. Suddenly I caught another tantalizing glimpse of the bay horse. My heart clenched as I realized the direction in which it was being led – back across the open sewer into the labyrinth of streets that I now knew to be called Jack Ketch's Warren . . .

1

I took to my heels again. My right ankle was still complaining from where it had been manacled the evening before, but none of that mattered: I had to rescue Archimedes from the clutches of whatever evil butcher was surely about to slaughter him.

As I reached the ditch, I came to an abrupt halt. Slowly rumbling towards me was a wall of heaving muscle, fur and horn. Several drovers in filthy smocks and gaiters were driving a column of cattle to market. As I watched, I realized that I was slowly sliding down the bank of the ditch. In fact I was heading straight for a deep, icy puddle in which a dead cat was floating, its teeth set in a grotesque grin.

I couldn't scrabble back up the bank behind me – and I didn't fancy being trampled into the ditch below – so I simply ran full pelt down the hill. Just as I was sure I would fall head first into the mire, I leaped up and grabbed the back of a hansom cab that was galloping past. My iron fingers clamped round the luggage rail at the back, but the carriage was travelling too fast for my legs to keep up. For a moment they scampered helplessly till I found myself being borne along, surfing through the mud behind the cab.

For a fleeting second I allowed myself a grin, pleased at my new mode of transport. But all too soon I spotted Archimedes ahead of me. Unfortunately my carriage had another direction in mind, suddenly veering sharply to the left.

There was nothing for it. I squeezed my eyes shut, fearing the worst, and let go. To my delight, I continued straight on, gliding effortlessly to a halt. By now, Archimedes – if that's who it was – was lost from sight, so I began frantically searching for him again.

This was no easy task: a steady stream of people was coming the other way, bustling in and out of shops. Finally, just as I thought the trail had gone cold, I caught a glimpse of a horse's tail disappearing down an alleyway.

By the time I reached it, I discovered that the passage was eerily familiar. Sure enough, a few more crooked back streets led me to a sign that made my blood run cold: BLEEDING HEART LANE.

I was within a few passageways from where I had lost the kidnapper the evening before.

As my eyes adjusted to the darkness, I made my way deeper into the gloom of the warren. The air smelled stagnant, as if something had died and rotted. Gradually the furore from the streets behind faded to a murmur. I reached the end of the alleyway and took a right, into the charmingly named Pissing Alley. This was the impossibly narrow passageway where the kidnapper's hearse had become stuck. Two eyes stared suspiciously at me from the shadows of a doorway, then slipped back into the darkness.

A few more paces and I found myself back in the dingy, airless courtyard, staring up at the tavern as I had the night before. Hanging above the door was the blackened sign: THE FORTUNE OF WAR. Above sat the plump little figure of the cherub, staring down at me with an impudent grin.

Was this where the kidnapper had fled with Lord Davenport's daughter, as Welch insisted? Or had he found some other escape route?

Sensing I was being watched, I looked round to be sure I wasn't about to be clubbed again. But the courtyard was spookily empty – or appeared to be. I swallowed hard and approached the tavern for the second time . . .

Pushing open the door, I was hit by a familiar fog of stale air and body odour. Several pairs of eyes were staring at me suspiciously from under an assortment of caps and tricorne hats – the triangular, pointed style favoured by Saunders Welch and the military. They belonged to various groups of men with sharp, fox-like features who were huddled in dark corners.

As my eyes grew accustomed to the smoky atmosphere, I saw that the ceiling was propped up by several ancient, rotten timbers. I could almost hear them groaning under the weight of the floors piled higgledy-piggledy above. A fire was burning in an open grate, while the floor was littered with straw. A chicken fluttered its way past my legs and began pecking at some crumbs.

Looking around, I was startled to see that several of the men were missing limbs. One or two had wooden stumps where their legs had once been. Another had a patch over one eye.

Perched at the bar, snoring loudly, was what appeared to be a little old man. A large, filthy admiral's hat was pulled down over his head, and a tankard lay upturned beside him. Sniffing around by his elbow was a rodent of some sort tied to a piece of string. Closer inspection revealed that it was, in fact, a weasel.

Feeling the weight of everyone's eyes bearing down on me, I moved nervously towards the bar, where the fat, greasy landlord appeared. He wiped his hands on his filthy apron, then turned to squint at me malevolently from his only good eye. The other was just a black hole.

'And who the deuce are you?'

'My name's Thomas Fielding,' I faltered.

'Well, what's your business, Thomas Fielding?' he asked gruffly.

For the moment, any notion of finding my uncle's horse had vanished. All I could think about was the Undertaker.

'Last night . . .' I cleared my throat, which was now stinging from the smoke and gin fumes. 'Did a gentleman come in here with a young lady? Dressed like an undertaker?'

The landlord squinted at me even more suspiciously. 'What's it to you?'

'I – I work for Henry Fielding, the magistrate,' I stammered, trying to keep the nerves out of my voice. I thought it best to make myself sound as officious as possible.

It was a mistake. No sooner had the words left my mouth than the place fell silent and I felt every pair of eyes in the room drilling into me.

'Bit young, aren't you?' the landlord asked, raising a sceptical eyebrow above the black hole where his eye should have been.

'I'm new,' I blustered.

'Well, we told the constable everything we know. You can ask him.'

At that moment I felt something lift up my left hand and set it down again with a clank. I turned to find that the figure next to me, the one I'd previously thought was asleep, was prodding my iron hand curiously with the tip of a knife. His pet weasel began to gnaw at the metalwork inquisitively.

'Now what would this be?' the figure asked from under the shadow of his hat. His voice had a soft Irish lilt to it – almost a lullaby quality. It was a common accent in my home town.

'Well, bless my breeches!' the landlord declared. 'I've seen a few amputees in my time, but that takes the biscuit and no mistake. How did you lose it?'

I withdrew my hand self-consciously, much to the weasel's annoyance. It stood up on its hind legs and produced a shrill, keening whine.

'Saunders likes it too,' the figure next to me chuckled.

'*Saunders?*' I asked, startled. 'As in . . .'

'Saunders Welch. I named him after the high constable. Figured they was similar types, if you take my meaning.'

At this point he tipped up the brim of his hat, and I saw that he wasn't an old man at all, but a wiry youth, maybe a year older than me. A tangle of curly black hair flopped forward over his face, which was dirty and pockmarked. The dirt was ingrained in his skin, like the flecks of Clay Snipeman's gunpowder in mine. Most striking of all was the colour of his eyes: they were a shimmering, silvery green, almost like liquid glass.

'So if you work for Mr Fielding, I'm guessing you and Saunders Welch must be big chums,' the landlord said, narrowing his one eye coldly. I saw his right foot slyly push a tatty old rug over to hide a trapdoor in the floor.

'I'd hardly say that' – I sniffed – 'seeing as he clubbed me over the head just three yards from this door last night.'

The Irish boy suddenly brightened. 'Give over! *Really?*' A thin hand shot out from the cuff of his filthy jacket.

'Malarkey De Vaux,' he announced, beaming from ear to ear.

'*De Vaux!*' the landlord said with a mocking snort. 'He only calls himself that because they say it was on the brandy box they found him in when he was a baby—' He suddenly froze. Fast as a flash, Malarkey's knife had found its way to his throat. The tip pressed against the coarse stubble just above where his Adam's apple was bobbing nervously.

'You were saying?' Malarkey asked coolly. His accent didn't sound so soft anymore.

The man stared down at the knife, a bead of sweat forming on his upper lip. Then, in the blink of the landlord's one eye, Malarkey had withdrawn the knife and slipped it inside his coat pocket.

I glanced down at his hand, and my eyes widened: it bore the same inky tattoo I had seen on the boys hanging around the market. It was a little faded, but even in the smoky half-light I could make out a crudely inscribed number *30*.

'Your tattoo – I've seen it before . . . at the horse market.'

Malarkey hastily stuffed his hand inside his sleeve. 'So what was you doing there?' he asked. 'Pladding a prig?'

'Pladding a what?' I asked, confused.

'He means izzying a horse – stealing,' the landlord explained.

'I wasn't stealing anything. I was trying to retrieve it. It was stolen from my uncle.'

'By this Undertaker fella you was talking about?' Malarkey asked.

'No – that was something different. He's kidnapped Lord Davenport's daughter. I thought he might have come in here last night.'

'Not here,' the landlord grunted, shaking his head. 'Believe me, if that supernatural demon had dragged himself in here, we would have burned him alive. If he *is* alive, of course.'

'Tell you what,' Malarkey announced, scooping up Saunders, the weasel, and nestling him in an inside pocket. 'Seeing as we're going to be such great pals, I can show you where you might find your gee-gee.'

'Archimedes? You know who might have stolen him?'

'I never said that. Just where you might be able to buy him back. Come on.'

He was already halfway out of the door. I hesitated, unsure whether to follow, then reasoned that he was probably my only lead.

Once outside, I paused to glance up at the little bronze cherub peering down from above the sign.

'That's from when the tavern had a different name,' Malarkey explained. 'It was called the Golden Boy. They say the Fire of London burned everything down the other side of it. Guess the fire couldn't make its way across the ditch.'

'So why's it called the Fortune of War now?'

'The new landlord called it that, on account of his injuries from some naval battle.' Seeing the perplexed look on my face, he continued. 'You of all people must know what a Fortune of War is . . . That,' he said, nodding towards my iron hand. 'It's when you've had one of your limbs blown off in battle.' I glanced at my hand, realizing that everyone had assumed I must have lost it at sea. 'No word of a lie. It looks dead nifty. Handy for stealing wipes.'

'*Wipes?*'

'Handkerchiefs. All the kids round here are snotter haulers. That's what they call pickpockets in these parts.'

'So you . . .' I began. 'You were in the navy?'

'From the age of twelve. Ran away from an orphanage back in Galway.' He shuddered. 'Terrible place.' His expression abruptly changed again. 'Ah, but the sea . . . Wouldn't have missed that for all the tea in China. Rose from cabin boy to the ship's surgeon, don't ya know. Could have gone right to the top, me.'

He suddenly remembered himself. 'But tell me.' He wiped his nose with the back of his hand then rubbed it down his jacket. 'Why would old Saunders Welch be so interested in our tavern? Surely he doesn't think the Undertaker's a regular.'

I hesitated, uncertain how much to admit to a complete stranger, especially one I had just met in the very place that Welch suspected of harbouring the suspect.

'He said the tavern has a lot of secret passages – hatches that open out into the sewer,' I told him. 'He thought the kidnapper could have disappeared down one.'

'Well, if he did, he must be more of a ghost than they say he is, because I was here last night and didn't see hide nor hair of him.' Malarkey's face suddenly brightened. 'Now, before we find this old nag of yours, we need a tot of cock-my-cap. That's gin to you.' With that, he marched briskly away. Deciding I had nothing to lose, I scurried after him.

In one of the adjoining passageways we came to a shop

with no name. The only thing that distinguished it from its neighbours was a small statue of a cat carved in bronze beside the door.

'Chuck us two pennies then,' Malarkey said, snapping his fingers.

My father was a staunch opponent of gin, and I had heard stories of how hundreds of thousands of people were entirely enslaved to the spirit.

'I – I'd rather not, if it's all the same to you,' I stammered.

'Suit yourself. But I'll still need you to stand me a penny.'

Curious to know how he would buy the gin, I decided to lend him the money from a small purse my mother had given me. I'd managed to change some of it for English money when I'd got off the boat. No sooner had I handed it over than he slipped it into a slot in the cat's mouth. He then produced a tiny pewter cup from his side pocket and held it under the cat's upturned paw.

For a moment nothing happened. Then there was a gurgling sound of liquid making its way through pipework, and suddenly a filthy viscous substance dribbled out of the cat's mouth and into his cup.

'Try some,' Malarkey said, offering it to me.

The smell alone was so rank, I had no intention of letting it past my lips.

'Suit yourself.' He shrugged, before downing the shot with one sharp jerk of his head. '*Slainte!* That's Irish for "cheers", in case you was wondering.'

He wiped round the edge of his cup with his fore-finger, then let his weasel lick it clean. After a loud satisfied smack of his lips he set off again.

We plunged back into the warren of back streets, Malarkey leading me first one way then another. Just as I thought we'd surely gone round in circles, we came out onto Fleet Lane, the steep, muddy street full of garish silk handkerchiefs – or *wipes* – hanging from the windows and balconies.

Suddenly he dived into a shop doorway and pulled his hat over his eyes.

'What is it?' I asked. He was clearly avoiding someone. He nodded across the street to where two men in sober-looking coats and tricornes were heading the other way.

'Turpy officers,' Malarkey hissed.

'*Who?*'

'Scum of the earth and no two ways about it! They're paid by some posh do-gooders to go scouring the streets seeking out the homeless. Yer man, Lord Davenport – Grace's *oul fella* – he's one of the bigwigs that pays them.' *Oul fella* was clearly an Irish expression for 'old man', meaning father.

'What do these "Turpy officers" do when they find them?'

'The homeless? Why, arrest them, of course, then cart them off to the workhouse.'

I looked across the street. Considering they were supposed to be on charitable business, the men looked uncommonly like thugs. After a few minutes they passed on their way, and Malarkey urged me on.

We hurried across the road and ducked down another side street. A few more turns brought us to a flight of wooden steps leading down towards the Fleet Ditch. To the right was a passage leading to a set of rickety old doors – the entrance to a disused warehouse. An ancient gantry stuck out high above with a large winch and rope dangling.

Malarkey had already begun to head towards the doors when he saw that I'd stopped. I'd been blindly following him for some time now, putting my trust in him. Now I had my doubts.

'Don't start getting shy on me now. It's just down here,' he reassured me.

'What is?' I asked cautiously.

'The fence. The fella that's going to get you your nag back.'

'He's lying,' came a deep growl I knew at once. I spun round to see a figure hidden in the shadows. He stepped into the light and I saw that it was none other than Saunders Welch – the real one this time. 'He's leading you into a trap.'

101

'Prove it,' Malarkey sneered at him. His cheery demeanour had vanished in a flash.

Saunders yanked on a rope, and suddenly, out of the shadows behind him, a boy in rags tumbled forward. I recognized him immediately: he was one of the lads I had seen watching me at Smithfield.

'He was waiting for you with this,' Welch told me, producing a large wooden club. It had several rusty nails embedded in it.

I threw an accusing look at Malarkey.

'On me mam's life, he's got nothing to do with me,' he protested.

'His mother's dead,' Welch retorted.

'Fine, on the Holy Mother then.' Malarkey turned to me pleadingly. 'I swear. I've never seen him before in my life.'

'Is that so?' Welch asked. 'Then perhaps you could explain why you both have the same tattoo on your hands. The sign of the Thirty Thieves.'

'The *what*?' I asked.

'It's a gang of smugglers and robbers. They normally prey on victims down by the docks, but I'm guessing times must be hard, what with all the ice. That's why they've strayed this far north.'

'I had nothing to do with this,' Malarkey insisted.

'Liar!' Welch roared.

'I haven't been in the Thirty Thieves for years,' Malarkey continued. 'I promise you, I was trying to find your horse. Take a look if you don't believe me.'

'Perhaps we should give him the benefit of the doubt,' I suggested to Welch. But the moment I turned my back, Malarkey suddenly bolted, sprinting towards the wooden doors.

Welch calmly drew his flintlock pistol and aimed it.

'No!' I shouted, rushing forward and shoving his arm into the air.

There was a flash of gunpowder as his pistol fired; but thanks to my efforts the shot went far higher than intended. The lead ball crunched into timberwork above Malarkey, splintering it into fragments, and causing a section of the balcony to come crashing to the ground. As the dust settled, a groan could be heard from somewhere within the wreckage.

Cursing, Welch hurried towards the pile of fallen timber. Underneath, barely conscious, lay the crumpled figure of Malarkey. As he shoved a piece of timber off his arm, there was a muffled squeak. Suddenly Saunders, the weasel, forced his way free of Malarkey's coat and poked his twitching whiskers into the air, shaken but alive.

8

I stood in the courtroom with my back to the fireplace, trying to warm myself as I waited for my uncle to pass judgement on Malarkey. It had been three hours since Welch had arrived to rescue me. Since then, Malarkey had been dragged into the courthouse and locked in the cells.

As soon as I returned from my adventure, Percy had bounded up to me like an overexcited puppy.

'Is it true you nearly got garrotted by the Thirty Thieves?' He sounded far too eager for my liking. Welch had indeed pulled a length of wire out of Malarkey's pocket soon after dragging him free of the rubble in the alleyway.

Percy was now standing beside me, stuffing his rosy cheeks with the remains of a pork pie and some piccalilli. The front of his waistcoat was caked in crumbs and a new sticky yellow blob. He let out a contented belch, then lifted the tails of his coat so he could roast his backside by the fire.

'Here, try one of these,' he said, pulling out a paper bag and offering its sticky contents to me.

I eyed them warily. 'What is it?'

'Candied liquorice. Delicious.' He shoved one of the sticks in his mouth along with the leftover pie and began to chew on it.

Despite my hunger, I decided against the liquorice. I hadn't been able to touch a thing since I'd got back – partly because of what I'd seen at the horse market; partly because of the adrenalin coursing through me after my narrow escape.

The door creaked open and Esther hurried in looking cross.

'You're in for it now,' Percy said, jamming another piece of liquorice in his cheek. 'Mr Fielding gave her a right ear-bashing for letting you out of her sight.'

I braced myself as Esther joined us, but to my surprise she seemed more concerned than angry.

'What were you thinking of, following that *animal* . . . what's his name?'

'Malarkey,' Percy put in helpfully.

'You're sure you're all right?' Esther asked me, ignoring Percy.

'I'm fine. In fact I feel like a bit of an idiot.'

'You *are* an idiot,' she scolded me. 'Didn't you learn from last night's little adventure how dangerous that place is?'

'How about you?' I asked, changing the subject quickly. 'Did you manage to find anything?'

'About what?' Percy asked.

Esther gave him a hard stare. 'Haven't you got some accounts to be adding up, or whatever it is you do?'

Percy swallowed his remaining mouthful and moved out of earshot.

'As it happens, I *did* find something interesting,' she continued. 'Look . . .' Turning her back to Percy, who was craning to see over her shoulder, she held up a small pewter tankard. At the bottom was a lump of ice floating in a little puddle. Seeing my baffled expression, she held the fragment of ice up to the candlelight. 'I had to chip it out of one of the cracks in the paving. See? Frozen in the centre?'

I peered closely and saw that there was a flake of blue paper entombed in the ice. 'What is it?'

'I have absolutely no idea. But there were loads of them sprinkled under the snow.'

'Have you shown it to your father?'

'And have him banish me to my embroidery for the

next week?' she said witheringly. 'I'll tell him as soon as I've worked out what it is.'

Before I had the chance to ask any more, the door at the end of the room creaked open. A court orderly, a frail, grey little man with a shambling gait who went by the name of Squibb, brought Malarkey in, his ankles shackled. As he was led up the steps onto the raised plinth where the defendants stood, he broke away and shuffled over to me.

'Please – just listen to me. Maybe I was *considering* robbing you—'

'You admit it?' I said, astonished at his brazenness.

'But I swear, if you give me a second chance, I can help you.'

'You really think I'd believe anything you say now?'

The orderly grabbed his arm and tried to pull him back, but Malarkey stood his ground. 'I can help you find that missing girl.'

'Like you did my father's horse?' Esther scoffed.

But Malarkey fixed me with a chilling stare. This time I could see something different in his watery green eyes. He was terrified.

'If Fielding finds me guilty, I'll be hanged!'

'He's lying,' Esther said, seeing my shock.

'He'll hang me all right!' Malarkey insisted. 'He warned me as much last time. Please. Give me one more chance and I won't let you down.'

'You tried to kill me,' I protested.

'*Me?* A God-fearing Catholic from Limerick? I would never do that!'

'Hold on. You said you were from Galway!'

Malarkey didn't bat an eye. 'Ah sure, I was born there. I moved to Limerick later.'

I was beginning to wonder if *anything* that came out of his mouth was true. 'Why should I believe a word you say?'

Before he could answer, my uncle and Welch swept into the room.

'Get that odious toadflax behind the bar or I will have you pilloried in the street!' Welch roared.

The orderly tried to push and cajole Malarkey back, but he was completely ineffectual.

'I swear I can help you find her!' Malarkey hissed to me. He wasn't able to say any more because Welch had crossed the room in three huge strides to land a crushing blow across his legs with his truncheon. Malarkey crumpled to the floor, wincing in pain. As my mouth fell open in shock, Esther turned furiously to Welch.

'You *brute*! You have no right!'

'On the contrary, Miss Esther, I have *every* right,' he snarled.

'Mr Welch!' my uncle shouted sharply. 'Need I remind you that it is customary to wait until *after* the accused has been found guilty before carrying out the punishment?'

Welch turned and made a small, insolent bow. 'My apologies, your honour,' he muttered, sounding not in the least apologetic.

For the next ten minutes or so my uncle listened intently as Welch recounted how he had learned that I had left the Fortune of War with Malarkey, a colourful petty criminal and confidence trickster he knew all too well. It was only a matter of time before he caught him hatching his wicked plan to rob me.

'And what say you to this charge, Mr De Vaux?' Henry asked him. I was surprised by his respectful tone, considering that Malarkey was such a frequent visitor to his courtroom. I was slightly less surprised, however, when I spied him surreptitiously sip at a glass of port under his desk.

'There must be some mistake, your honour,' Malarkey insisted. 'I was never trying to steal from him. As if I'd do such a thing! I was trying to help him find your gee-gee.'

'*Archimedes?*' Henry exclaimed, suddenly looking up and spilling his port. He hurriedly dabbed his lap with a handkerchief. 'And did you find him?'

'We searched the property where the accused claimed his contact would be waiting,' Welch interrupted. 'The only animal we found was one of his accomplices.'

On and on Malarkey battled to clear his name, protesting that he was entirely innocent of all charges, and was in fact the victim of a cruel vendetta by Welch. But with every passing minute the case against him grew more compelling. As the orderly read out a catalogue of Malarkey's past crimes, my mind kept racing back to what he'd whispered to me. Was it true that my uncle would have him hanged? Even if his intention *had* been to rob me, the last thing I wanted was for him to forfeit his life! What's more, not once in the vast encyclopaedia of misdemeanours was there mention of him ever trying to *kill* anyone.

And what of Lady Grace? What if he really *could* help find out what had happened to her? Or was this yet another of his cunning ploys?

'Thomas?'

My head was spinning so much I didn't even hear my uncle when he suddenly addressed me. Esther shook my arm and I realized the whole courtroom was staring.

'What is your opinion on this matter?'

'My – my *opinion*?' I stammered.

'I presume you have one. Do you believe this young man was trying to rob you or do you believe that he is telling us the truth?'

As my uncle waited expectantly, I glanced at Esther and then across at Welch, who was glowering at me impatiently. Finally I turned to look at Malarkey himself. He held my gaze unwaveringly – his whole life hanging in the balance.

The next words that came out of my mouth could decide his fate one way or the other—

'*Aarghhh!*'

For a moment I wondered if the agonizing cry had come from my own lips – till I saw Percy flapping frantically at his bottom, which was now smouldering. He'd leaned so close to the hearth he'd set his breeches on fire. Luckily Esther grabbed a jug of water and threw it over his backside. Poor Percy stood there, dripping wet and blushing, in a puddle of water.

9

'*What?!*'

Welch's voice echoed off the walls like a giant anvil being struck. With the fire in Percy's breeches finally extinguished, I had delivered my verdict.

Welch was now staring at me with a mixture of disbelief and fury. He wasn't the only one in the courtroom looking at me astonished – Malarkey was too.

I cleared my throat. 'If you please, sir, I said it is my opinion that he should be given the benefit of the doubt.' I saw a ghost of a smile spread across Malarkey's face.

'This is an *outrage*!' Welch roared, but Henry was quick to silence him.

He turned to me enquiringly. 'Perhaps you could enlighten me as to why you have arrived at this conclusion . . .'

My mouth opened, but nothing came out. What could

I say? Malarkey had already admitted that he meant to rob me. But if there was even the slightest possibility that he could help me find Lady Grace, it was worth a try.

'You asked me my opinion, Uncle,' I said simply. 'Well, my opinion is that he is to be trusted.' As I spoke the last words, I looked Malarkey straight in the eye, daring him to break his word.

'It seems you are to be believed on this occasion, Mr De Vaux,' my uncle announced. 'Use this opportunity wisely, and do not let me see you in front of this court again.'

'You won't, your honour. I give you my word on it,' Malarkey assured him, beaming broadly despite the assortment of bruises he'd sustained in the course of the day. Saunders, his weasel, poked his little furry snout out of his inside pocket and echoed this with a squeak.

Enraged, Saunders Welch glared at me, then swept out, leaving the door swinging on its hinges.

As the orderly began to unlock Malarkey's manacles, I seized my moment.

'You said you could help me. *How?*'

Malarkey looked around to see if anyone was listening. Esther and Percy were helping my uncle down from his chair.

'I heard a little rumour that Lady Grace was taken by resurrectionists,' he began in a low voice.

'*Resurrectionists?*' I repeated, baffled. 'What are they?'

'Ask Saunders Welch. Word is they might be about to strike again. But you need to move double-quick and no mistaking. If she's alive, she won't be for long.'

Squibb was beginning to bundle him out of the door. He threw open the side entrance and a gust of icy wind swept through the courtroom, sending official documents dancing into the air.

'*That's it?*' I said, suddenly feeling like I'd been cheated.

'Don't worry,' Malarkey called over his shoulder as he stepped into the snow outside. 'You have my word – and Malarkey De Vaux always keeps his word.'

'I saved your life!' I hissed.

'And I'm grateful. Honest I am. Now you have to trust me.'

'But how will I find you again?'

'You won't. I'll find you. You'd be surprised how I can pop up in the most unexpected places.'

With that the door slammed shut and he was gone – as far as I knew – for ever.

For a moment I stood there, speechless. Malarkey had lived up to his reputation, all right. I had well and truly been played for a fool.

Almost immediately I heard raised voices from somewhere higher up the house. Henry and Welch were having a furious argument. Sensing I might be the cause, I hurried up the rickety staircase. Once I reached the landing I pressed my ear to the study door. On the other side, Welch was complaining bitterly.

'You trust the word of a boy you barely know over me? People already think you're too soft. What will they think now that you've let that sewer rat get away with it?'

'That it is never too late for them to see the error of their ways?' Henry retorted.

Welch let out a snort of derision. Suddenly the door swung open and he was staring straight at me.

'Ah, my dear boy,' Henry said. 'Please, come and join us.' He lifted a stack of discoloured legal files off a stool and blew the dust away.

Welch glowered at me, then grudgingly stepped aside to let me enter.

'You realize that guttersnipe you just spoke up for would have slit your throat without a second thought?' he said bitterly. 'Perhaps you'd like to explain what you were thinking of to his next victim.'

'You may well be right, Mr Welch,' I said as humbly as I could. 'My mother has often said I am too quick to see the good in folk. But he had information about Lady Grace.'

Neither of them seemed to be expecting this.

'What kind of information?' my uncle asked, leaning forward intently.

'He said he had heard a rumour that the kidnapper was a resurrectionist – whatever that means.'

'It means a grave robber, my dear boy,' Henry explained. 'Sadly there is a small band of the truly depraved who will dig up the recently deceased for profit.'

'For *profit*?'

'To sell to the anatomy schools. The city is teeming with them. Every eminent surgeon, and quite a few less eminent ones, runs his own college to train the next generation. But to do so they require cadavers – dead bodies – to dissect.'

'Except that there are so many of the damned places, they run out of bodies, even in this infernal weather,' Welch added. 'So grave robbers – or *resurrectionists* – will wait for someone to be buried, then dig them up again.'

'The anatomy schools are known to pay up to ten guineas for a fresh corpse,' Henry continued. 'It seems to be quite a growth industry.'

'But you told me all the Undertaker's victims were taken alive . . .' Suddenly the full meaning of what Malarkey had said was dawning on me. 'Unless . . .'

'I fear your new friend Mr De Vaux thinks the kidnapper intends to murder Lady Grace and then sell her body,' Henry said grimly.

For a moment my mouth hung open in disbelief.

'*Cock and bull!*' Welch growled.

'Is it?' Henry asked, raising a quizzical eyebrow.

'You mean to tell me you believe that scoundrel?' Welch said. 'You saw the tattoo on his hand. He's nothing more than a smuggler and a thief.'

'He said he left the Thirty Thieves years ago,' I volunteered, a little feebly.

'Then why was he still drinking in the Fortune of War, the most notorious smuggler's den in London? If you ask me, he concocted this entire story to throw us off the scent. He's probably trying to cover up for the real suspect.'

'You may well be right,' Henry said evenly. 'But we cannot afford to dismiss what he says. Speak to your informants. See if they've heard anything that could add credence to his claims.'

'It will only waste more time we haven't got,' Welch protested.

'All the same, humour me.' A steelier tone had crept into Henry's voice. 'Bring in every grave robber we know of. If there's a grain of truth in this, someone will know.'

Welch snatched up his leather gloves from the side table, then left without another word.

'I'm sorry, Uncle,' I began, as soon as the door had closed behind him. 'I thought Malarkey could help.'

Henry silenced me with a wave of his hand. 'You don't

know yet that he won't. If I hadn't believed in your judgement, I would never have let him go. And don't worry about Saunders. He may have a fiery temper, but he is a good man at heart. Now come,' he said, levering himself out of his armchair. 'We have an appointment.'

'Where are we going?'

'To speak to Lord Davenport again. I want to go over every detail of what happened when Lady Grace disappeared.' His eyes twinkled at me from under his bushy eyebrows. 'As you were in the street nearby, you may be of some use.' He dragged his wig off the manikin next to him and blew some white powder off it. 'Confound these things . . .' As he put it on the wrong way round, I saw a large brown moth crawl out of one of the grey curls. It twitched its antennae, clearly wondering why it had been woken up.

There was one outstanding matter before we left. 'Your horse, Archimedes . . .' I began. 'I was sure I saw him. That was why I went off with Malarkey.'

'Then there is still hope. But first we must find poor Grace. Not to mention the Undertaker's other victims.' My uncle picked up his cane and turned his wig the right way round. The moth fluttered off and settled on one of the shelves. 'Let us hope we're not already too late.'

When we reached the bottom of the stairs, Esther was waiting for us.

'Ah, my dear child,' Henry said. 'Young Thomas and I have to pay Lord Davenport an urgent visit.'

'I'll get my coat and bonnet,' Esther replied, turning to head down the back stairs.

'That won't be necessary. You have an important appointment of your own.'

'Oh . . . ?' Her face brightened.

'I have taken the liberty of asking Lady Cynthia Allbright to call with her daughter. They should be here presently.'

Esther's face fell immediately. 'No – you cannot do this to me!'

'Now, now, my dear. At least meet them.'

'The woman is poisonous. And as for her *child*! Not to mention her stupid little dog.'

'All I ask is that you are polite. This could be a wonderful opportunity for you.'

'To be a governess to that *brat*? I won't do it! I refuse.'

Henry sighed, vexed, then gently lifted Esther's chin with one of his inky fingers. 'Humour your old father and meet her. *Please?*'

Esther's face, until now contorted in fury, gradually softened into a look of resignation. Henry planted a kiss on her forehead before pulling his cape around him against the cold.

'Come, come, Master Thomas, we have a case to solve!'

As he strode out of the front door I glanced at Esther. To my surprise her eyes were full of tears. She didn't look angry any more; just crushed. She wiped her cheek and hurried downstairs.

For a moment I felt a pang of guilt: it seemed unfair that my uncle was favouring me, a 'nephew' he had known all of a day. But he called sharply from the street and I had to set my qualms aside.

Outside, the light had taken on an eerie yellow tint as a flurry of snowflakes eddied around us. A bitter breeze was gusting through the pillars of Covent Garden, ruffling the skirts of ladies as they passed. I looked up and saw that a bank of ominous, heavy clouds was about to blot out the last of the afternoon sun.

'I fear there will be no end to this winter for some time,' my uncle sighed, turning up the collars of his cape. He waved to a passing hackney carriage, which swerved across the road, its wheels cracking the ice on the puddles.

'After you, my dear fellow,' he urged me, opening the door.

Moments later we were weaving our way towards the residence of Lord Davenport. His was one of the most modern and grand homes in Grosvenor Square, out to the west. Just behind it was the huge expanse of Hyde Park, separating the West End from the pastureland that lay beyond. The park was a lawless area plagued by highwaymen, who would hold up coaches at gunpoint.

Suddenly our carriage was forced to veer straight through a heap of stinking manure in the middle of the road. A large clot of dung splattered the window, inches from my face.

'Why doesn't anyone clear up all this horse dung?' I complained.

'My dear boy, why would they clear it up? They went to great lengths to put it there!'

Sure enough, I could see more heaps of steaming excrement all the way down the road. It looked like some kind of giant mole-field.

'But surely it's a health hazard?'

'Observe the way the steam is rising from it,' Henry said. 'Just beneath the surface of the road there are water pipes stretching all the way from the reservoir in Hyde Park. The pipes are made out of elm trees, sharpened at the ends so that they lock together. It's a disastrous system because they leak so much. What's more, the rotting wood makes the water taste infernally rank.'

'And the heaps of manure . . . ?'

'They stop the pipes from freezing.'

I glanced out at the road again, astonished by the

simple ingenuity of it. If it hadn't been so repulsive, I might have been tempted to use something similar on my left hand, the stump of which was now throbbing from the cold. It was marginally less painful than my ankle, which was still stinging from where the manacles had dug in.

Henry saw me rubbing my iron hand. There was still a large indentation where the Undertaker's bullet had ricocheted off it. Rust was beginning to corrode the edge.

'Does it bother you in the cold?'

'It's nothing,' I replied, not wanting to draw attention to it.

'Your father must have been a very gifted inventor to create such a device,' he said, smiling.

'Did you know him?'

'Sadly not. I lost contact with his side of the family some time before I left for the Colonies. I'm afraid I was not a very popular figure,' he added.

'Really?' I tried to look like this was news to me.

'Come, come,' he scolded me. 'I'm sure young Persimmon has filled you in on my chequered history. Suffice it to say that when I was younger, I was very resourceful at raising funds to spend on life's little *amusements*. Unfortunately I was even more talented at losing it all again. Leaving for the Colonies was my only hope of escaping my creditors and starting afresh.'

'And did you?'

'Let's just say I wasn't really cut out for running a sugar plantation. But I have my beautiful daughter to show for it. I now have the good sense to entrust the household expenses to her,' he said with a knowing wink. 'But enough of me. What made you decide to take up my offer and come back to the Old World.'

'My mother hopes I will become a lawyer.'

'And you?'

'I can't think of anything more boring,' I declared.

'Quite right!' Henry snorted, not the least bit put out by my bluntness. 'Mind you, if I'd been better at it myself, I wouldn't be doing this infernal job for a living.'

'So why did you become a magistrate . . . if you don't think that's too impertinent to ask?'

'I thought it would pay off all my debts,' he answered candidly. 'Does that shock you?'

'I just assumed you did it for the public good.'

'My, you're quite the idealist, aren't you? I'm sorry to disappoint you, young Thomas, but my intentions were entirely cynical. You see, when I returned from the Colonies, I was even more in debt than I was when I sailed there in the first place. I hoped my plays would pay me something. For a while they did.' His expression darkened. 'Till that dog Walpole shut down the theatres.

I had to do something if I was to feed and clothe my daughter. Being a magistrate seemed as good a way as any.'

Our carriage turned a corner and bounced its way past a row of grander-looking houses before lurching to a halt.

'Ah,' Henry announced. 'We've arrived.'

I peered out to see a polished plaque announcing the residence of Lord Davenport. Two giant pillars flanked a flight of steps leading to a pair of gleaming front doors, where a butler in white stockings and gloves was waiting for us.

A few moments later we were shown into a vast library at the back of the house. The room was lined with dark mahogany bookshelves, with two marble pillars on either side. Against one wall was a vast fireplace, where a fire was crackling and spitting. In front of it, sprawled on a colourful Persian rug, lay a huge grey deerhound. It glanced up curiously as we entered, its droopy eyes and long grey whiskers giving it the look of a distinguished elderly relative. Then, uninterested, it returned to its snoozing.

Hanging on the wall above the fireplace was a huge oil painting in a gilt frame. It showed a haughty-looking man in his mid-fifties sitting stiffly next to a very beauti-ful smiling woman. Beside her stood a girl of about seventeen.

'That's Lord and Lady Davenport with Grace,' Henry informed me.

I looked at the painting more closely. Like her mother, Grace had a small, rounded face like a bird, with skin so smooth it seemed to be glowing. Her soft brown eyes stared at me longingly, but there was no joy in them: they looked haunted, as if she was carrying the burden of some terrible secret.

After a moment I glanced around the rest of the library. Side tables bore brightly painted porcelain vases and a china horse decorated in yellow and green.

'Where does all this come from?' I whispered.

'Lord Davenport made his fortune running the East India Company. They trade in the Far East, mostly in luxuries like tea, spices and silks.'

As I approached the horse to inspect it more closely, I knocked it with my clumsy iron hand. It would surely have smashed to a thousand pieces on the floor had my uncle not caught it in the nick of time.

'Careful. It's from the Tang dynasty in northern China. If I'm not mistaken, it dates back more than eight centuries.'

'In fact it's over a thousand years old,' a voice announced from behind us. I spun round to see a tall, willowy man with a chiselled, haughty-looking face. I recognized him from the painting over the fireplace. He pulled off his wig to reveal strands of thin, sandy-coloured hair, smoothing them across his head before studying us with narrow, hawk-like eyes. His nose was long and poker-straight, his lips thin and unsmiling. He immediately struck me as someone with a military bearing.

He stretched out a long knobbly hand to my uncle. 'Fielding,' he said, managing to make the greeting sound like a sneer. 'If only we could be meeting under less tragic circumstances.'

'Let us hope not *tragic*, my lord,' Henry replied. 'I have every intention of finding your daughter alive and well. May I introduce you to my nephew? Thomas, this is Lord Davenport.'

Davenport's gimlet eyes slid sideways. There was something calculating, almost cruel, about the way he studied me.

'Thomas was the young fellow who attempted to apprehend the kidnapper,' my uncle continued.

For a moment his lordship's eyes seemed to soften. 'I am indebted to you, young man. Please – sit.' It was more of an order than a request. He waved us to the chairs by the fire. As he sat down stiffly, he flicked aside the long black tails of his frock coat. 'My wife is too distraught to join us. As you can imagine, this terrible business has left her entirely broken and she has taken to her bedchamber. What news do you have?' he asked.

'I can assure you that every possible resource has been made available in the search,' my uncle began.

'In other words, next to nothing,' Davenport growled under his breath.

'But if you will permit me,' Henry continued, 'I wanted to ask you a few more questions, in case it throws up any new leads we haven't covered.'

'What else do you want to know?'

'I assume you haven't received any kind of ransom demand?'

'None whatsoever. You think that's why she was taken? For money?'

'If she was, I feel sure they would have contacted you by now.' My uncle shifted awkwardly in his seat. 'I hate to ask this . . . but is it possible that someone could be doing this for revenge?'

'What kind of a damn question is that?' Davenport snapped.

'One I have to ask, my lord,' Henry replied calmly.

His lordship sighed heavily before reconsidering. 'You're right. You don't get to my position without putting a few noses out of joint . . . But to kidnap my daughter! She's still a child, for God's sake . . .' His voice caught and he looked away to hide his emotion.

'Lord Davenport . . .' I asked. Both he and my uncle

regarded me curiously. 'I gather you are one of the founders of something called the Turpy?'

Davenport grunted mirthlessly. 'That's a rather vulgar term used on the streets. Its official name is the Clerkenwell Institute for the Suppression of Moral Turpitude. And no – it is one of my *wife's* charitable follies. She sits on their board of governors. For what earthly purpose is beyond me. To salve the conscience of various bored ladies, no doubt. What of it?'

'What exactly does it do?'

'I've asked the same question myself. Helps the poor and wretched out of their moral malaise, supposedly.'

'By putting them in the workhouse?' I asked bluntly. My father had told me of such places; they were cruel and despicable, with the poor forcibly interned and made to do manual labour for upwards of ten hours a day.

Lord Davenport stiffened at my impertinence. 'Let me assure you, Lady Davenport has only the best interests of these wretched parasites at heart. Much to my regret. But enough of this idle chatter,' he said, turning to Henry impatiently. 'All I care about is finding my daughter. If you need more men, I'll pay whatever it takes. But mark my words' – he lowered his voice to a sinister growl – 'when you find whoever did this, I want him dead.'

For a moment my uncle stared at him, unblinking.

'I will find your daughter, Lord Davenport. And when I do, he will face the full force of justice.'

I couldn't be sure, but I sensed that he was making a point. Letting Davenport know that he would not be pushed around. Either way, his lordship's stony stare showed that he was not reassured.

He tugged on a red silk bell rope hanging by the fireside. Moments later the door opened and in stepped the young black footman who had fired the blunderbuss.

'You will have met Gabriel,' Davenport muttered.

'Of course.' I nodded cordially. Gabriel was evidently unused to being shown such courtesy. His eyes darted between me and my uncle warily before he gave a bow.

'I purchased him on a trading trip to North Africa. Generally I have a poor opinion of the moral fibre of the natives there,' Davenport continued matter-of-factly. 'But Gabriel has proved surprisingly loyal.'

As his master spoke about him, making him sound little more than a commodity, Gabriel kept his gaze rooted on the floor.

'He tells me that he unloaded an entire barrel at this fiend as he took flight with my daughter,' Davenport went on. 'Yet it had no effect. Tell me, do you believe this nonsense they're spreading in the papers that he's some kind of *ghoul*? What is it? A "vampyre" – risen from the dead?'

'The public are highly superstitious, my lord,' Henry replied. 'They are wont to believe anything the papers tell them.'

'As is my wife,' Davenport said with a scowl. 'She is convinced that this villain is some kind of phantom. I, however, do not share her view.' He turned his ruthless gaze on me. 'You are the fellow who gave chase. Did you form any kind of opinion as to who this animal could be?'

'He was too well disguised. His face was camouflaged by a white mask of some sort.'

'But we are pursuing a number of lines of enquiry,' Henry added optimistically.

'You mean you haven't the damnedest,' Davenport sneered.

'As we speak, my officers are interviewing a number of informants,' Henry persisted.

'Your *officers*? You mean that shower of drunken wastrels? This isn't just *anybody's* daughter you're dealing with, man. I want her found. I won't be made a fool of, do you hear? Not by anyone. And especially not by someone pretending to be a *phantom*!' He thumped the table, making Gabriel jump. I could see the veins on Davenport's temple throb. After a moment he regained his composure. 'I'm sorry. As you can imagine, I've been under a lot of strain.' He dabbed his brow with a hand-kerchief. 'Now if that's all—'

'Actually, there was one further request,' my uncle announced. 'I wondered if we could take a look at Grace's room. In case it throws up any clues.'

'Of course. I'll ask Miss Jardine to show you up there.'

As Davenport rose from his seat, my uncle leaned across and whispered to me under his breath. 'Miss Jardine is Grace's governess. She was with her in the chapel when she was kidnapped.'

Davenport faltered for a moment. 'It's strange . . .' he said, his expression softening for a moment. 'The last time Grace and I spoke it was in anger.'

'In *anger*?' Henry asked, surprised.

'My daughter could be quite . . . how should I say? Strong-willed.'

'I have one much the same,' Henry sympathized.

'Probably her age. She was seventeen only a few months ago. In truth, she has been angry with me for some time.'

'May I enquire why?'

'A year ago she had a riding accident. The damn fool of a stableman failed to tighten the girth on her saddle and she fell off. She could have died! Naturally I dismissed the oaf. Grace never forgave me. For some reason she seemed attached to the toothless old dolt . . . Just find her,' he finished, then strode purposefully out of the room.

A few minutes later Gabriel was ushering us up the main staircase and along a corridor decorated in a delicate shade of duck-egg blue with gold leaf along the picture rail. The governess was waiting for us at the end of the passageway, next to an open door.

'Ah, Miss Jardine,' my uncle said. 'May I say how fetching you look today.'

The woman sniffed disapprovingly. She knew as well as we that *fetching* was the last thing she intended to look. She was a thin, drawn-looking woman dressed in black from head to toe. Her face was set in a severe grimace, with coarse, blotchy skin that looked like it had been scrubbed too vigorously with carbolic soap and a yard brush. Her forehead was enveloped in a large bandage – presumably where Grace's assailant had attacked her – while her jet-black hair was drawn back severely under a small bonnet.

'I trust you have recovered after your ordeal in the chapel,' Henry continued.

'I'm more concerned about what has happened to that poor girl,' she replied sharply in a slight Scottish accent. As she spoke, her tiny black eyes darted between us suspiciously.

'Of course. As are we. Perhaps if you could show us into her chambers now . . .'

'Mind you don't touch anything.' She pushed the door open and we stepped inside.

I'm not sure what I expected, but I certainly hadn't anticipated anything quite so neat and ordered.

'Has someone tidied this up?' Henry asked abruptly. 'I particularly wanted the young lady's effects to be left untouched.'

'Everything has been left exactly as it was,' the governess replied. 'Lord Davenport has always insisted that the house should be kept in order. In that we are both of one mind. Slovenliness is the devil's work.'

'You wouldn't want to look at my private chambers then,' my uncle snorted.

Miss Jardine's nostrils flared disapprovingly.

Five minutes of careful combing through Grace's room turned up nothing unexpected . . . Until, as we were leaving, I noticed something shining underneath the cast-iron bedstead. Reaching down, I managed to retrieve the object. Turning it over in my hand, I saw that it was a miniature bottle. It smelled of some kind of ammonia – perhaps a medicine.

'What is this?' I asked.

As soon as Miss Jardine saw what I was holding, her skin paled even more.

'Nothing. After Grace's riding accident she was prescribed laudanum to help with the pain.' She made to snatch the bottle, but my uncle beat her to it.

'If it's all the same, we'll keep it. Even the most

innocuous object can prove useful.'

For a moment the governess looked unnerved. 'As you please.'

'Tell me,' my uncle enquired. 'The stableman – I should like to speak to him. Do you have an address?'

'Even if I did, I wouldn't tell you. His lordship wants nothing further to do with him. Now, will that be all?'

'Thank you. You have been most . . . *obliging*,' my uncle replied, his voice heavy with irony. The governess tutted to herself and bustled away.

'Strange, don't you think?' Henry mused. 'Her being Grace's governess. She never once asked if there was any news about her.'

Moments later, my uncle and I stepped out into the street and hailed a hackney carriage. Snow was falling steadily and coating the dung heaps with a light dusting that made them look like sugared meringues.

'I'm sorry,' I said as we clambered up into the carriage. 'I didn't mean to speak out of turn about the workhouse. It just sort of came out.'

'What you need to understand, my dear boy, is that his lordship has friends in very high places,' Henry explained. 'No less than the Home Secretary himself. The Duke of Newcastle is looking for any reason to shut my office down to save money. The last thing we want to do is give him an excuse.'

I suddenly felt like a complete dunce. If I'd been hoping to impress my uncle, I couldn't have got off to a worse start.

'Are we going back to the courthouse?' I asked glumly.

'So soon?' He raised a quizzical eyebrow. 'I haven't shown you the scene of the crime yet.'

'Where the poor cabbie was shot?'

Henry shook his head. 'That was where the Undertaker made good his escape. I am talking about the chapel where he kidnapped Grace in the first place.'

10

I stared at the vast pillars of the church and gulped.

'Hard to fathom, isn't it?' Henry said. 'To think that, only a few years ago, this was one big stagnant swamp. Some of the locals used to let their pigs roam in the mud.'

'How was it possible to build something like this?' I asked, astonished.

'Easy if you have a large purse. And Lord Davenport most decidedly has that.'

'I didn't realize he was so religious,' I said.

'He isn't. His wife is the pious one. He just wanted the King to make him a lord. Come on.' Henry began to climb the steps towards the chapel.

I looked out across the neighbouring area. It was mostly a forbidding, unlit warren of slum housing. Just to the east was the street where I had first encountered the kidnapper and his hearse. It was quiet now, abandoned for fear the Undertaker might return – perhaps from the grave. Beyond, I could see the streets leading towards the riverside, where I had pursued the fiend across the ice. The glow of the braziers had faded now, the circus having moved on.

Feeling a gust of arctic wind whistling round my neck, I tugged my collar up and scaled the steps after my uncle.

Inside the church I was forced to squeeze through the locals pressed into the chapel. So this was where everyone had come – a church service. The vicar was a man with vast grey sideburns that sprouted out above his white ruff. They swirled around his cheeks like a sea fog as he castigated his parishioners.

'And our Lord said unto the people of Canaan that if they did not cease their sinful ways, their fornicating and their lying with others in moral turpitude, then Satan would visit them in the form of a fearful daemon.' He turned from his book, glaring down from the pulpit at his cowering congregation. 'I ask you now, is this day not upon us?'

'Amusing, don't you think?' Henry whispered as I wormed my way through the crowd to join him. 'Until yesterday this place was deserted. Now suddenly it's standing room only. Funny how people discover religion when there's a vampyre about.'

A cross-looking woman with a face like an old cabbage scowled at us and gave a loud '*Shush!*'

'*Shush* yourself, you foul-looking toad-pool!' Henry hissed back at her, making her shrink in shock and cross herself. 'The woman's so confoundedly ugly, they should have used her as a gargoyle,' he whispered to me.

After a great deal of pushing and shoving, we found ourselves in a quieter section behind the pillars. In front of us steps led down into the dark.

'What's down there?' I asked as I felt a draught of cold dank air.

'That, my dear boy, is where they keep the skeletons.'

My uncle grabbed one of the candles off a side altar, then plunged down the stairway. I swallowed hard and set off after him.

It wasn't long before we reached the bottom step and peered into the darkness.

'When you say *skeletons* . . .'

Henry took the candle and lit a torch fixed to the wall. It flared into life, illuminating the low vaulted ceiling. 'I mean these . . .' he said.

I felt my chest tighten as a hundred – no, a thousand – eyeless sockets stared back at me from behind iron railings. There was a mass of skulls and bones piled to the ceiling.

'Aren't they a sight for sore eyes?' Henry marvelled,

enjoying his pun. He held the torch close to one of the skulls. A rat poked its whiskery snout out of the eye socket and sniffed us suspiciously. 'Come on, my good fellow,' Henry cooed, encouraging the rat to take a crumb of leftover pie he'd produced from his pocket.

'I don't understand. I thought you said the church was new?'

'It is.'

'So where have all these skeletons come from?'

'Ah . . .' Henry clearly relished what he was about to reveal. 'When the engineers started excavating the foundations, they made a fascinating discovery. The whole area, up to twenty feet deep, was thick with skeletons. What no one had realized was that it had been used as a mass grave during the plague.'

I recoiled in horror. 'You mean to tell me that all these people died . . . from the *plague*?' I tugged a handkerchief from my pocket, covering my nose and mouth for fear of infection. I hadn't survived a month at sea, a cudgel to the head and manacles to my ankles, only to die from the bubonic plague!

'What are you doing?'

'Surely we shouldn't be down here. We could catch it . . .'

'Relax, my young friend.' Henry grabbed one of the skulls and held it next to his own head. Both sets of eyes

— his dancing with mischief, the skull's eerily empty — stared back at me. 'If you remembered your history, you'd know that the Great Fire of London burned everything to a crisp. Killed off all trace of the infection around here.'

To emphasize his point, he planted a light kiss on the skull, only to grimace and spit on the ground. 'Probably shouldn't have done that.' He tossed the skull back into the pile before wiping his hands clean. When he looked up again, he saw that I was standing as still as a ghost . . . or as if I'd seen one.

'What is it, dear boy?'

I couldn't bring myself to admit what had flashed through my mind.

'Tell me. No matter how absurd it is.'

I sighed. 'All this talk of a vampyre . . . The crow skull he wore that looked like a plague doctor's mask . . . You don't think . . .' I looked around at all the skulls.

Henry knew exactly where my mind was leading me. 'You think the Undertaker might have been one of these poor fellows? Risen from the dead?'

'It just seems a coincidence, don't you think? That Lady Grace was kidnapped right *here*?'

'It's an interesting theory,' Henry mused. 'Yet in all my studies I have never found one iota of proof that man can survive beyond the grave. Perhaps our villain simply has a fascination for plague victims.' He fixed me with a solemn look. 'Now, to the matter in hand – and the real reason I brought you here.' He struck the stone floor with the tip of his cane. 'This, young Thomas, is the very spot where poor Grace was abducted.'

'She was kidnapped from the crypt? But why would she have been down here?'

'A good question. And one I will attempt to elucidate. Grace was attending the funeral of the family's beloved housekeeper. During the service, the casket lay open at the front of the altar . . . roughly here.' He held the flaming torch aloft and pointed to the ceiling with his cane to indicate the place in the chapel above. 'Poor Grace became so overcome with emotion, her mother wanted to take her outside for some air. However, Grace, not wishing to create a scene, refused and said she would be fine accompanied by Miss Jardine.

'Her father agreed that this was a capital idea, and Grace was ushered out of her pew towards the nearest door . . . here.' Henry used his cane to point to the area above our heads, not far from the entrance to the crypt. 'At this point Miss Jardine testifies that there was a change of plan. They decided it would be better not to attract the attention of the public outside. Instead, they chose to slip down into the crypt and use the back door so that Grace could collect herself, free from gawping onlookers. However, what Grace would not have known was that someone was already lying in wait down here. And I don't mean our friends the skeletons.'

'The Undertaker?' I surmised.

'Exactly.' My uncle indicated a paved ramp that led up to a set of large double doors. 'This allows real undertakers to bring their hearses in from the street. The kidnapper used it to get inside, then waited until Grace and her governess appeared. As soon as they descended the stairs, Miss Jardine claims she was attacked from behind. She was knocked unconscious and fell precisely here.' He tapped a spot on the flagstone floor with his cane.

'What happens next is a little hazy, since our only witness had passed out. But what we do know is that upstairs, at this exact moment, the young footman, Gabriel, asked Lord Davenport if he should go and check on Grace. His quick thinking, alas, was to prove a matter of seconds too late.'

'What happened?'

'If we are to extrapolate from what the footman saw, in the seconds after Miss Jardine was attacked, the kidnapper grabbed Lady Grace and dragged her to the waiting hearse. When Gabriel appeared at the bottom of the steps, he saw Grace being manhandled into the coffin. The Undertaker then leaped aboard and whipped his horses to flee the scene. Gabriel recalled that he had left a blunderbuss upstairs in case of any trouble. He raced up and sounded the alarm. As Lord Davenport and various members of the congregation rushed to help, young Gabriel gave chase.'

As I listened to all this, something was troubling me. 'It's weird, don't you think? The Undertaker waiting down here . . . How would he have known that Grace would come down?'

The thought clearly hadn't occurred to my uncle yet. 'Perhaps Grace was not his intended victim after all: he was waiting here for whoever he could seize. But let us now follow the route he took to escape the scene of our crime.'

We climbed the ramp and emerged into the alley. A sudden gust of icy air froze me to the marrow, but I set my face to the wind and hurried after my uncle.

Soon we were back in the narrow lane leading off Wych Street, where I had stumbled upon the Undertaker the night before.

'This, I believe, is where you pick up our story,' Henry announced. 'Perhaps you could describe it to me once more.'

'My carriage was heading up through here,' I said, pointing to the narrow street, 'when the hearse suddenly burst out. Gabriel appeared behind and fired after it.

The Undertaker turned in his seat and loosed off a shot from his flintlock.'

'This would be the ball that lodged itself in your unsuspecting cabbie's head.'

'Exactly. Except I don't think he meant to shoot him. His gun was jolted.'

'I see,' Henry said, contemplating. 'Then what?'

'I grabbed the reins and set off after him.'

'What was Gabriel doing at this point?'

'Looking pretty shocked that he wasn't dead, as I recall. I sent him off to summon Mr Welch before I made after the hearse.'

Suddenly Percy came bounding out of the shadows, his face white as a sheet.

'Good God, Persimmon, whatever brings you here?' Henry asked, startled.

I had to prop Percy up as he started to speak, gasping for breath.

'Slow down, man,' Henry urged him. 'You know you aren't supposed to run.' He turned to me to explain. 'Persimmon has a weak chest. The doctor has insisted he shouldn't take too much vigorous exercise.' Judging by the size of Percy's belly, he had clearly taken the advice, I thought.

At that point Percy retched, just missing my boots. I gave him my handkerchief to wipe his mouth, and he recovered sufficiently to explain his urgency.

'Begging your pardon, but Mr Welch expressly asked if you would meet him at the Goose and Grapes Tavern.'

'Did he say why?' my uncle demanded.

'He thinks someone's about to snatch a body, your honour. He thinks the crew behind it might know who the Undertaker is. Might even be in league with him.'

11

Less than half an hour later, our carriage entered the parish of Spitalfields. The area to the north was dotted with scrubby pastureland, but Spitalfields was a densely packed neighbourhood of homes belonging to Huguenot weavers. The Huguenots, Henry explained, were a group of Protestants who had fled persecution in France at the turn of the century. Famed throughout the world for their skill at weaving fine silks, they had set up their looms in the only part of London they could afford.

Suddenly our carriage crunched to a halt. We had arrived at the Goose and Grapes. Unlike the neighbouring houses, which were flat-fronted brick terraces with wooden shutters, the tavern looked like an old country inn. It straddled the corner of a junction where its occupants would have a clear view down each of the approaching roads. Its stooped wooden front was barrel-shaped, with small irregular window frames.

On the other side of the muddy lane squatted a rickety little hut. This, I discovered, was a watch house – the makeshift office of the night watchman or 'Charlie'.

'Let us see what we might wake up inside,' my uncle said with a wicked glint in his eye. He struck the door loudly with the end of his cane. There was a sudden rumpus inside and the box rocked from one side to the other.

'*Adzooks!* Who the deuce has come knocking at this ungodly hour?!' came a rasping voice from inside. Suddenly the little hatch at the front was flung open to reveal a toothless, grizzled old reptile. Seeing the chief magistrate directly in front of him, his rheumy eyes bulged like saucers.

'Mr Fielding, your *honourableness*,' he spluttered. 'Begging your pardon, sir, I had no idea it was your venerable self.'

'What, pray tell, is that distinct smell I can discern . . . ?' Henry asked with a wry smile. 'Would it be rum, by any chance?'

'That, m'lud? That would be something I just con-fiscated off some rowdy young coves,' the old Charlie said craftily.

'In that case you won't mind if I take it into my charge.'

Seeing he had no alternative, the old watchman reluctantly handed over his bottle.

'Come along now, Master Thomas,' Henry told me, squirrelling the rum away in his inside pocket and heading towards the warm glow of the inn.

As we were about to go inside, I heard a snort. For a moment I thought it was the old Charlie breaking wind, but then I looked up the alleyway leading round to the back of the tavern. In the moonlight I saw a cloud of hot breath in the freezing air.

'Uncle . . .' I whispered. He looked round and I pointed. Two horses were tied to a post. But it was what was behind them that made my blood run cold: a gleaming black hearse. It had the same large black plumes jutting from each corner that I had seen on the Undertaker's carriage. The same crimson curtains were drawn across the oval window on each side.

'It's identical to the one that took Grace,' I said breathlessly.

'A coincidence perhaps,' Henry murmured. 'This type of hearse is not uncommon.' One horse whinnied, unnerved by our presence. As it shook its head, the ornate metal decorations on its reins jingled. Instinctively I offered my hand for it to sniff.

'What should we do?' I asked my uncle.

'Go inside and see if we can find the driver.' He turned

to Percy, who was waiting timidly at the end of the alleyway. 'Wait here. Under no circumstances are you to let this hearse leave.'

'But it's freezing, your honour,' Percy protested, then looked like he wished he hadn't said anything. My uncle threw him the bottle of rum he had confiscated from the old watchman. 'Take a nip of this. It should warm you up.'

Inside, the pub was heaving.

At one end of the public room was a huge inglenook fireplace, large enough for a grown man to stand up in. In front of it, an assortment of important-looking dignitaries were sitting at a large trestle table.

In the middle was a tall gangly gentleman. His head was so narrow it looked like it had been squeezed in a vice that had made his eyes pop out with a wild, staring intensity.

'He's the chairman of the local parish council,' Henry whispered. 'He's also the supervisor of Lady Davenport's workhouse, and as slippery and self-interested as they come. All he cares about is getting re-elected and lining his purse.'

Nearby, at a separate table, sat his secretary. She had beady eyes and a neck so scrawny she looked like a vulture. Beside her, leaning against the fireplace, stood a short, stocky figure with a face like a boiled ham. He was wearing a full-length frock covered in ornate braiding, and clutched a huge mace that suggested he must be very high up in the order of things. In fact, he wasn't.

'That's the local beadle. He helps oversee the parish workhouse and likes nothing better than to make people believe he's important. In truth, he's a half-witted oaf.'

'And on the other side?' I asked. A third stooped figure sat hunched beside the chairman. Slight and bookish-looking, he wore a pair of wood-framed spectacles as he scratched away at some parchment with a quill. 'That is the coroner. It's his job to decide what the cause of death was.'

Death. I suddenly remembered why we were here. Squinting to see through the fog of smoke, I'd failed to spot the most prominent object in the room – an open coffin. Whoever was inside was obscured behind a post. I edged closer, peering over the heads of several people perched on a table in front of me. Inside lay the thin, ghostly figure of a lad of about fifteen. He had been dressed in what was clearly his Sunday best suit. It looked somehow out of place in the simple wooden box that was his final resting place.

'Can you see the kidnapper?' Henry hissed in my ear.

My eyes scanned the room for a glimpse of the culprit. 'No,' I whispered.

Henry nodded to a few empty seats at a table in the

corner. 'We can sit here and see out of the window in case anyone tries to make their escape.'

As I sat down, I noticed a figure leaning against one of the pillars, his face hidden by the shadows.

It was Welch. I slid along the bench to make room for his muscular frame, squeezing into the corner.

'One of my informants told me that a crew of resurrectionists may be planning to snatch the body this very night,' he informed us.

'That I would care to see,' Henry said with surprise. 'To steal the body from under the noses of the coroner and the family. Not to mention ourselves.'

But something was bothering me.

'What is it?' he asked, seeing my uncertainty.

'It's just . . . well, you said the Undertaker has only ever kidnapped people who are still alive. So why would he take a *dead* body?'

'Once we've caught him, we'll ask him,' Welch said snidely. 'Besides, it was your idea to listen to that Malarkey rogue.'

'Perhaps the Undertaker only kidnaps living people when he can't find someone who's already dead,' Henry suggested more helpfully. I didn't say it, but I couldn't help feeling that this was daft. Why would the Undertaker go to such lengths to snatch people who were still alive if he just wanted corpses?

'Who is the boy who died?' Henry asked, changing the subject.

'He was the local bricklayer's apprentice. That's the man he was apprenticed to.' Welch nodded towards a grizzled man in his fifties, squeezed into expensive breeches and overcoat. 'O'Callaghan. Originally from County Cork, Ireland. He claims that the boy was killed by accident when part of a wall collapsed on him.'

'Are the parents here?' my uncle asked, looking around.

'The boy's father is dead, but that's the mother and uncle up at the front.'

I saw a woman in a black bonnet and mourning clothes, silently weeping into a handkerchief as her brother consoled her. His eyes were red with tears as he listened to the parish chairman droning on at the front. Clearly the inquest into the boy's death was nearing its conclusion.

'It seems to me eminently clear from the facts laid before us,' the chairman announced, 'that this was a most tragic accident and that our esteemed local businessman Mr O'Callaghan can be absolved of all responsibility. In fact, he should be praised for his great care and diligence in the preservation of this young boy's life, which was so tragically cut short.'

At this, the boy's poor mother let out a gasp of grief.

The chairman looked aghast and hastily pressed on. 'Therefore I move to record a verdict of accidental death ...' He paused, remembering himself quickly. 'That is, if his majesty's coroner agrees.' The coroner nodded awkwardly, shuffling in his seat. 'Good,' the chairman declared, satisfied. 'Then I see no further obstacle to allowing the body to be given back into the custody of his family so that he may be buried at a place of their choosing.' With that, I saw him share a private nod with Mr O'Callaghan, who gave a relieved smile.

'Ask me, the whole thing's a complete sham,' Welch grunted. 'O'Callaghan has probably paid the chairman off.'

'That's not important now,' Henry insisted. 'What is important is what happens to that body.'

As the inquest began to break up, the boy's uncle tried to comfort the mother. At the same time the beadle nodded towards the corner, where a figure emerged from behind a curtained-off area.

My heart lurched as I saw him. He was wearing an almost identical outfit to the kidnapper. A tall, crooked hat shaped like a chimney pot was perched on his head, while his face was obscured by the high collars of a long black funeral director's coat.

'Is it *him*?' my uncle pressed me impatiently. I craned to get a view of the undertaker's face. With all the comings and goings it was impossible to see him clearly, but one thing was certain – he wasn't wearing the Undertaker's trademark crow mask.

Welch was on his feet, ready for action.

'Wait!' my uncle instructed. 'We need to catch him in the act. We need proof.'

I watched the undertaker approach the coffin and produce a hammer, ready to nail down the lid. Before he could do so, the boy's uncle whispered something to him and he stepped back to allow the mother to say goodbye. She reached into the coffin and stroked her son's hair, then turned and buried her face in her brother's chest. He nodded to the undertaker, who stepped forward and began to nail the coffin shut as the uncle led the distraught mother outside to the waiting hearse.

After hammering down the last nail, the undertaker nodded to three assistants. They lifted the box onto their shoulders and began to carry it out to the hearse.

'We must act now!' Welch protested.

As gingerly as we could, we slipped out of the side door. Outside, we lurked in the shadows, watching as the coffin was loaded onto the hearse. I saw Percy hiding behind the wall at the end of the alleyway, desperately trying to keep himself warm. The freezing air must have been playing havoc with his chest, and I could see him trying to stifle his wheezes.

Beside him was the stooped figure of the night watchman, suddenly more sober. Surely if the hearse took flight now, there would be little, if anything, two such sickly specimens could do to stop it . . .

Still, we waited for a sign – evidence that the undertaker was Grace's kidnapper.

The dead boy's uncle passed him a note – probably directions for where to take the body. Meanwhile I noticed that the mother had dropped her handkerchief. As she stooped to pick it up, something suddenly caught my eye. It was only a glimpse, but I was certain I'd seen a tattoo on her hand.

My mind immediately started to race. Why would the mother of a bricklayer's apprentice have a *tattoo*? Could it be the same one as Malarkey's? A hundred different thoughts crowded through my mind at once.

'Uncle . . .' I stuttered, tugging at his arm.

'Not now,' he hissed back.

'But the woman . . . I think she's a *man*!'

For a moment my uncle was speechless as he tried to understand what I'd told him; then he turned calmly to Welch. 'Arrest them immediately!'

Welch looked thrown. 'Even the *mother*?'

'Especially the mother!'

Without another word, Welch pulled out a double-barrelled flintlock and stepped into the alleyway.

'Take one more step and you'll be needing a coffin of your own!' he boomed. Immediately the undertaker, the uncle and the boy's mother looked up in shock.

'What is the meaning of this?' the uncle cried.

'I am arresting you on the charge of abducting a corpse,' Welch declared. 'Percy, secure these people.'

Percy looked astounded, his mouth hanging slack.

'Now!' Welch growled, and Percy shuffled down the alleyway, producing a pair of handcuffs.

'I told you they was acting suspicious,' the old watchman croaked. 'Soon as I saw them.'

'Silence, you dog!' Welch roared, and the old man shrank back inside his overcoat.

'I don't know who you think you've come to arrest,' the uncle began, 'but surely you would not detain a poor grieving mother.'

With that I stepped forward and snatched the bonnet off the mother's head. There, plain for all to see in the light of Welch's flaming torch, stood a young ferrety-looking lad. For a second I saw his eyes widen as he thought about running. Then he felt the cold steel of the flintlock press against his temple and he had a change of heart.

12

'I swear to you, Mr Welch, on my mother's life—'

'You never knew your mother, you lice-ridden dunder-head!' Welch spat. The boy winced as Welch's spittle landed on his face. His bonnet had been removed, but he was still wearing a dress and overcoat.

'Why is Saunders attacking that woman?' Esther asked as she joined me in the corridor. We were in the back of the courthouse, directly above the holding cells. The stench from the cesspit was suffocating.

'It's not a woman,' I explained. 'His name's William Smirke. He's a grave robber.'

Esther eyed the culprit, intrigued. 'She's a *he*?'

'*She* was in disguise.'

'And my father thinks that's the Undertaker?' Esther asked dubiously.

I shook my head. 'Maybe he works with him. If he

157

knows who he is, he might be able to lead us to him.' I looked down and saw that Esther had been carrying a bucket. 'What's that for?'

'Ask Lady Cynthia Allbright,' she replied, her eyes narrowing. 'Her horrid little dog relieved itself on the back stairs.'

I tried to suppress a smirk.

'It's not funny. It took me half an hour to scrub it clean. Why I bothered when the place stinks so much!'

Inside the interrogation room, Smirke was still protesting his innocence.

'Please, Mr Welch, sir, you have to believe me. I admit we were going to prig the thing.'

The *thing*. I realized that this was a quaint euphemism for a dead body.

'But we would never have taken this girl, Lady Bobs-your-uncle,' the whelp continued. 'We ain't murderers!'

If the lad was acting, he was good at it: he looked horrified at the idea.

'So where were you taking this body then?' Welch demanded.

'To Sir Montagu Gibbons's dissecting house in Poland Street, sir.'

At the mention of this name, Henry's face went white. Sir Montagu, I would soon discover, was Lord Davenport's personal physician. He was also one of London's most celebrated surgeons and ran his own dissecting school. Up to three hundred medical students a year passed through his establishment, learning the finer points of anatomy.

'You can imagine,' my uncle told me later, shuddering, 'just how many corpses are required there.'

Back in the interrogation room, his eyes searched Smirke's suspiciously. 'Did Sir Montagu ask you to bring him a dead body?'

'He never asks, your honour. He gets one of his porters to leave a basket outside the school. It's like a secret sign. We dump the dead body in it, then the porter pays us.'

'How much?' Henry asked, appalled.

'Depends on how fresh the body is. The more recently deceased, the more money they give us. Trouble is, there ain't enough bodies to meet the demand.'

'All the more reason for you to kill someone,' Welch said accusingly. 'Like Lady Grace Davenport.'

'No, I swear we would never do such a thing. But there are rumours . . .' The boy fell silent, looking like he had said more than he should have.

'What kind of rumours?' Henry asked.

Smirke seemed reluctant to say more, till Welch began to apply pressure to the manacle around his ankle.

'All right, all right! I heard there was a surgeon willing

159

to pay more if he could be given a thing that wasn't dead yet. So it was fresher.'

'Who?' Henry demanded. 'You mean Sir Montagu?'

Smirke looked genuinely unsure. Welch pressed even harder on his manacles. 'Give us his name!'

'I don't know, Mr Welch, I swear,' Smirke pleaded. 'Like I said, it was only a rumour. But if you can find *him*, maybe you'll find the real Undertaker.'

'Keep hold of Smirke and his accomplice till we can be sure that what he's telling us is the truth,' Henry ordered. 'I myself will pay Sir Montagu a visit tomorrow.'

Squibb, the ancient orderly, hobbled back down to the cell while Henry eased his aching foot onto a stool in his study. The evening's excitements were wreaking havoc with his gout.

'You can't really think that Sir Montagu Gibbons is buying *live* victims . . .' Welch said in disbelief. 'He's Lord Davenport's own physician.'

'It could be one of the junior doctors in his school,' I suggested. 'Maybe one of them is paying the Undertaker to bring him fresh victims to dissect.'

'Do you realize what you're suggesting?' Welch said gruffly. 'Every one of those young men comes from a powerful, moneyed family. You start throwing around accusations like that, you'll have us shut down by dawn.'

'What about the undertaker we arrested at the coroner's inquest?' Henry asked. 'Do we know *he* isn't the fiend?'

'I checked out his credentials, your honour,' Percy put in. 'He's genuine. He had the paperwork to prove that the hearse is his.'

'More to the point, he has an alibi for the time when Lady Grace was taken,' Welch went on. 'Unsurprisingly he was at a funeral. In Cheapside, to be precise.'

'So we are no better off than yesterday,' Henry sighed despondently.

'Begging your pardon, Uncle,' I interjected. 'Can I suggest that you *don't* visit Sir Montagu Gibbons tomorrow.'

Henry looked at me, bemused. 'Why ever not?'

'Even if Sir Montagu knows where these dead bodies come from, he'll never admit it to you. But he might to *me*.'

'To *you*?' Welch nearly choked on the words.

'And why, pray, would that be?' Henry asked.

'Because I plan to go in disguise,' I replied coolly.

'Disguised as what?'

'A resurrectionist. I'll tell them I may be able to get hold of a live body and see if they're interested.'

'If anyone is going to ask him, it should be us!' Welch said, outraged.

'Wait,' Henry said. 'The boy makes a good point. We

can't just accuse Lord Davenport's personal physician without proof. If he's been procuring kidnap victims from this felon, we need evidence.'

So against Welch's better judgement, it was decided that the following morning I would approach Sir Montagu Gibbons's anatomy school and make my enquiries.

It had been a long and arduous day so I decided to get some rest before my early start. As I stepped out of my uncle's study, he appeared behind me.

'Here . . .' he said, flipping open a catch on the tip of his walking cane. Inside there was a secret compartment full of a sweet, fruity liquor. 'A few drops of my finest brandy should fortify you for tomorrow. I keep it in here so Esther won't confiscate it,' he added with a wink.

I was going to tell him that I didn't touch alcohol – my father had always been very stern about its ill effects – but I decided to accept the gift just this once.

'Thank you,' I said and took a swig. Henry joined me in a draught before snapping the lid shut again. I was turning to head up the crooked steps to bed when he put his hand on my arm.

'You serve your father's memory well. He would be very proud.' He smiled, then shuffled back into his study, dragging his bandaged foot.

For a moment I let his words hang in the air. I had rarely talked about my father's death. Thinking about it made my heart ache too much. As I felt tears threaten to betray me, I hurried upstairs.

A little while later there was a light rap on the door.

'Come in.' My voice echoed in the cold, sparsely furnished room. The door eased open to reveal Esther standing there with a basin of water and a towel.

'Papa asked me to come and see to your hand. He said it was hurting from the cold.' She glanced towards my iron fist.

'It's nothing,' I said, suddenly self-conscious. I was proud of my father's cunning invention, but I would never let anyone see what it concealed. It felt ugly and shameful.

I shuffled slightly and winced from where my leather boot was still chafing my ankle. Esther immediately noticed.

'You've hurt your ankle, too?' Before I could answer, she was laying out a towel and bandages.

'Show me.' It was more of an order than a statement.

As I pulled off my boot, I saw that my stockings were caked with dried blood from the wound caused by the manacles.

Esther gave a gasp. 'You do realize that this could become infected. Here . . .' She began to carefully peel away the stocking. I tried not to show the pain, but it was impossible not to flinch.

'It's still got rust in it. That animal, Welch,' she cursed.

As she continued to bathe my foot, I watched a curl of her biscuit-coloured hair fall across her eyes. She tucked it back behind her ear, only to catch me studying her. I hastily pretended to be fiddling with the wires of my metal hand. I did that when I felt awkward.

'Papa tells me you were born here – before you left for Virginia,' she said presently. 'He said that your father died during a robbery.'

'A man called Clay Snipeman held up the store we were shopping in.'

'He shot your father?'

I shook my head. 'He pointed a pistol at him and Papa keeled over. They said his heart gave out.'

'I'm so sorry.' All Esther's brittleness was gone. Instead I saw that her soft amber eyes were glistening with tears.

'Afterwards, I just sat there on the floor. I did nothing,' I continued.

'And you blame yourself?'

'I should have gone after the man. Done *something*, at least.'

'But you stayed with your father. Surely he would have wanted that.'

'I stayed with him because I was frightened,' I said, ashamed of my cowardice that day.

'You were a boy . . . he was armed.'

'I still should have done something,' I replied hotly. '*He* would have done something.'

After a moment she nodded towards my iron hand. 'Did he make that?'

'Straight after I lost it.'

'How did it happen?' She quickly checked herself. 'Sorry, I'm being too nosy – I've been told it's one of my many vices.'

'When I was six, I was playing in my father's workshop. I was trying to make a sword, but when I put it under the metal press . . .' My voice trailed off as I recalled the moment.

'It must be very . . . practical,' she said uncertainly.

'He made loads of attachments. Look . . .' I reached into my trunk and retrieved various tools. 'There's a knife for eating, a screwdriver that clips on . . . even a corkscrew.'

'All you need is an attachment for a pistol and you'd have everything.'

'Before my father died, I never thought I'd need one,' I said darkly.

Esther looked solemn again. 'Did they ever find the man who killed him?'

'They found him hanged near his logging cabin.'

She shuddered and I decided to change the subject.

'The etching in your room – it's your mother, isn't it?'

'So you *were* snooping?' She narrowed her eyes at me teasingly. 'My father drew it just after they'd fallen in love.'

'How did they meet?'

'She was a slave on a plantation owned by my father's uncle. Papa set about trying to free her, but that didn't go down very well.' She pulled a face. 'My great-uncle was a brute of a man. Not long after this my mother fell pregnant with me. You have to remember, she was his property, so any child of hers would be his property too.'

'You would have been a slave?' I asked, shocked. 'What did your father do?'

'He saved up every penny he could until he was able to buy my mother. Then he left the plantation and came back to London.'

'What happened then?'

'Papa was a gentleman; she was a black ex-slave. You can imagine the scandal it caused. But apparently my father didn't care. In fact, I think he thrived on it. The thing you have to understand about him is that he hates the establishment; he hates being told what to do by anyone.' She arched an eyebrow wryly. 'A bit like me.' Then her face clouded. 'It's why he makes so many enemies.' For a moment she looked care-worn, older than her years, till she remembered herself and carried on tending to my foot.

'The trouble was, buying my mother had cost him every penny he had. He tried to make money from writing, but he was poking fun at too many people in high places. In the end, the Prime Minister shut down the theatres just to silence him.' Her brow furrowed. 'That was when things started to go wrong. He fell into debt. Then, when I was born . . .'

'Your mother died,' I said, finishing her sentence.

She nodded. 'The rest you know.' She sighed heavily. 'So, it would seem we have both lost a parent.'

'And we have both left the Colonies for a new start in London.'

We shared a smile, surprised to discover that we weren't so different after all. In fact, there was a very real danger that we might even become friends.

13

Before dawn I was up and dressed in the foulest clothes I had ever come across. They had been borrowed from Smirke and stank of sweat and gin. There was something else too: I couldn't place it at first, but then I recognized the smell of death.

I slipped silently out of the courthouse and made my way through the deserted streets to the corner of Golden Square. Here I perched, shivering, under the canopy of a shopfront that advertised itself as AUBREY CROUCH; RAG, FAT AND BONE MERCHANT; PURVEYOR OF CANDLES AND SOAP. I wondered grimly whether the fat was connected to the trade in corpses. A cart was wheeled past bearing the words CLOMPEY DOGGERILL, CHIMNEY SWEEP AND CARPET BEATER. Trotting along behind was the sweep's sooty-faced assistant, a boy no older than six.

I turned my attention back across the road to Sir

Montagu Gibbons's anatomy school and rubbed my arms vigorously to warm myself up. There was still no sign of a basket in the side alley – the signal that I could approach the porter.

'Mary and Joseph! You don't half pong!' came a sudden voice in my ear.

I spun round to find Malarkey smirking at me. 'What are you doing here?' I asked, startled.

'You thought you'd seen the last of me?' He pretended to be offended. 'I told you, old Malarkey never goes back on his word, Iron Hand.'

'*Iron Hand?*'

'That's what I'm going to call you from now on, seeing as we're going to be spending a bit of time together. What do you think, Saunders?' His weasel poked his snout out of an inside pocket and squeaked approvingly.

I wasn't sure if I should be offended or flattered by my new nickname – though it did have a certain ring to it.

Malarkey glanced across the road at the anatomy school. 'I see my tip-off about the resurrectionists was on the money.'

'That depends on what I find in there,' I sniffed. 'But for your sake, I hope you're right. I can always tell my uncle I've changed my mind about letting you off.'

For a moment Malarkey looked a little unnerved; then

his face brightened. 'About that nag of your uncle's – *Archi*-whatsit . . .'

'*Medes*.'

'That's the fella.'

'You've found him?'

'Not *found* as such. But I might have a lead.'

I gulped, fearing the worst. 'He hasn't been sold for horsemeat?'

'Get away! He's far too valuable for that. They usually wait until they're near dead from starvation and disease before they turn them into pies.' As my empty stomach began to turn at the thought of this, something behind me caught Malarkey's eye.

'That what you've been waiting for?'

I spun round to discover a large wicker basket had appeared in the side passageway while we had been talking.

Considering the school occupied such a grand double-fronted house, the side door was surprisingly mean. Malarkey and I slipped across the road and I lightly tapped on it.

At first there was no answer, so I knocked more loudly. Still no one came. I was about to try round the front when Malarkey opened his jacket and revealed a range of tools – everything from screwdrivers to tweezers to hairpins. He slid out a long thin scalpel with a deadly-looking blade.

'Out you come, my little beauty.' He gave me an approving wink. 'This should do the trick.'

He carefully slid it between the doorjamb and the lock, and after some careful fiddling the door clicked open. Saunders, the weasel, popped his whiskery snout out again and sniffed expectantly.

'Best you stay out of harm's way,' Malarkey said, encouraging him back inside. 'After you,' he added, turning to me with a satisfied smile.

As the door eased open, my first impression was of hot, humid air. My second was of darkness. As I put a hand to the wall to guide myself, I found that it was wet with condensation.

I edged along the corridor until I made out a light under a doorway. A faint bubbling noise was coming from just the other side. I sniffed. Something smelled horribly familiar. At first I couldn't place it; then it hit me. It was the same stench I'd come across in the abattoir at Smithfield market.

'Reckon someone's having a bath in there?' Malarkey whispered.

'Somebody or *something*.'

I pushed the door open gingerly and saw that the room was white and low-ceilinged, with old flagstones on the floor, grooved by years of use. A window faced out onto the pavement above, but the glass had been boarded up to stop anyone seeing out. Or to stop anyone seeing *in* . . .

Stacked against the brickwork were more wicker baskets – but more important was what lay in the centre of the room: several huge copper bathtubs. A fire underneath kept the liquid inside bubbling furiously.

Malarkey gave me a nudge, and I stepped closer. Peering down, I saw a fatty froth on the surface of the water, obscuring whatever was boiling away. On the floor, a mound of old rags and clothes lay discarded in a pile.

'It's only some oul fella's drawers being washed,' Malarkey said, visibly relieved.

Suddenly I heard footsteps accompanied by a dull thumping noise. Whoever was approaching was seconds from entering the room.

'In here,' I said, lifting the lid of one of the baskets and clambering inside. Malarkey climbed into another and we closed the lids with seconds to spare.

Through the wickerwork I could just make out a blurred image of the door. It swung open and a tall, spindly figure entered the room. It was all I could do to stop myself gasping out loud, for whoever was standing there was wearing a skeletal white mask. I held my breath and peered through the basket's tiny holes. Was it the mask the Undertaker had worn? It was impossible to be sure.

For a moment the figure stood completely still, examining the room. My heart began to pound against the inside of my chest. Did he suspect that we were there? If he did, he seemed to dismiss the thought. He stepped briefly outside before reappearing, dragging something behind him. Was it just a sack of old clothing? I wondered.

As I watched, I already suspected the answer.

The figure began to yank on the end of the sack, and something heavy dropped out onto the floor with a dull thump.

It was the body of a young woman.

I struggled not to retch. Was I witnessing this vile creature disposing of *Lady Grace's* body? I was about to burst out of the basket and confront him when he suddenly paused. He seemed to change his mind and left the room abruptly. Moments later I heard his footsteps head back up the stairs.

'*Iron Hand?*' came a whisper from the next basket. 'Did you see what I just saw?'

Without wasting another moment, I threw the lid of the basket back and clambered out. Malarkey did the same.

'Is it *her?*' he whispered. 'The *toff's* daughter?'

Hardly daring to look, I approached the body lying on the floor. The young woman's face was partly hidden by the sack she had been carried in, but I could tell immediately that something didn't add up. Whoever she was, she was wearing filthy grey rags and looked gaunt and emaciated.

'This isn't Lady Grace,' I muttered as I pulled the sack away. From the painting in Lord Davenport's library, I remembered that she had a pretty, rounded face with delicate, rose-petal skin – the skin of someone from a genteel background. The poor woman I was now looking at was old and haggard, her face scarred from disease and malnutrition.

'Who do you reckon she is?' Malarkey asked.

'She must be another of his victims.' I laid the sack back over her face.

'Ask me, he was going to stick her in here . . .' Malarkey grabbed a large wooden spoon that was hanging beside the copper vat and scraped some of the scum off the surface of the water. The instant he did so, we both sprang back in horror.

An eyeball was staring back at us. There was another body lying under the murky water!

At the same moment the door swung open and the masked figure burst back in – only this time he was levelling a flintlock pistol directly at my head.

'Who are you?' came his high-pitched voice.

For a moment neither of us could say a thing. We were both too shocked.

I suddenly realized that the figure wasn't wearing a mask after all. It was his own gaunt, skeletal face that was white. As white, in fact, as a ghost. But more surprising than this was the colour of his eyes.

They were red. And they were staring straight at me.

'I said, *who are you?*' His voice was strangely nasal and shrill.

Before I could find the words to explain, Malarkey's weasel clambered out of his pocket and leaped towards the man's face, scratching his cheeks. He staggered backwards, screeching in pain. Quick as a flash, Malarkey twisted his arm and disarmed him in one clean and well-practised move.

Suddenly the tables had been turned, and it was we who had the gun, now trained on the man with the red eyes . . .

14

'*What in God's name do you think you are doing?*'

The exclamation came from an astonished-looking gentleman in a fine silk waistcoat. Enormous silver side-burns sprouted from either side of his face, making him look uncommonly like a badger. He was poised, scalpel in hand, over a dissecting table.

Lying on the bench in front of him was a body – only it had had all the flesh peeled back to reveal a mass of muscle and sinew. Its teeth grinned eerily at the ceiling. Gathered around the table were about ten young men, all wearing fine waistcoats covered with blood-stained aprons.

Malarkey and I had frogmarched the ghostly figure with the red eyes up the stairs and had emerged straight into the main dissecting room.

'I asked you a question, you scoundrel!' the man

said in rich, superior tones.

'I am acting on behalf of the chief magistrate, Henry Fielding,' I announced importantly. 'And I am arresting this . . . *creature* for the kidnap of Lady Grace Davenport and others.'

The badger gentleman snorted with derision. 'I knew Fielding employed some dubious fellows, but even he would stop short of employing a pair of *blackguards* like you. Yates, seize these two immediately.'

A young assistant took a step forward, but Malarkey immediately trained the pistol on him. 'I wouldn't do that if I was you,' he said calmly. 'My finger might just slip. Then you'd have one more body to dissect.' The weasel squeaked his own threat at him.

'You do realize I could see you hanged for this!' the surgeon blustered.

'I think that is unlikely,' said a voice I knew instantly.

I spun round to see that Henry himself, the real Saunders Welch at his side, had entered the room.

'Mr Fielding, please have these two ruffians arrested immediately.'

'On what charge?' Henry enquired.

'For holding my porter at gunpoint for a start. For breaking and entering; and for passing themselves off as officers of the law.'

'I'm afraid I can't do that, Sir Montagu,' my uncle

replied almost apologetically. 'You see, my nephew is telling the truth.'

'Your *nephew*?'

'I'm sure he has arrested this man on good grounds,' Henry continued, turning to me hopefully. 'Thomas, perhaps you'd be so good as to enlighten us.'

Taking centre stage, I cleared my throat and pulled myself up to my full height. 'I have reason to believe that this is the . . . *person*,' I began, nodding towards my prisoner, 'who abducted Lady Grace Davenport. We found him boiling up the bodies downstairs.'

'He's right,' Malarkey chipped in. 'He's the vampyre, all right. Just look at the eyes on him.'

'Well, Sir Montagu?' Henry turned to the surgeon for some sort of explanation.

'This poor man is no vampyre, as you call it,' he fumed. 'His eyes are like that because he has a condition called albinism. It's a defect of his skin that means he doesn't have the usual pigment. As for kidnapping Lord Davenport's daughter, it's not only absurd, it's impossible. He was working with me.'

'What about the body downstairs?' I protested.

'It is customary to boil the flesh from the bones after we've finished dissecting. It's the only way to stop them rotting.'

Suddenly I began to feel the ground underneath me was a little less solid.

'I think you'd better give me that,' Welch said gruffly, holding out his hand to Malarkey. I nodded and he reluctantly handed over the flintlock.

Soon we were all standing in Sir Montagu Gibbons's private study. The room was considerably taller than it was wide, with dark mahogany bookshelves reaching up to an ornately carved ceiling. The top shelves were so high they could only be reached with the aid of a ladder attached to rails running round the edge. By now the sun had come up and was streaking in through a blind that partly obscured the window onto the street. On the other side of the room, behind the vast walnut desk bureau, stood a locked cabinet. This, it transpired, contained a vast selection of medicines and preservatives in a series of miniature glass bottles.

As we entered the room, my uncle had found himself entangled with a potted plant in the corner.

'*Chlorophytum comosum*,' Sir Montagu announced crisply.

'More commonly known as the spider plant,' Henry replied.

'Bravo, Mr Fielding. You clearly know your Latin terms. I wonder, though, did you know that as well as being extraordinarily ugly, they're remarkably useful for filtering bad odours. I find it helps to counteract the smell from the bodies.'

'We should keep one down in our cells,' Henry observed drily.

Meanwhile Welch was growing impatient with the idle banter. 'Sir Montagu, you said that you could vouch for the movements the day before yesterday of that *thing* outside?'

Following my outburst in the dissecting suite, the ghostly porter had been kept outside in the hall. Malarkey was waiting with him in disgrace.

'His name is Gregor,' Sir Montagu replied evenly. 'And yes, I was with him here the whole time.'

'*Gregor?*' my uncle asked, intrigued. 'Is that Russian?'

'East European. I came across him on a little fact-finding mission some years ago. The poor wretch had been shunned by the rest of his village because of his rare condition. You have to understand, superstition is very strong in those parts.'

'As it seems to be here,' my uncle added.

'His parents pleaded with me to bring him back.'

'To cure him?'

'In the hope that he would have a better life. He's a fascinating specimen. And most diligent about his work.' Sir Montagu sat back in his leather armchair and steepled his fingers under his chin. 'Now perhaps I may be permitted to ask a question of my own?'

'Please, feel free,' Henry replied courteously.

The surgeon glanced over at me. 'Why would this young' – he looked uncertain of quite the right word – '*gentleman* choose to break into my anatomy school?'

'Forgive me, Sir Montagu,' Henry began. 'We were given some information that led us to believe someone from this establishment had been looking to acquire . . . how shall I put it?' This time it was his turn to struggle for the word. 'A *fresher* corpse.'

If Sir Montagu was taken aback by this accusation, he took it in his stride.

'Mr Fielding, I don't think I need tell you that our work here is vital if we are to find cures for the diseases that afflict mankind. Finding cadavers to teach our students is essential to their training. The fresher the better.'

'Does that include someone who *isn't* dead?' The words had sprung out of my mouth before I could stop them.

Sir Montagu stared at me, more bemused than offended. 'Dear boy, I think your imagination has entirely run away with you.'

'So you never use the services of *resurrectionists*?' Welch asked bluntly.

The physician sighed deeply and pushed his chair back before heading to the door. He picked up a small china jug and carefully watered his spider plant.

'I am aware of the unscrupulous reputation some of

our fellow anatomy schools have acquired for the services of *resurrectionists*, as you call them. In truth, there are not nearly enough bodies to supply demand. Perhaps if our judges were a little more stringent in imposing the death sentence . . .' he added with a smooth smile that showed his teeth. It was clearly intended as a subtle dig at my uncle. 'Nonetheless I will admit that we take these . . . *gentlemen* who supply us a little too much at their word. But I can assure you most forcibly that we would never condone the taking of a life. That, of course, would be murder.' His eyes flashed with anger as he glared at me.

'So why would our two informants tell us otherwise?' Welch demanded.

'Because, by their very nature, grave robbers are the lowest of the low. Almost an entire sub-species, in fact. You can sometimes tell just by the shape of their heads, you know. They would say anything if it got them out of a tight corner. I myself would gladly have nothing to do with them,' he said haughtily, 'but, alas, they are a necessary evil.'

'So the bodies downstairs . . . how did you come by them?' I asked.

'Twin sisters from the Clerkenwell Institute for the Suppression of Moral Turpitude, if you had paused for a second to ask.'

'The *Turpy*?' I said, taken aback.

'I believe that is the vulgar name for it, yes.' Sir Montagu turned towards my uncle. 'As you may know, Lord Davenport's wife is on the board of governors. We have an agreement whereby the bodies of deceased inmates are turned over to us. For a fee, naturally.'

Welch gave a snort of derision. 'Must be rather difficult for them to spend their fee once they're dead.'

'I beg your pardon?'

Henry held up his hand to placate the surgeon. 'We have taken up more than enough of your time, Sir Montagu.' He pushed back his chair and hauled himself to his feet. 'We will of course still need to interrogate Gregor to confirm his alibi.'

'Good God, man! Is my word as a gentleman not enough?'

'If we took every gentleman at his word, there'd be even fewer hangings,' Henry replied drily. 'Naturally, if Gregor's alibi is corroborated, we will release him without charge.'

'Please,' Sir Montagu entreated, his tone softening. 'Gregor is vulnerable. He barely steps outside these doors. If people suspect him . . . well, you know what the mob can be like . . .'

'You have my word,' Henry assured him. 'No harm will come to him.'

As he turned to leave, he gave a wince of pain. Sir

Montagu immediately glanced down at his bandaged foot. 'Gout, I assume?'

'The cross I have to bear,' Henry replied ruefully.

'Perhaps this will help.' The physician unlocked the medicine cabinet behind his desk and took out one of the glass bottles. 'Laudanum. Extracted from the latex of the poppy plant.'

'*Opium*.'

'You'd be astonished at its properties. A few drops at night with your brandy should help you get a good night's sleep. But be careful,' Sir Montagu warned. 'Too much will render you fit for nothing. You'll be like the walking dead. The Chinese are addicted to the stuff, I gather.'

As he handed over the tiny bottle, I started with surprise. 'Uncle, the bottle . . .'

'What about it?' he asked, before suddenly peering at it and making the connection.

'Is there a problem?' Sir Montagu enquired.

'Only that we found a bottle exactly like this one in Lady Grace's bedchamber,' Henry explained.

Sir Montagu let out a snort. 'I very much doubt that.'

'You mean you *didn't* prescribe it for her?' Henry asked, confused.

'I think I would remember if I had. And seeing as I was her physician, no one else could have done either.'

'*Am* her physician,' Henry corrected. Sir Montagu

looked at him, baffled. 'You said *was*, as if she were already dead.'

'Of course,' he blustered awkwardly.

My uncle thanked him once more for his time and we were shown to the door. Outside, my worst fears were confirmed. Malarkey had fled the scene, no doubt to avoid the wrath of Welch for leading us on a fool's errand.

'Young man.' I spun round to find that Sir Montagu was addressing me. 'If you're so keen to attend one of our dissections, please feel free to come back and I will be only too happy to let you sit in. But perhaps not in disguise next time.' He smiled – a little too smugly for my liking – and disappeared back into his study.

Moments later, Gregor was bundled out of the basement door, his head covered by Welch's overcoat to avoid the glances of any curious passers-by. As I waited to speak to my uncle, I noticed that another wagon had pulled up next to Henry's carriage. It was an old delivery cart drawn by two black ponies. A short, effeminate-looking youth with elegant features and a sweep of lank, raven-black hair was unloading large glass jars of clear liquid. I quickly surmised that this must be alcohol for preserving the bodies in the anatomy school, as well as various other medicines.

Welch returned from the carriage, his face puce with

anger. 'Now perhaps you'll believe me about that rodent Malarkey!'

'I'm sorry,' I said weakly to my uncle as he hobbled down to join me. 'When I saw Gregor's face . . . the bodies . . .'

Henry took a deep breath and smiled philosophically. 'The fault is more mine than yours. Had I stopped for a moment, I would have realized that Sir Montagu's point is a powerful one. Even if he were in the business of buying bodies from a murderer, he would hardly have colluded in the kidnap of Grace, his own patient, not to mention the daughter of a close friend.'

'More to the point,' Welch seethed, 'Sir Montagu has given Gregor a cast-iron alibi. He's insisting he was with him on the night Grace was abducted.'

'Until we have evidence to the contrary,' Henry concluded, 'we have nothing to go on. As for the bodies of the two unfortunate twins, it appears that they were bought and signed for, with Lady Davenport's own blessing.'

I felt my shoulders slump in defeat. My father had always warned me that I needed to think first, act later. And now, yet again, I had made things infinitely worse.

15

'What do you expect, you foolish boy? You should know better than to wear yellow breeches! Coco *detests* yellow!'

The shrill exclamation came from a tall, imperious-looking woman with an absurd blue wig piled up on top of her head and a large 'beauty' mark on her cheek.

Lady Cynthia Allbright had returned in all her splendour to discuss Esther's position as companion to her daughter. It was her snappy little dog that had fouled the back stairs the day before. Lady Cynthia was now occupying the entire hallway, her nostrils flared like trumpets as she blocked our entrance.

Dressed in the finest silks from the looms of the Huguenot weavers in Spitalfields, she looked like a vast blue wedding cake as she fanned her powdered cheeks in irritation. Meanwhile her absurd French pug, Coco, had its jaws firmly clamped onto the bottom of Percy's breeches. He spun round to shake it off, causing the dog to leave the ground, its eyes out on stalks. Lady Cynthia's plump nine-year-old daughter, Cassandra, promptly opened her mouth and let out a continuous ear-shattering note.

Immediately Lady Cynthia began to swat Percy furiously with her fan. 'Desist, you wretched creature!'

Poor Percy was forced to fend off her blows while simultaneously trying to shake the snarling pug off his leg. The horrid little dog once again relieved itself all over the floor, whereupon Percy slipped and fell flat on his backside in the putrid yellow liquid.

As the creature continued to tear at Percy's trousers, Esther gave it a well-aimed boot up the backside. The dog yelped and scampered between Henry's approaching legs, straight out into the street and very nearly under a passing carriage.

'*Coco!*' Lady Cynthia wailed in alarm. She spun round to glare at Esther – 'How dare you assault him!' – then turned to unleash her fury on Henry. 'To think I was trying to do your daughter a service by elevating her position in society! But I can see that she is nothing short of a savage! You will be hearing from my lawyers. Good day, sir!'

She grabbed her daughter's arm, stuck her chin in the air, and stalked out of the door with as much dignity as she could muster. But seeing as her vast hooped dress filled the entire doorway, this was no easy matter. We were forced to plaster ourselves against the wall until she finally wrestled her way between us, catapulting herself out onto the street.

At last my ears stopped ringing from the commotion and her odious daughter's squeal. Percy, meanwhile, had managed to clamber up out of the puddle of dog wee and was sniffing at the damp patch on his breeches.

'Well,' Henry sighed, turning to Esther, 'I think we can safely say that you won't be going to work for Lady Cynthia any time soon. In which case, I think I will take a well-earned forty winks.'

'That may be difficult, Papa,' Esther said gravely. 'The Home Secretary is waiting for you upstairs.'

Henry went grey. 'Sir Montagu must have contacted him sooner than I thought.'

He passed Esther his walking cane and cloak and began to mount the staircase to his study, looking more like a condemned man climbing the scaffold than the magistrate who had sent him there. To make matters worse, his face contorted with pain each time he stepped on his bandaged foot. He paused halfway and turned to his daughter. 'Perhaps if you could bring me a hot posset, my dear . . . ?'

'You know wine will only make your foot worse, Papa.'

Henry smiled weakly. 'Just the spiced milk then.' With that, he began to clamber up the stairs again.

I saw Welch lead Gregor through the felons' entrance and down the back stairs. But as I made to follow them, he suddenly turned to block my path. 'Where do you think you're going?' he asked brusquely.

'To question Gregor, of course.'

He took a step closer, his slate-grey eyes drilling into me. 'I think you've *helped* quite enough today, don't you?' He then turned his back and disappeared into the interrogation room.

I thought about going after him – telling him that Malarkey was getting closer to finding Archimedes. But then I realized I only had Malarkey's word on that, and he was nowhere to be seen.

So, instead, I dragged myself up the crooked staircase to my room. When I reached the first landing, I paused. I could hear a heated conversation taking place in the study.

'Two nights now that poor child has been missing!' the Home Secretary was saying furiously. 'Two nights and not one single credible lead. Except that you allow your nephew – little more than a *child* – and accompanied by a criminal ruffian, no less – to break into the anatomy suite of one of our most eminent surgeons!'

'We have detained a suspect,' I heard Henry protest.

'That freakish *thing* downstairs? He hasn't stepped out of Sir Montagu's school for the last four years. Even you must acknowledge that's quite an alibi!'

'We have only Sir Montagu's word for that.'

'That's where you're wrong. My own son happens to be training at the school. He was there himself on the night in question. Or are you calling *him* a liar too?'

As I pressed my ear to the door, I failed to notice Esther appear at the top of the stairs with the warm milk.

'What are you doing?' she hissed.

'I should say something. It was my fault.'

'No. My father is more than a match for that mean little goblin. Now go.'

With that, she knocked and entered the room. As the door opened, I caught a glimpse of the Home Secretary standing with his back to the fireplace. Dressed all in black, except for white stockings over his short, stocky calves, he was a dark, bear-like man. He had discarded his wig, revealing a thin cover of receding black hair. His face was grey and his thin lips turned downwards in a grimace. In the firelight, his stooped shadow loomed against the curtains, making him look like a hunchback – or a gargoyle, I thought.

'If I had the budget to employ some more officers, I wouldn't need to recruit my nephew,' my uncle complained.

'You really think I would waste yet more public funds on this incompetent menagerie?' the gargoyle scoffed, waving towards the stuffed monkey. 'Let me make something very clear.' He jabbed a finger towards my uncle. 'Unless you find this Undertaker before the week is out, you will have your budget for this shambolic circus slashed . . . to precisely nothing!'

Esther stepped out of the room and closed the door softly.

'There must be something I can do,' I sighed guiltily.

'There is. Find Lady Grace. Even the Home Secretary won't be able to fire Papa after that.'

'But Welch doesn't want me anywhere near the case.'

'And you listen to what that oaf says?'

'He's right,' I said gloomily. 'He's been right all along. I was an idiot to believe anything Malarkey said.'

Esther stared at me in disbelief. 'So that's it? You're just giving up? Who *cares* if you got it wrong this morning? You should be out there trying to put it right, not feeling sorry for yourself.'

For a moment her rebuke left me tongue-tied.

'Sir Montagu has given this Gregor an alibi, correct?' she continued.

'The Home Secretary's son, no less, has confirmed it.'

'Then we need to find some other hole in his story. The bodies – the ones he was boiling . . .'

'What about them?'

'Sir Montagu insisted that they had been bought and paid for from the workhouse. Did he prove it?'

'All we have is his word as a gentleman.'

'Then maybe we should go and find out for ourselves.'

'*Ourselves?*' I asked, startled.

'You hardly think that after the mess you made of things this morning I'm leaving you alone, do you?' Esther replied, with a hint of mischief.

'Find out *what?*'

We turned in unison to see that Percy had been listening to our every word.

'None of your business,' Esther said sharply. Then she wrinkled her nose. 'Oh, and I'd change my breeches if I were you.'

A smug smile spread across Percy's face. 'So you won't mind me letting Mr Welch know what you're up to?'

Esther took three strides towards him and he shrank back. 'If you so much as breathe a word of this . . .'

His cocky swagger evaporated in an instant. 'This is about L-Lady Grace, isn't it?' he stammered.

'What if it is?'

'Then let me come with you.'

'Out of the question,' Esther snapped.

'Besides, it could be dangerous,' I added, thinking that any mention of danger would discourage him.

Instead, an absurd smile appeared on his lips. 'Danger and I are old bedfellows,' he said, raising an eyebrow in a way he obviously thought made him look daring and inscrutable.

Esther and I stared at each other, then burst out laughing.

Half an hour later, our cab pulled up outside the Turpy. This was a vast and imposing structure built about thirty years earlier to house the poorest and most destitute members of the local parish – so Percy prattled in my ear. Since we had allowed him to tag along, he had taken it upon himself to be my unofficial tour guide.

It was here, he continued enthusiastically, that those who had fallen on hard times could receive a bed, hot food and medicine. In exchange, inmates would be given a sharp pointed tool called a *spike* and set to work unpicking rope covered in tar. This was then sold off to shipyards to pad the beams inside new cargo vessels.

'Who exactly have we come to arrest?' Percy asked excitedly as he leaped out onto the pavement.

'We're not here to arrest anyone, you booby sap!' Esther berated him. 'We've come to look at their records. We need to know if Sir Montagu was telling the truth about buying the bodies from here.'

A few minutes later we were waiting in a draughty, mean little office. Through a glass partition I spied a short, stout woman bustling towards us. Her vast bosom looked like it was armoured plated under a stiff, tight-fitting jacket that buttoned up to her chin. Under her bonnet her hair was frizzy, as if someone had passed several hundred volts of electricity through it.

'*Adzooks!*' Percy squeaked. 'It's the *matron*.' The very sight of her was making him wilt like a lettuce leaf and he dropped half a pork pie onto the floor.

'Leave her to me,' Esther said, rising and brushing some of Percy's crumbs off her dress.

'*Yes?*' asked Matron, glaring up at us severely as she burst in.

Esther held out her hand formally. 'Good day to you,' she said, managing to sound extremely business-like and important. 'I am the chief magistrate's daughter. We're looking for a new housemaid and my father has asked me to inspect suitable candidates.'

The matron did a double-take. 'You want to find a housemaid *here*?'

'Is not the purpose of this charitable institution to help rehabilitate the less fortunate?'

'Well . . . I . . .'

'Good,' Esther said crisply. 'Then you will oblige me immediately.'

'This is most irregular,' the matron spluttered. 'I'll have to speak to the *master*.'

'Do that. But don't take too long. My time is most valuable.'

The woman glanced between us, flustered, then gave in. 'If you'd like to follow me.' She turned and hurried through the door, leaving Percy staring, open-mouthed, at Esther.

'That was . . . *amazing*! For a moment you actually sounded like a real lady.'

'Imagine that,' Esther replied pointedly before lowering her voice to a whisper. 'Now listen, both of you. As soon as I give you the nod, slip away. I'll try to make some excuse to cover for you. But don't take too long!' With that, she hurried off to catch up with the matron.

Percy and I stood watching her for a moment.

'She's very bossy, isn't she?' I observed.

'She's a goddess,' Percy sighed, a big dreamy smile on his face.

'Come on,' I said, shoving him quickly through the door.

Once we'd crossed a grim courtyard, we entered a long vaulted room supported by pillars and dotted with wooden benches. Leading off to one side was a cramped kitchen, thick with steam, where some of the more elderly inmates helped. Ahead of us stood a forbidding set of

panelled doors with a plaque that read: NATHANIEL
STURGIMAN ESQ., MASTER.

'Wait here,' the matron said haughtily. She tapped
lightly on the door and then slipped inside.

'Quick,' Esther hissed. 'Go to the records office. I'll
hold them off for as long as I can.'

'But I have no idea where it is,' I protested.

'I do,' Percy said cunningly. 'I've accompanied Mr
Fielding here on many an occasion. There's a short cut
through the kitchens. Come on.' There was no time to
argue – he was already hot-footing it through the door.

I scurried after him. Just in time, as it turned out: the
matron was already emerging from the master's office.

Percy and I dived into the kitchen, fighting our way
through the steam rising from two huge pots.

'What are you two doing in here?'

I turned to see a haggard old woman scowling at me,
her face hideously deformed by scars.

'We're here to perform a spot inspection,' I replied,
blurting out the first thing that sprang into my head.

'No one told me about no inspection,' she complained.
But before she could ask any more questions, we had
hurried past her towards the back staircase.

As we did so, I spied a large pot steaming on the stove;
I dipped my finger in and licked it. 'More salt,' I called
back to the astonished cook.

Leaping up the back stairs – or waddling, in Percy's case – we soon found ourselves on the next floor. Across the corridor was a schoolroom. About forty children dressed in rags, some without shoes, were perched on benches reciting the alphabet.

'Here!' Percy said, indicating a small side room marked RECORDS.

We slipped inside to find what looked like a broom cupboard stacked to the ceiling with large leather-bound volumes.

I stared at them in dismay. 'We'll never have time to work our way through this lot.'

Percy spread out his fingers and cracked them one by one. 'Leave that to me,' he said with relish. 'Files are my forte.'

With that he began to sift through the volumes, carefully leafing his way through the pages as I kept watch through a crack in the door.

I could hear a large clock ticking ominously from somewhere further down the hallway. Suddenly there was a whirr of clockwork followed by twelve deafening chimes. Moments later, eighty little feet scampered out of the schoolroom opposite and down the back stairs.

'Hurry,' I hissed to Percy, whose head was buried in one of the ledgers.

'Here,' he said at last. He blew the dust away and I

peered over his shoulder at an immaculately inscribed entry.

Knatchbull. Emily. Miss. Also Katharine. Miss. Sisters. Cause of death the Flux. No known next of kin. Bodies to be donated to Sir Montagu Gibbons.

'So Sir Montagu was telling the truth.' I couldn't hide the disappointment in my voice.

'Unless he poisoned them,' Percy suggested hopefully.

'If he did, we've got no way of proving it. He's probably boiled them down to bones by now.'

Suddenly I heard raised voices further along the corridor. I eased the door open a crack and peered out. To my alarm, Esther had appeared at the top of the stairs with the matron and cook. They were joined by the master, the gangly chairman of the parish I'd seen at the inquest.

'Young lady,' he was saying pompously, 'I don't care on whose authority you are here, you cannot call without a prior appointment. Now I demand you tell me the whereabouts of the two young fellows who accompanied you.'

I pushed the door shut quickly. 'Time to leave.' I hurried over to help Percy put the volumes back on the shelf. But as I did so, I suddenly caught sight of an entry under 'J' in one of the other books. Leaning closer, I read out a familiar name:

'*Jardine. Chastity. Miss. Place of Birth: Scotland.*'

'What about her?' Percy asked.

'It's the same surname as Lady Grace's governess.' I squinted to read the tiny handwritten entry etched next to her name. 'According to this, she was admitted here nineteen years ago, aged twenty-two.'

'Fascinating as I'm sure that is,' Percy said impatiently, 'can I suggest we leave now?' His taste for espionage was beginning to wane as the voices outside grew louder.

'Wait,' I said, still peering at the entry. 'According to this she had a baby. *Delivered of a boy. Edmund. Father unknown. Child given up for adoption. Apprenticed to Greaves and Pilcher Esqs.*'

The voices were now only feet from the door.

'They're going to find us!' Percy squeaked, panicking. He was beginning to wheeze again.

I ripped the page from the ledger and stuffed it in my pocket.

'You can't do that!' he gasped, but I was already peering through the tiny window behind him. Down below in the yard, I saw a large bin full of laundry.

'Quick! Through here.'

'Surely not . . .' he gulped, eyeing the drop nervously and going pale.

'You want the master to find us? He could get you fired. Then what will Welch do to you?'

It was all the encouragement Percy needed. He clambered out of the window as fast as his portly frame would allow, only for his bottom to get caught on the window frame. With a few sharp pushes I managed to dislodge it and he tumbled, head over heels, into the bin below. Moments later I thumped down beside him.

16

It took two cupfuls of hot chocolate and a stick of candied liquorice before Percy regained his colour. His first exploit as an undercover agent had clearly been too much for his delicate constitution. So as soon as we had met up with Esther again, we paused at his favourite coffee house, Buttons, to steady his nerves. Fortunately it was not far from the workhouse.

Unlike him and Esther, I had chosen to drink coffee. I had acquired the habit from my father, who used to drink it strong and black like oil. But taking a sip, I winced and spat it back out into the cup. It wasn't just strong – it was like soot mixed with water.

'What were you thinking of, telling the cook you were conducting an inspection?' Esther tutted.

'It was all I could think of,' I told her.

Percy looked up from his hot chocolate. 'Do you

think they'll say anything to your father or Welch?'

'Probably. But my father thinks the master's an odious little stoat, so it won't be too hard for me to think up some excuse.'

Percy's colour gradually returned, and he was soon reprising his role as tour guide. He lifted his head, sporting a large frothy moustache of chocolate, and resumed his potted history of coffee shops.

'This particular establishment was founded by a news-paper editor called Joseph Addison,' he said importantly. 'He set up a paper called the *Guardian* and edited it at this very table.'

As he wittered on, I looked around the room. At one end there was a small wooden counter where a little wizened old lady in a bonnet was ladling out coffee and hot chocolate. The remainder was filled with rows of wooden tables where men from all walks of life sat cheek by jowl studying the latest halfpenny newspaper: gentlemen, lawyers, poets, playwrights, doctors and journalists sat side by side with fishmongers, butchers and labourers. Those who couldn't afford the newspapers simply leaned over the shoulders of those who could.

At the other end of the coffee shop, fixed to the wall, was a marble lion's head, its mouth gaping open. As we watched, one of the customers placed a small folded piece of paper in its mouth.

'What's he doing?' Esther asked, curious.

'Anyone can put suggestions in the lion's mouth and the newspaper editor will print it. Mostly it's just limericks or gossip,' Percy said, adding rather grandly: 'I sometimes think *I'm* wasting my talents being a clerk. Plenty of papers would pay me handsomely if they knew half the stories that come through Mr Fielding's courthouse.' He suddenly glanced at Esther and remembered himself. 'Not that I would *ever* divulge such information.'

But Esther was preoccupied with what we had unearthed about Grace's governess. 'I keep thinking of that poor woman having to give up her child.'

'If it is her, then Lord Davenport did her a favour by taking her in.' Percy picked at a piece of liquorice that was stuck in his teeth. 'Most women would be ruined by having a baby out of wedlock.'

'Yes, thank you, Percy,' Esther said sarcastically. 'Not all of us *need* to be reminded.'

However, I did not share Percy's faith in Lord Davenport. After Welch, he was the least compassionate person I'd ever met.

Having successfully dislodged the liquorice, examined it and then eaten it, Percy looked around expectantly. 'So what are we going to do now?'

'I want to know why Miss Jardine lied about the bottle of laudanum we found in Grace's room,' I said. 'Sir

Montagu insisted he'd never prescribed it for her, so what was it doing there?'

'Let's ask her,' Esther said matter-of-factly.

'Is that a good idea?' Percy asked nervously. 'Didn't Welch forbid us to interfere?'

'Then we'd better make sure he doesn't find out,' she replied, a glint of devilment in her eye.

Percy's thirst for adventure was returning. 'Is this another secret mission?'

'Not for you,' I grunted. Seeing the hurt on his face, I quickly added, 'That is, you have a far more urgent mission. I want you to find out who Greaves and Pilcher are. I want to know if the boy they took in really *was* Miss Jardine's son.'

'What does it matter?' Esther asked.

'Maybe it doesn't. But if it *is* her son, what else has she been keeping from us?'

Percy visibly swelled in stature. 'If there is anything to be discovered, be sure I will sniff it out.' He grinned absurdly. 'Information is my currency.'

The ride to Lord Davenport's house took longer than it had the previous time: one of the new squares under construction in Mayfair was completely flooded. The frost had finally thawed a few degrees – and with it the frozen water pipes buried underground. In spite of the mounds of steaming horse dung piled along the route, the wooden pipes had cracked, and the streets surrounding the square now resembled a shiny lake.

Our cab was forced to take a more roundabout route, circling north along Oxford Street, and we were soon impeded by a huge crowd.

'What have they come for?' I asked, peering out at the hordes.

Esther shuddered. 'The hanging.' It was then that I saw what was known locally as the Tyburn Tree. This was a wooden scaffold designed to support three poor wretches when they were hanged. A wooden spectator's gallery had been erected, where more wealthy spectators could pay for a better view. In front of the jeering crowd, a wagon had pulled up and a convict was being escorted to where the executioner was waiting.

Suddenly I noticed a familiar figure holding back the crowd. 'It's Sir Montagu! What's he doing here?'

'Protecting his property,' Esther explained distastefully. 'Once they've been hanged, the dead bodies belong to him. It's the only way he can get enough corpses to chop up.'

'Except that now someone is willing to kill for them,' I murmured grimly.

'Want me to wait here so you can see him fetched off?' our cabbie shouted down. *Fetched off* meant being killed, evidently.

'Certainly not!' Esther rebuked him.

'Suit yourself,' he replied, snapping the reins sharply. A few moments later there was a sudden roar from the crowd behind us. Neither of us said anything; we knew what it meant.

Esther stared out of the window, then turned to me. 'Do you think she's really dead? Grace, I mean? I can't stop thinking about her.'

I considered her question. 'I don't know. The worst part of it is that there may never even be a body. If the grave robbers *did* take her, she probably ended up in one of those vats.'

Esther closed her eyes; when she reopened them, I saw that they were filmed with tears.

'Something I've been meaning to ask . . .' I said, hoping to lighten the mood. 'How did someone like Percy come to work for your father?'

'Percy may be clumsy,' Esther replied, 'and he's certainly not the bravest, but he's very loyal.'

'And he's clearly got a talent for filing.'

She smiled. 'Percy lives with his aged aunt. She was terribly poor – Papa took Percy on so she wouldn't have to go into the workhouse. He's become very fond of him. Besides,' she said, rolling her eyes, 'Papa loves nothing better than collecting *odd* specimens.'

Looking out, I saw that we were approaching Lord

Davenport's Grosvenor Square address. Suddenly a team of four gleaming horses drawing a sleek black carriage galloped past.

'That was Lord Davenport,' I said, pulling out my spyglass to peer after him.

'Well, that makes it easier to snoop around,' Esther pointed out.

I paid the driver and jumped down beside her; she was wrapping a large shawl around her shoulders to protect herself from the chill wind.

We mounted the steps and tugged on the bell. The door was opened by Gabriel, the footman, who looked taken aback to see us.

'I'm afraid you've just missed Lord Davenport. He's out at an important meeting.'

'Actually, it's Miss Jardine we've come to see,' I explained.

For a moment he looked thrown, but then he showed us in. As he led us towards the library, he stopped, nervously checking that no one could overhear. 'Please . . . Is there any news of Lady Grace?' He fell silent as one of the maids shuffled past before disappearing down a back staircase. 'It's not my place to enquire, but I heard my master mention that you had arrested a suspect.'

I was surprised to see how anxious he seemed – was he feeling guilty that he hadn't been able to do more to protect Grace?

'Mr Fielding is questioning someone as we speak,' I told him. 'I'm not at liberty to say any more.'

We heard footsteps approaching, so Gabriel ushered us quickly into the library. 'I'll tell Miss Jardine you're here,' he said, before bowing his head and slipping away.

Once he'd gone, Esther gazed around at the ornaments and vases in awe. 'For someone so devoutly Christian, Davenport certainly flaunts his wealth.'

'Your father said he made his fortune in shipping. Something to do with trading in China, I think—'

I broke off as the door was suddenly flung open and Miss Jardine appeared. 'You shouldn't be here,' she snapped in a brittle voice. 'Lord Davenport was most specific.'

'Miss Jardine, we're trying to find his daughter,' I said, feeling my hackles rise.

'By accusing his lordship's own physician of ordering her murder? Yes, we've heard all about that,' she said haughtily. 'Now please leave.'

'As soon as you answer a few more questions,' Esther replied coolly.

The governess looked her up and down contemptuously. 'Who gave a *slave* the right to question me?'

I saw a wave of outrage and hurt pass across Esther's face. 'You are mistaken, Miss Jardine,' she said, biting back her anger. 'I'm Mr Fielding's daughter.'

The older woman curled her lip. 'Of course. It was your mother who was the slave. Well, whoever you are, if you don't leave now, I'll be forced to send word to the Home Secretary's office.' She saw us both tense at her threat, and smiled. 'That's right – Lord Davenport left me specific instructions in case you caused any more . . . *problems.*'

Something about her determination to get rid of us was making me suspicious. 'Before we go, perhaps you can explain why you lied about the medication we found in Lady Grace's room. Sir Montagu told us he never prescribed laudanum for her. Why say that he had?'

Suddenly the governess's steely resolve faltered. 'Lord Davenport is a very private man. He does not appreciate his family's personal health being discussed with strangers. Perhaps the doctor was merely being discreet. Now I must ask you once more to leave.'

But Esther wasn't going anywhere. 'I can see why you would be loyal to his lordship,' she said, her voice heavy with meaning.

'What do you mean by that?'

'Given everything he's done for you. There can't be many women who have risen to a trusted position such as yours . . . after having a baby out of wedlock.'

For a moment Esther's words hung in the air like the smell of cordite after an explosion.

'I don't know what you're talking about . . .' the governess murmured.

'We saw your name,' I said. 'On the register at the Turpy.'

'Don't call it that!'

'You had a son. Edmund, wasn't it?' Esther continued.

Miss Jardine pursed her lips, but quickly regained her composure. 'Young woman, I don't know what you're trying to suggest, but you have clearly mistaken me for quite another sort of woman. Just because your own father sired an illegitimate child by a slave, do not dare to insult my good name. Or indeed the honour of Lord Davenport's household. Rest assured the Home Secretary will hear of this outrage!' With that, she turned and marched out. The door slammed behind her, making the porcelain figurines rattle.

'Well, that couldn't have gone much worse,' Esther said with a groan.

'She's lying,' I muttered. 'But *why*?'

Esther, however, was beginning to have her doubts. 'Has it occurred to you that she might actually be telling the truth? She can't be the *only* unmarried Scots woman called Jardine. Maybe it was another woman who had the baby.'

But I was already heading towards the door. I eased it

open and peered out into the hall – to see Miss Jardine pulling a shawl over her head. Esther joined me in time to watch her hurry out of the front door, her footsteps echoing away down the street.

'What's the betting she's gone straight to the Home Secretary?' she sighed.

'Then we have no time to lose,' I said.

Moments later I was on all fours, peering under Grace's bed. As my fingers searched the cracks in the floorboards, a pair of shoes suddenly appeared inches from my nose. At first I thought it might be Miss Jardine. The shock made me crack my head on the bed frame. Rubbing it vigorously, I looked up to find Esther standing there.

'Are you trying to get my father arrested and sent to Newgate?' she hissed. 'We need to warn him.'

'And we will. But Jardine's hiding something about Grace's laudanum.' I stood up and started rifling through the bureau drawers.

'What in Heaven's name are you hoping to find?' Esther sounded more exasperated than ever.

'I'll tell you when I find it.' I continued to sift through various items of stationery, but my metal hand was making me clumsy.

Esther rolled her eyes and pushed me aside. 'Here. I'll do it.' She began to empty the tiny drawers, tipping out their contents and tapping the wooden bottoms.

'What are you doing?' I asked, bemused.

'Old bureaus like this always have false bottoms so people can hide their love letters. Honestly! Boys know *nothing*.' As she continued her search, my iron hand pressed a little too firmly on the top edge of the bureau. To my surprise, a small panel suddenly clicked out. Esther and I glanced at each other, then she slid her fingernail behind the panel and eased it open. As she did so, an avalanche of tiny bottles cascaded onto the floor.

'They're the same as the one I found,' I gasped, picking one up and turning it over in my hand. 'Except that these ones are still full.'

Esther studied one and then another. 'Not one of them has been used. But why have they been hidden in here?'

I twisted the lid off the bottle in my hand and sniffed. To my surprise, it didn't smell of ammonia like the last one. This just looked like water. Then I spied something scratched in ink on the underside. Peering at the spidery writing, I realized it was a signature. It was Sir Montagu Gibbons's.

'So he lied,' Esther said. 'He *did* prescribe it for her.'

'There's a date next to it . . .' I squinted to read it.

Esther noticed the surprise on my face. 'What is it?'

I looked at her, dumbfounded. 'It's from only a few weeks ago!'

17

As we hurried out onto the street, my mind was still whirring, trying to make sense of what we'd found.

'Sir Montagu said something about the Chinese being addicted to opium. That it made them like the "walking dead". You don't think Grace was addicted, do you? Perhaps he's trying to cover it up?'

'But wouldn't the bottles all be empty?' Esther reasoned. 'Why fill them with water? And why would someone like Sir Montagu Gibbons want to supply Lord Davenport's daughter behind his back?'

'Maybe he didn't know about it,' I suggested.

'You mean she was stealing it?' She looked even less convinced now.

Even I had to admit that the idea seemed fantastical. But then, so was a demon undertaker risen from the dead.

'Say she was addicted to the stuff – what does that have to do with her going missing?' Esther persisted.

It was a good question – one I didn't have the faintest clue how to answer. But before I could ponder the matter further, a movement caught my eye: a familiar figure had emerged from the mews behind Lord Davenport's house.

'*Malarkey?*'

'Surprised to see me again?' he asked nonchalantly as he sauntered over to join us.

I wasn't sure whether to be delighted or furious. 'How did you know we were here?'

'I was at the hanging at Tyburn when you drove past. Thought I'd follow you. When I got here, they wouldn't allow me in, surprise, surprise. So I decided to take a little sniff round the back. That's where they keep the gee-gees.'

'With a view to stealing them, no doubt?' Esther said pointedly.

Malarkey turned and gave her the once over. 'This your girlfriend?'

For once, Esther was speechless.

I quickly put him right. 'Esther is my cousin several times removed.'

'Is that right? Well, let's hope if you ever take over from Mr Fielding you'll be just as charitable,' Malarkey said to her with a smirk.

'You're friends with this *criminal*?' Esther asked me.

'This *criminal* happens to have found you a very important piece of information,' Malarkey told us.

'You said that last time,' I reminded him.

'Fine. If you don't want to hear it . . .' He turned and began to walk away.

'Wait. What information?'

'Surely you're not going to trust him?' Esther asked me incredulously. 'He's a liar and a thief.'

'I didn't have to come and find you,' Malarkey pointed out. 'It would have been a darn sight easier for me to do a runner. Have you any idea what people would do to me if they found out I was informing to the *beak's* daughter?!'

Even Esther couldn't deny that he had a point.

'So, if it's that dangerous, why *are* you here?' I asked.

'Because I'm obviously a soft touch. And because the fact is, well . . . I owe you.'

Esther rolled her eyes. 'I told you – my father would never have hanged you. He never hangs anyone.'

'Maybe not. But he would have *transported* me. Last thing I need is to be sent off to them Colonies.'

Every instinct told me not to trust him. But if he was conning me, he was making a very good job of it.

'OK. What is this vital piece of information?' I asked grudgingly.

'I got nattering to one of the chambermaids,' Malarkey began, his chirpiness returning. 'Very obliging too, she was.' At this, Esther sighed again, assuming he was being vulgar. 'Not in that way,' he insisted. 'Mind you, she was a comely little thing.'

'What did she tell you?'

'After this Lady Grace had her horse accident a few years back, she starts slipping out the house on little expeditions. Always when Daddy's out. Obviously didn't want him finding out what she was up to.'

'What *was* she up to?' Esther asked.

'That I can't tell you. But she was always accompanied by that dark-skinned footman of theirs.'

'*Gabriel?*

'That's the one.'

'Maybe she was trying to get hold of more laudanum,' I said, trying to piece everything together.

'Or she was visiting the old coachman. The one her father blamed for her riding accident,' Esther ventured.

'Claybourn. Did this maid say what happened to him?' I asked.

Malarkey shrugged. 'Only that he'd been turfed out onto the street. Her and yer man, the coachman, were dead close. Looked up to him like a sort of uncle figure, by all accounts. The maid reckons that's why Lord

Davenport was so keen to get rid of him. Didn't like his precious princess mixing with the unwashed commoners. Bit like you,' he added, turning to Esther and winking.

'Oh, it's not just because you're unwashed that I don't like you,' Esther replied icily.

'Is that all this maid told you?' I pressed Malarkey.

'There was one other thing,' he recalled. 'Apparently it wasn't just her father Grace hated after he kicked out the coachman. She couldn't stomach her governess either. In fact, the maid reckons she was terrified of her.'

'Are you sure?' I asked, confused. 'According to Lord Davenport, Grace was devoted to her. Why else would she have asked for her when she felt unwell at the funeral?'

Esther turned to Malarkey with a triumphant grin. 'Looks like your comely maid took you for a fool.'

'Unless you're the cotton heads for believing his lordship,' Malarkey replied coolly.

Suddenly my eyes went as wide as saucers. 'Quick! Hide.' I pushed them both down the steps into the basement of one of the neighbouring houses.

'What are you doing?' Esther complained furiously.

'It's Gabriel.' Sure enough, the footman had appeared and was glancing up and down the street furtively. He hailed a cab and quickly climbed aboard. 'Where's he off to in such a hurry?' I wondered as the cab sped past us.

'One way to find out,' Esther said. She gave a loud wolf whistle, just as she had at the horse market, and another cab immediately pulled up next to us.

Malarkey glanced at me, full of admiration. 'She's a feisty one, your girlfriend.'

'I am *not* his girlfriend,' Esther seethed, before turning to speak to the cabbie. 'Follow that cab.'

'First I'll need to see you're good for the money,' the cabbie replied suspiciously. He hawked up a gobbet of phlegm and spat it onto the snow.

Esther wrinkled her nose in disgust. 'We are on official business for none other than the Chief Magistrate,' she told him haughtily.

'For that old goat!' he snorted. 'Fined me two farthings last month for driving without due care and attention. All because some little blackguard ran into the street and gets caught under my wheels. Well, you can keep your money.'

He cracked his whip and the carriage lurched forward, all but driving over Esther and forcing her into Malarkey's arms. By the time she'd disentangled herself from him, the cab was long gone and there was no sign of another.

'Great. Now what do we do?' I groaned.

18

'At last!' Percy said as we burst through the side door of number 4 Bow Street. Having dismally failed to halt another cab over an hour ago, we'd been forced to give up any hope of pursuing Gabriel. For the moment, at least, his secret destination would remain just that – a secret. 'I was about to summon a party of watchmen to look for you,' Percy said, his face looking pale and clammy.

As he spoke, I noticed that something about the court-house was different. It was eerily quiet. Too quiet.

'Where is my father?' Esther asked.

'That's what I needed to tell you,' Percy blurted. 'A messenger came from the Home Secretary's office sum-moning him there immediately. Welch has gone too.'

Esther looked like she'd been winded. 'So it's finally come. They're going to sack him.'

'That's where Miss Jardine must have been going,' I

sighed. 'I'd hoped she was bluffing.'

'There's something else.' By now Percy was wheezing loudly. 'I found out about Greaves and Pilcher. They were the employers her son was apprenticed to.'

'It's too late for that now,' Esther said dismissively.

'But you don't understand.' I'd never seen Percy so agitated before. 'They're a firm of undertakers.'

I felt a shiver run up the back of my neck. 'Miss Jardine's son was apprenticed to an undertaker?'

'Hold on,' Esther interrupted. 'We don't know for certain that he *is* her son yet.'

But I was more convinced of it than ever. 'You saw the way she looked when you asked her. She was terrified that we were on to her.'

'So what?' Esther persisted. 'Even if Edmund *is* hers, what's he got to do with anything?'

'That's what I'm trying to tell you,' Percy cried, puce with frustration. 'I spoke to the owner, Mr Pilcher. He said they had to fire him because they found him cutting up the bodies.'

If I had been astonished before, I was speechless now.

'A more arrogant and deviant young villain I have never had the misfortune of employing!'

The words came from the large, slobbering mouth of Mr Pilcher himself. The weight of his vast jowls dragged his eyelids down, giving him the look of a bloodhound. He had just been settling down to his evening meal of pigeon pie and jelly when we burst into his back office. He was perched at a little dusty bureau hidden behind several coffins.

'Persimmon said you found Edmund cutting up the corpses,' Esther pressed him, trying to hide her disgust at the cranberry jelly dribbling down his chin.

'He had this absurd notion that he could train to be a surgeon,' Pilcher snorted, spraying pigeon and pastry in all directions. Percy recoiled as a piece landed on his tunic. Then, thinking better of it, he picked it off and popped it in his mouth with an approving nod.

'Of course!' I gasped. 'That's why he was dissecting the bodies. So he could learn about surgery.'

'As if someone with his *low birth* would ever be accepted into an anatomy school,' Pilcher scoffed. Suddenly his face contorted and went bright red as he thumped his chest several times. For a moment I thought he was choking, but after two more thumps he produced a belch so loud that it rattled the windowpanes. Then, his face its normal hue again, he resumed his feast.

'I don't suppose you know where Edmund is working now?' Esther asked, grimacing with disgust.

'Last I heard, he had procured a position as a delivery boy for Brandyman and Sons.'

222

'Delivering what exactly?'

'Medical supplies to all the dissecting schools. The deluded wretch obviously thinks it will get him one step closer to being accepted into their hallowed halls.'

The moment he had uttered the words, my mind raced back to that morning – to the raven-haired youth who had been unloading bottles from the back of his wagon. Could it be that I had already seen Edmund outside Sir Montagu Gibbons's school? There was no time to lose.

'Mr Pilcher, you have been most useful,' I told the undertaker.

'Perhaps you can do me a favour in return,' he called after us, waving a fork at Esther. 'I told this girl's father that I'd been robbed some six months gone, but as usual he has done absolutely nothing about it. I would be obliged if you would *jog* his memory for me.'

Esther and I shot each other a look. She was clearly thinking the same as me.

'What precisely was taken?' I asked, but I'd already guessed the answer.

'One of my older hearses. Damned thing was worth a small fortune. Fortunately they didn't take the horses or I would have been put clean out of business!'

Esther, Malarkey, Percy and I bundled ourselves back out onto the icy street.

'Smirke – the grave robber,' I said breathlessly. 'He

told us there was a surgeon who wanted fresher bodies. But what if it *wasn't* a surgeon? What if Edmund stole Pilcher's hearse and has been kidnapping people so he can dissect them . . . ?'

'You think Miss Jardine's son is the Undertaker?' Percy gasped, going very pale. '*He* kidnapped Lady Grace?'

'I know it sounds crazy . . . but have you got a better explanation?'

He didn't. None of us did.

'There's something else you should know,' Malarkey announced. 'The delivery company Edmund works for – they do loads of jobs for the East India Company.'

'Wait,' I said, astonished. 'Doesn't that belong to Lord Davenport?'

'That's the one. After his ships have finished all their trading in India and China and the like, they come back loaded down with opium. Then they stick a label on it and sell it to the fancy toffs as laudanum.'

'How do you know?' Esther asked suspiciously.

'Because me and the rest of the Thirty Thieves used to rob their ships at low tide,' he replied casually.

I couldn't believe what I was hearing. '*Edmund* was delivering laudanum to Sir Montagu Gibbons's anatomy school?'

'Why is that such a big deal?' Esther asked, confused.

'Don't you see? The bottles we found in Grace's room

. . . Sir Montagu insisted he hadn't prescribed them. But what if Edmund gave them to Miss Jardine instead?'

'Why on earth would he do that?' Percy asked, completely lost.

'It's obvious! He wanted her to drug Grace so he could kidnap her.'

'Oh, *please*!' Esther said, exasperated. 'Don't you think your imagination is running away with you just a bit? You still don't know for sure that Edmund *is* Miss Jardine's son. Now you're saying she's in on it?'

But this time I was sure I was right. 'You heard how hostile she was when we asked about her son. The woman is evil!'

Suddenly all – or at least *some* – of the pieces of the puzzle were falling into place. I turned to Percy urgently. 'Where is Gregor?'

'The albino? He's in the holding cell. Mr Welch told me I had to get him back to the anatomy school without anyone seeing.'

Even before the words were out of his mouth, I was leaping across the frozen ruts in the road, sprinting back to the courthouse.

When I opened the door to Gregor's cell, I found him cowering in the dark. Light seemed to hurt his red eyes, for he shrank back as if in pain.

'It's OK,' I assured him. 'I know you didn't do this. But you have to help me.' He looked at me uncertainly, his eyes searching mine to see if this was some sort of trap. 'The boy who was delivering the preserving jars this morning – he delivers the laudanum, yes?'

Gregor looked from me to Percy.

'Please,' I urged him. 'Someone's life is in danger.'

After a moment Gregor nodded cautiously.

'His name – is it Edmund?'

He looked confused and shrugged, and I feared we had hit a dead end – till Esther took a step forward.

'Gregor, listen to me,' she said gently. 'Do you know where the wagon comes from? Is there an address?'

Gregor stared blankly at us again.

'It's no use. He's obviously half-witted,' Malarkey grunted.

'Wait,' Percy said. 'Look.'

I turned to see Gregor fishing a scrap of paper out of his pocket. I took it from him and began to flatten out the creases. Looking closely, I realized that it bore a long list of surgical items, including twenty units of laud-anum.

'It's some sort of receipt,' I said.

Then I saw it. At the top of bill of sale was the name Brandyman and Sons. Underneath was an address.

* * *

A matter of minutes after Gregor had given us the address of Edmund's employers, we were hurrying off towards the docks at Limehouse.

'Thank you,' I said to Esther as we weaved our way through the crowded streets. 'For helping with Gregor.'

'I didn't do it to help *you*,' she said matter-of-factly. Then her expression softened. 'If you're right, let's just hope we're not too late.'

Soon we were on the docks where Lord Davenport's cargo ships from the Orient were unloaded – and frequently robbed by Malarkey and the Thirty Thieves. Trouble was, the toothless old clerk at Brandyman and Sons immediately recognized him as one of the gang who'd carried out the raids. There was no chance he was going to help us – until Esther stepped in, adopting the same tones she had used at the Turpy. She threatened to have Welch impound all Brandyman's delivery wagons for being unroadworthy. This seemed to do the trick: the old man hastily consulted with his colleagues before giving us a rough description of where Edmund lived.

It was enough to make us hail another hansom cab and head back across London – to an area I now knew well: Smithfield market. Meanwhile Percy was dispatched to raise the alarm with Henry and Welch at the Home Secretary's office.

We were silent as our cab rattled along the uneven

streets: we were all too shocked by the evening's revelations. Eventually Esther turned to me. Something had clearly been preying on her mind.

'Do you really think Miss Jardine could have helped Edmund to kidnap Grace?'

What kind of a person would help to snatch her own pupil? I wondered. But the more I thought about it, the more it all added up.

'Might explain why Grace was terrified of the old bat,' Malarkey suggested. 'Maybe she'd got wind of what Jardine was up to and reckoned she was next for the chop.'

Moments later we pulled into Smithfield's main square. The place was deserted now, apart from a few scavenging dogs and drunkards.

Suddenly I glimpsed something that made my skin crawl – crows picking over some rotting entrails. A 'murder' of crows, they were called. How fitting the term was! If Edmund really was the Undertaker, was this why he wore a mask like a crow's skull? In some gruesome way, was he like them – picking the flesh off dead carcasses?

Our cab turned right down a filthy back street.

'There!' I said, seeing something looming out of the darkness. We lurched to a halt outside the entrance to a derelict yard. It perfectly matched the description the clerk at Brandyman's had given us. To my astonishment, we were only a few streets from the abattoir where I'd seen the horse about to be butchered a few days earlier. To think that I had come so close to stumbling across Edmund's lair . . .

We paid off the cabbie and edged our way through the rusty old gates into the tumbledown courtyard. Peering through the darkness, I made out a peeling sign on the wall. It was the name of an old brewery. Above it, a tree had grown up through a hole in the roof and jutted into the night sky. Just to our left was an entrance to what must have been the front office. I eased the rotten door open as silently as I could – to find that it was almost pitch dark inside.

Malarkey whispered in my ear. 'If this Edmund fella really *is* the Undertaker and he's hiding here, we need to find that flintlock he used.'

'Why?' I asked dubiously.

'We used to see it on board ship when someone was shot. When you dug the lead ball out of their wound, it had this marking on it from the barrel of the weapon that fired it. Like a sort of signature. If we find the gun, we can match it to the bullet that killed the cabbie.'

I could just make out the look of disgust on Esther's face. 'You're saying we dig the bullet out of the cabbie's head? Hasn't the poor man been through enough already?'

'He's dead. He's not going to be complaining now, is he?'

I shushed them both. 'Before we cut open anyone's head, let's see if Edmund's here, shall we?'

I turned to head further inside when Malarkey froze.

'Something just ran past me foot.'

'I'm pretty sure it was a rat,' Esther replied. Suddenly she saw the look of horror on his face. 'Surely you're not afraid?'

'Give over! Of course not,' Malarkey blustered. 'Saunders doesn't like them.'

'Well, Saunders isn't here.'

'This one is.' He opened his jacket and his pet weasel poked his nose out.

'You brought your own rat?' she said, recoiling.

'He's not a *rat*. He's a weasel.' Even Saunders sounded put out, grinding his back teeth. 'He does that when he doesn't like someone,' Malarkey added pointedly.

'I should try that next time we meet,' Esther said with a smirk. 'Though with any luck, we won't have to after tonight.'

'What's up with you?' Malarkey asked. 'Or are you this snotty with everyone you fancy?'

'*Fancy?*' Esther nearly choked on the word.

'Both of you, shut up,' I whispered. I'd heard a voice coming from somewhere overhead. Listening more closely, I realized it belonged to a woman. But not just any woman. It was Miss Jardine . . .

'When she left Lord Davenport's this afternoon,' Esther said under her breath, 'she wasn't going to see the Home Secretary at all. She was coming here!'

Eager to get closer, I started up the staircase leading to the next floor. The woodwork immediately creaked under my weight.

I froze on the spot, heart thumping. Had Miss Jardine heard? By now my eyes were adjusting to the darkness and I could see the whites of Esther and Malarkey's eyes.

I carefully edged my foot onto the next step, where I figured the wood would be less rotten. Easing myself a few inches higher, I was finally able to peer over the top step.

Sure enough, Miss Jardine was standing on the far side of a room across a corridor. Another figure was warming himself beside a glowing stove. His back was turned so I couldn't see his face, but I recognized the lank mop of jet-black hair. It was the same stooped, effeminate creature I had seen delivering the bottles to the anatomy school.

Edmund.

'They know,' Miss Jardine told him anxiously.

'Know *what*?'

'About us. That I'm your mother.'

Esther tugged at my elbow. 'What are they saying?' she

mouthed. I put a finger to my lips and craned my head to hear the rest of their conversation.

'All they know is that you had a bastard,' Edmund continued, sneering.

'Don't use that word!'

'Why? Does it offend your Christian virtue?' he asked, mocking. 'Should have thought of that when you gave yourself to the first man to show an interest in you.'

Miss Jardine made to slap him across the face, but her son had seized her hand. Despite his slight frame, he seemed to possess almost unnatural strength. She let out a whimper, clearly terrified. For a moment I thought he was going to strike her; then he let her hand go in disgust.

'Please . . .' Miss Jardine's voice was hoarse with emotion. 'For me – stop. It's too dangerous.'

'And give up everything I've worked for?'

'But they could find you. I can't lose you. Not again.'

Suddenly Esther let out a tiny cry: Malarkey's weasel had given her a nasty nip on the finger.

Miss Jardine immediately glanced over, forcing me to duck into the shadows. 'Someone's here,' she hissed.

Peering over the top of the step, I saw Edmund turn to look in my direction. His black eyes scanned the darkness, his head tilting to one side. Even without a mask, he looked like one of the sinister crows I'd seen in the market place.

After a moment he appeared to relax. 'It's the rats. Now go. You should never have come.'

'Promise me you won't take anyone else,' his mother begged him. Her words sent a shiver down my spine. There was no doubting it now: Edmund, Miss Jardine's illegitimate son, was the Undertaker – and she was protecting him.

But if he had kidnapped Grace, was she somewhere in this building? Could she still be alive?

As these and more questions flashed through my mind, I suddenly realized that the governess was heading straight towards me. Within a matter of seconds I would be exposed.

I frantically waved the others back and we crept down the steps before diving behind the counter in the front office.

Squinting under the bench, I watched Miss Jardine's boots descend the stairs and cross the room. At the door, I heard her give a cry of disgust, then boot several rats out of her path before hurrying off.

A moment later a second pair of boots descended. This time they were long, black and pointy, the soles almost worn through. I edged back and held my breath as Edmund seemed to sniff the air with his beaky nose. Could he tell that we were there? I saw Malarkey clamp a hand round Saunders's snout to stop him squeaking at a rat that scurried past.

If Edmund sensed our presence, he didn't show it. Instead, he took out a large set of keys and disappeared through a small door leading off the office.

When we were sure he was not about to return, we emerged from our hiding place. Dusting herself down, Esther grimaced to find that she was covered in a silky veil of cobwebs.

'We should wait for your uncle and Welch,' Malarkey whispered. 'Percy must have got a message to them by now.'

'There isn't time,' I told him. 'If Grace is alive, she may not be for much longer.'

I put my ear to the door through which Edmund had just disappeared, and listened. Nothing. I turned the handle and edged the door open.

On the other side was a stable, presumably where Edmund kept the wagon he used for his medical deliveries. Two black horses were bedded down in the straw – but far more important was what stood on the far side.

The Undertaker's hearse. The sinister black bodywork gleamed in the moonlight . . .

19

'I don't understand,' Esther whispered. 'The Undertaker abandoned his hearse after you chased it. Papa has kept it as evidence. So how can it be sitting here?'

'He must have stolen another,' was all I could deduce.

'Forget the hearse,' Malarkey said. 'Where does he keep the bodies?'

I squinted through the gloom and saw a pair of trap doors set into the floor. Above them, hanging from a beam, was an old, rotten pulley. When the yard was a brewery, this must have been where the barrels of beer were winched up for delivery.

Suddenly a gruesome thought struck me: what if Edmund now used it to hoist up the bodies of his victims . . . ?

I felt my pulse quicken with dread. Were Grace and the other poor victims being held somewhere below us?

I was about to reach for the trap door when I caught a flicker of movement. I wheeled round and saw, out of the corner of my eye, another door standing ajar. On the other side, the room was dimly lit by an oil lamp.

Steadying my nerves, I beckoned to the others, then edged closer.

The room was furnished like a little parlour. There was an armchair by the fire, a desk and several bookcases. Everywhere, books lay open. It almost reminded me of Uncle Henry's study.

It was also empty. If Edmund had been here, he was now nowhere to be seen. Yet there was no other way out. Had I just imagined the movement?

As I surveyed the room, I saw that it was littered with anatomical sketches. I picked one up, holding it under the table lamp to study. It showed in meticulous detail the muscle structure and tendons of a human arm. For a fleeting moment I thought of my own hand, now partly mechanized. From another sketch, an eye glared out at me, the eyelids peeled back.

All at once I spotted something on a side table that chilled me to the bone. I recognized it from the illustration Henry had shown me.

It was the skull of a crow. The same sunken eye-holes I'd seen on the Undertaker's mask stared lifelessly at me.

Next to it lay various sketches. Looking closer, I saw that they were designs for a mask. A pot of white paint sat open beside them.

By now Esther and Malarkey had joined me.

'What a freak!' Malarkey muttered. He picked up the skull and peered at the beak. 'What is this thing?'

'A dead crow.'

He grimaced as Esther sifted through the sketches – every one of them showing some sort of raven. 'Talk about obsessed . . .' she murmured.

'Your father said it was a mythical symbol for death,' I explained. A fly crawled out of the eye-socket of the skull Malarkey was holding. He shuddered and dropped it on the table.

I picked up one of the books lying beside me on a chair. It was a textbook on human anatomy, its author none other than Sir Montagu Gibbons. Several more were stacked beside it, all manuals on surgery.

'We were right. He's studying to be a surgeon,' I said. 'He wasn't kidnapping his victims to sell on to Sir Montagu. He wants to dissect them himself.'

Esther shivered and tugged her shawl tightly around her neck. At the same moment the flame in the oil lamp flickered.

I narrowed my eyes and peered around the room. 'That draught – where did it come from?'

'The whole place is falling down,' Malarkey said. 'It's hardly a surprise if it's a bit nippy.'

'It doesn't make sense,' Esther said. 'There are no other doors or windows. So how is the draught getting in?'

'Do you have any face powder?' I asked.

'Now's not the time to be doing your make-up,' Malarkey joked.

Esther produced a little tin and I took it over to the wall. Taking a generous pinch of powder between my forefinger and thumb, I tossed it into the air, watching it fall.

'Careful,' Esther complained. 'That stuff is expensive.'

Suddenly the powder caught a current of air and eddied away.

'The draught is coming from somewhere behind the bookcase,' I said. 'Help me.'

Esther and Malarkey joined me in pulling away the books.

'What are we looking for?' Malarkey asked.

No sooner had he spoken than there was a *click* and the bookcase edged forward an inch.

'That,' I said.

As I made to draw it back, I saw that more flies were crawling through the gap and were now buzzing around our ears.

'*Eugh!*' Esther shuddered in disgust.

'Only two places you get blowflies,' Malarkey noted chillingly. 'One's round horse turds. The other's round rotting meat.'

The thought sent a prickle of fear down my spine. Trying to ignore it, I pulled on the bookcase and it swung open to reveal a set of steps leading down. We all stared at it, daunted.

'You sure about this?' Malarkey asked warily.

'No,' I answered truthfully. 'But what if Grace is down there?'

Esther grabbed the oil lamp off the table and pushed past us. 'Come on,' she said, and began to descend into the darkness.

Turning the lamp down to its lowest flame in order not to advertise our presence, Esther lit the way as we sank into the bowels of the brewery.

Soon we reached a dank basement corridor. The ceiling was low and vaulted, not unlike the crypt in the church. To our right was a cobbled ramp leading to the trapdoors above. Just beyond, something glinted in the weak lamplight.

'Over there,' I whispered to Esther. She turned and held up the lamp. All three of us took a step backwards in shock when we saw what had been glinting.

It was the metal bars of a cage. The floor around it was strewn with old pewter plates . . . and bones.

'Please tell me those aren't human . . .' Esther's voice was trembling as she stared at them.

'They look too small,' I said.

Malarkey picked one up and sniffed it. 'Chicken.'

'He must have been feeding his victims to keep them alive,' I said, realizing the awful truth. 'He wanted to keep them fresh before he dissected them.'

Malarkey and Esther fell silent as the horror of what they were looking at sank in: this had to be where Edmund had been holding his victims captive. In which case, where were they now?

By this time the air had become thick with the buzz of flies. I had to keep swatting them away as they crawled around my eyes and nostrils. Was this because of the chicken bones, I wondered, or was something else rotting down here?

The air was thick with something else too. It was a confusing, overwhelming smell – something dead mixed with an almost intoxicating aroma of alcohol.

I saw that Saunders was fidgeting to get out of his master's jacket.

'He doesn't like it. Not one bit,' Malarkey murmured ominously.

Suddenly I craned my head to listen. Close by I could hear the faint *plop, plop* of dripping water. I took the lamp from Esther and peered through the darkness. Just ahead of us was a low wall made of crumbling brick.

'It's a well,' Malarkey said. I held the lamp over the rim, but we immediately recoiled from the smell of putrefying flesh.

'What *is* that?' Esther asked.

'More like *who*,' Malarkey answered darkly.

'You think someone's down there?' she gasped.

'If they are, I'm pretty sure they've been dead a very long time.'

Just above the well was a rope and pulley. I began tugging at the rope. Esther joined me, and then, reluctantly, Malarkey. Whatever was attached to the other end at the bottom, it was heavy.

Slowly we began to hoist it up. Finally a filthy old bucket appeared over the edge. Esther swung the lamp round so that we could see what was inside – and then clapped her hand over her mouth in horror.

It was a man's leather boot . . . but not just a boot. It had a section of bone sticking out of it, some of the flesh and muscle still attached.

My hand let go of the rope in shock and the bucket whistled back down the well, landing with a splash that echoed off the walls.

'Now we know what they used to flavour the beer,' Malarkey whispered wryly.

'*Sssh!*' Esther hissed. 'He'll hear.'

'If he didn't hear *that*, he must be deaf,' Malarkey muttered.

Suddenly our conversation was brought to an abrupt halt. A coarse rasping sound, like something being sawn, was coming from just around the corner. We edged our way closer and saw a wooden door ahead of us. Light was pouring through a crack underneath.

I glanced at the others, then decided that there was nothing for it. I turned and sprinted towards the door. As I crashed through it, I was blinded by the dazzling light of a thousand candles. Shielding my eyes, I squinted around the room. It was a mean, windowless chamber, its wooden panels crudely whitewashed. In the middle of the room was a long wooden bench, bleached with what smelled like strong disinfectant. I knew instantly what its purpose was. The livid red stains told me that it was some sort of improvised dissecting table.

As the others joined me and we stared at the walls, I saw they were sprayed dark red.

'Arterial blood,' Malarkey said grimly. 'It was the same in the operating room on board ship. Cut an artery, you might as well be spraying the walls with a hose.'

One wall, however, was stacked to the ceiling with large glass jars. Esther peered at one more closely, then let out a gasp.

Inside was a human heart. It was perfectly preserved

. . . almost as if it was still beating. Someone had clearly removed it with care and precision.

Glancing around, I saw that each jar contained a different specimen. Most chilling and heart-breaking of them all was the miniature figure of a baby, still not fully formed. It must have been taken from its mother's womb before it was born.

'*Does it shock you?*' a muffled voice suddenly asked from behind us.

We spun round and staggered backwards. There, filling the doorway, was a crooked figure wearing an undertaker's coat. But most chilling of all was the deathly white mask in the shape of a crow's skull.

There was no doubting it this time. We had finally come face to face with the Undertaker . . .

Slowly the figure lifted the mask to reveal the face of Edmund, beady black eyes studying us with cruel pleasure.

'So it *was* you,' Esther gasped, almost hoarse with fear.

Edmund gave a little bow before turning to Malarkey. 'I'm curious . . . How does someone like you know so much about surgery?'

'I used to be in the navy,' Malarkey answered coolly. 'Could say I had a lot of experience with chopped-up bodies.'

'*You* were a surgeon?' Edmund scoffed.

'An apprentice,' Malarkey corrected him. 'To a *real* surgeon.'

'Then we have a lot in common. Except that soon *I* will be a real surgeon too.'

'I very much doubt that,' Esther told him. 'They'll hang you first for killing all those innocent people.'

'But how will they know?'

'Because I'm going to make it my personal mission to tell them,' I told him coldly.

'No,' he corrected, licking his lips with relish. 'You're going to be my next experiment.'

Quick as a flash, he pulled the mask back over his face. With his other hand he snatched a glass flask of liquid from the side table and threw it down on the floor. It smashed instantly, releasing a cloud of vapour. My eyes immediately began to sting and my head swam as I choked on the fumes.

'Relax,' Edmund urged me. His voice was soothing. 'In a moment you'll be fast asleep.'

'What is this stuff?' Esther said, fighting for breath.

'I came upon it quite by accident. It's a completely colourless alcohol. Highly flammable, but with a most astonishing side effect that will revolutionize medicine.'

'Which is . . . ?' I asked, starting to feel the room spin.

'It paralyses you.'

I stumbled backwards, falling against the side table and knocking various saws and pliers to the floor. 'So this was how you kidnapped your victims without a fight. You drugged them – just like Grace. The mask stopped you breathing it in. Just like a plague doctor.' But by now my speech was growing slurred.

'I'm flattered,' I heard Edmund say, his voice muffled. 'But even I wouldn't be daring enough to abduct Lady Grace right under the noses of her entire family.'

'But if *you* didn't . . .' Esther tried to form the words, but it was hopeless. The vapour was working too fast and she slumped to the floor beside me.

Still I fought against the drug. I tried to pull myself to my feet, but it was no use: my limbs had become heavy and useless. I made one last attempt to lift my iron hand – if I could just clamp my grip round his throat . . .

But as I stretched my arm out towards him, Edmund looked down at me, an expression of pity on his face. Slowly he began to recede into a pinpoint of light as darkness crept in from the margins of my vision. He was slowly disappearing down a rabbit hole of darkness.

Suddenly, just as I thought I had finally passed out, there was a blinding flare of light followed by a deafening roar of gunpowder.

Instantly the tunnel of light rushed back and my senses

recovered enough to see that Edmund had crashed to the floor next to me. I saw his astonished expression as he put a hand to his right shoulder. There was a scorch mark from which a bloom of crimson blood was now flowing across his shirt.

Someone had shot him, and the bullet had torn clean through his shoulder. Glancing towards the door, I had to blink several times before I could take in what I was seeing. Was this some illusion brought on by the vapour?

Standing there, more shocked than anyone, tendrils of smoke still snaking out of the barrel of his flintlock, was Percy.

20

It was another half-hour before I had finally stopped retching into a bucket. Esther was little better, as we huddled together in the cobbled courtyard upstairs. To my astonishment, Malarkey was suffering no such ill effects – on account, perhaps, of his many years spent drinking cheap gin.

By now, the limp and groaning Edmund was being dragged up from the basement to a waiting carriage so that he could be taken into custody. It turned out that the lead shot from Percy's flintlock had passed right through him, narrowly missing his heart.

Henry and Welch had arrived seconds after Percy's dramatic appearance. In the aftermath, Henry had heartily congratulated his young clerk, even more astonished than the rest of us that he had managed to gun down the culprit.

Percy clearly couldn't believe it either, unused to being the subject of so much admiration. He began to shiver – a reaction to the freezing fog that was now rolling in, and the shock of what he had just done.

Welch was more grudging in his praise. While Henry announced that Percy would receive a pay increase of sixpence a week, Welch pointed out that neither he nor any of his men had been paid for at least a month. Henry waved this away as a trifling objection. He was sure the Home Secretary would find the funds to give them a raise after their spectacular success.

It seemed that Percy's arrival at the Home Secretary's office earlier that evening couldn't have been better timed. The minister had been giving Henry a furious dressing down when Percy burst in to tell them the news. Ignoring the Home Secretary's objections, Welch and Henry had raced across London, arriving with seconds to spare.

Edmund had now been clapped in irons and bundled into a carriage. Welch would escort him back to the courthouse while Percy was despatched to summon Sir Montagu Gibbons to tend to his wounds. It would not do, my uncle insisted, for the accused to die in custody before he faced a trial.

'I myself,' he announced, 'will hasten to Lord Davenport's abode in the hope of apprehending Miss Jardine before she discovers that the game is up.'

Esther voiced the question we were all too scared to ask: 'But if Edmund took Grace, where is she now?'

'In one of them huge pickling jars he keeps downstairs, I shouldn't wonder,' Malarkey answered grimly. 'Yer man's probably chopped her up into a thousand bits, along with the others.'

In the carriage, I heard Edmund struggling. 'I had nothing to do with taking the girl!' he cried.

With one bound, Welch caught him a crushing blow on the jaw with one of his granite fists, knocking him senseless.

My uncle rolled his eyes. 'Was that *entirely* necessary?'

Before Welch could justify himself, a cry came up from the ramp that led to the cellar.

'Mr Fielding, sir!' It was one of Welch's night watchmen, a rat-like, dishevelled creature. He was clutching a scrap of brightly coloured material and looked very green about the gills. Clearly what he had witnessed below had sickened him.

'Look!' he wheezed, his chest rattling from the exertion of clambering up the ramp into the freezing night air. 'I found it in that well, sir.'

Henry took the material and held it up to the light. It was a turquoise silk handkerchief. He turned it over in his hand, then froze.

'Well . . . ?' Welch asked expectantly.

All eyes were on my uncle as he cleared his throat. He had found a monogram embroidered in the corner. It said simply *GD*.

For a moment I thought Lord Davenport's legs would buckle and give way. He was clutching the handkerchief in his left hand. With the other he fumbled blindly for the mantelpiece. His fingers gripped the stone till the knuckles were white.

'Yes,' he said, in barely more than a whisper. 'It's Grace's.'

Minutes earlier, my uncle and I, accompanied by Welch and two other watchmen, had beaten on the door of the Grosvenor Square house. As soon as the butler opened it, we hurried inside. It was essential to catch Miss Jardine by surprise before she could flee. Welch had bounded up the stairs, with the two watchmen scurrying after him. Miss Jardine was soon apprehended in her chambers, vehemently protesting her innocence.

'Please,' she begged my uncle as she was led towards the door. 'I swear I would never do anything to harm Lady Grace.' However, her words fell on deaf ears.

Now Lord Davenport was trying to take in the shock of what my uncle had told him – that Miss Jardine had conspired with her son to abduct Grace, and that his daughter was most likely dead. Suddenly the door burst open and a ghostly figure appeared. I recognized her immediately from the painting above the fireplace. It was Grace's mother, Lady Davenport – though her face was now so pale, her cheeks so sunken, the skin seemed to have melted off her like wax. Her eyes frantically searched ours; then she saw the handkerchief and snatched it from her husband.

'*My poor, dear, darling girl!*' She held it to her cheek; then her face crumpled and an eerie, strangled cry rose up from somewhere within her. '*What have I done?*'

It seemed a strange question to ask. The next moment she collapsed on the sofa. Davenport called out for Gabriel, who came rushing in, startled, as Henry and I leaped forward to offer help.

'Leave her!' Davenport barked, before softening his tone. 'We can manage.'

Lady Davenport's lady-in-waiting appeared at the door, clutching her hand to her mouth in distress. Between her and a shaken Gabriel, Lady Davenport was lifted up and led from the room.

'Call Sir Montagu immediately,' Davenport ordered.

I threw a nervous glance at my uncle.

'Actually, your lordship,' he said falteringly, 'the doctor is at present detained.'

'With whom?' he demanded.

'The suspect sustained a serious bullet wound in the struggle.'

Davenport's eyes narrowed. 'You mean to tell me you're keeping that animal *alive*?'

'He will need to stand trial,' Henry explained.

'Is he likely to die from his wounds?'

'I have every faith in Sir Montagu's abilities.'

'Pity,' Davenport snarled. 'It might have saved me the effort.' He strode over to a side table and poured himself a large glass of brandy from a heavy cut-glass decanter.

'To think we trusted that evil witch Jardine!' He snorted in disbelief. 'You know it was my wife who hired her? I knew I should never have trusted her to choose a governess.'

Henry looked surprised. 'Lady Davenport *knew* about Miss Jardine's background – her illegitimate son?'

'Of course! It was all part of her infernal do-gooding with the church. She thought the damned woman deserved a second chance.' Lord Davenport laughed bitterly. 'And now see what she's done! Well, I will personally see to it that life in that institution of hers becomes a living hell for every one of those ungodly wretches!'

'You can't punish the rest of the inmates because of one woman!' I protested.

His lordship's eyes darted towards me, burning like molten lava. 'How dare you presume to tell me what I can or cannot do!'

'What about Edmund's job as a delivery boy?' Henry asked him quickly. 'Was that your wife's idea as well?'

'Jardine duped her with some sob story. I had no idea who he was or I would never have agreed to it.' He swallowed his brandy in one gulp. 'And this is how she has repaid my wife's compassion. By grooming our daughter to be the next victim of that brat of hers – that *fiend.*' He spat the words out before pouring another tot of brandy. I saw his hand tremble as it clutched the glass, threatening to shatter it. 'Someone should have drowned him at birth. Then my daughter would still be alive.'

I now understood why Lady Davenport had reacted in the way she had. She clearly blamed herself for taking on Miss Jardine, and the sordid plot that had followed.

Her husband sighed heavily and took a step towards the French windows. Beyond these I could see a mews and a coach house. 'There is one thing you haven't mentioned.' He kept his back to us, his voice icy calm now. 'If you think this animal was the one who abducted my daughter . . . where is her body?'

When my uncle didn't answer, Lord Davenport turned to glower at him. Henry lowered his eyes, unable to meet his gaze.

'What is it you aren't telling me?' His stare probed like a scalpel. '*You*, boy,' he said, his eyes darting to me. 'You were the first there tonight. What did you find?'

I glanced at Henry uncertainly. I could barely bring myself to say the words. 'There was a well . . .'

Davenport paused as he took this in. 'And what was in this well?'

I looked up and held his gaze. 'Human remains.'

For a moment I thought Davenport would be physically sick, but he steeled himself. 'Whose?'

'It's hard to say. More than one person.'

'Including my daughter?'

'We won't know for certain until Sir Montagu performs an examination,' my uncle interjected.

'But in your opinion?' Davenport demanded.

'I really don't think that I should speculate at this point.'

His lordship's eyes slid across to me again. 'What about you? Are you too much of a coward to tell me the truth?'

I took a deep breath. 'It's hard to be sure. But we found Grace's handkerchief amongst the body parts, so . . .'

Davenport held up a shaking hand to stop me. It was obviously all the confirmation he needed . . . or could bear to hear.

'Thank you,' he replied before slowly turning his back to us again. 'Now if you don't mind, my wife and I would like to be alone.'

21

As soon as Edmund's wounds had been seen to, he and his mother were charged and transferred to Newgate Prison until their trial a week later. Esther told me that Newgate was a terrifying, disease-ridden hellhole where inmates were often crammed thirty or more to a cell.

As their crimes were so monstrous – not to mention *newsworthy* – it was agreed that Edmund and Miss Jardine would be tried by the most senior judge in the city rather than Henry. This, it turned out, had more to do with making money. Even if my uncle had been deemed senior enough, the courthouse in Bow Street was far too cramped and vile-smelling.

The trial was turning into a feeding frenzy, hotly anticipated by the whole of London, from its finest drawing rooms and coffee houses to the filthy back streets of Jack Ketch's Warren. As it approached, journalists from

every halfpenny journal jostled with the rich and in-
fluential for ringside seats.

Henry would be presenting the case for the prosecution,
but in truth the governess and Edmund had already been
tried through the popular press. I myself would be called
as a witness to recount the conversation I'd overheard at
the old brewery. But my testimony was hardly necessary.
There was already the evidence of the hearse we had
stumbled across. Added to this there was the skull mask
Edmund had been wearing, his grisly 'museum' of pickled
specimens and the home-made dissecting suite.

Most gruesome of all, there were the human body
parts we had found in the well. As if this weren't enough,
Edmund's previous employers, Greaves and Pilcher, had
confirmed his obsession with dead bodies. His disguise
as an undertaker made perfect sense, given his previous apprenticeship.

But what of that mask? After my uncle had finished
interrogating him, I asked Edmund why he had chosen
the crow's skull. His answer couldn't have been more
sinister.

'People despise crows because they pick over the
carcasses of dead animals. I myself think they are beautiful
and noble creatures for precisely that reason. It is people
who should be despised.'

Thanks to his deliveries to Sir Montagu Gibbons's

anatomy school, Edmund had also come into daily contact with Gregor. Had it been his plan all along to make him look like the suspect? I felt sick remembering how I had accused the poor wretch based on nothing more than his pale skin and red eyes.

The final irrefutable piece of evidence against Edmund was that his own mother had worked as Grace's governess. Had she helped her son to find his other victims too? The prosecution – and the public – were convinced of it.

Clearly the laudanum bottles we'd found in Grace's bureau were part of the evil ploy – no doubt to drug Grace so that she wouldn't put up a fight. I realized that this must have been how she and Edmund had managed to smuggle Grace into the hearse waiting in the crypt.

One piece of evidence hadn't yet been discovered – the flintlock pistol Edmund had fired at the cabbie. Malarkey had been determined to see if he could match it with the bullet lodged in the poor man's head. But no gun was discovered at Edmund's secret lair.

If mother and son were found guilty, there could be no doubt that the judge would impose the death penalty: they would be ferried from Newgate Prison to the Tyburn Tree and hanged in front of a crowd baying for revenge.

In the meantime Sir Montagu Gibbons had been engaged by my uncle as what he called an *expert witness*: his evidence would be taken as gospel because of his skill as a surgeon. Over the coming days he began to examine every body part that had been retrieved from the well. Percy was drafted in to help, but he vomited the moment he saw the first one on the dissecting table.

Malarkey, however, suffered no such queasiness. In fact, he seemed to relish the task, so he and I were dispatched to help Sir Montagu in the grisly process.

Malarkey's experience with severed limbs and spilled guts, gained from his days in the navy, proved invaluable. The surgeon was dubious about his presence at first, huffing and puffing and generally looking down his bulbous nose at him. But as the days went on, he was forced to admit that Malarkey showed a real talent for sifting through gore. He even allowed him to grope around inside the bullet hole in the cabbie's head. After a great deal of prodding and fiddling, Malarkey withdrew his pincers. Squeezed between the tips was the dented lead ball.

After carefully washing it in alcohol, we peered at it under a large magnifying glass in my uncle's study.

'Fascinating,' Henry purred as he examined it.

Sure enough, just as Malarkey had predicted, the lead ball had distinct grooves down the side. Percy clambered down from the ladder carrying a huge tome. Blowing the dust off, Henry flicked through the pages until he found an etching of a similar piece of lead shot. It turned out that the miniature musket ball was used by British cavalry regiments.

'Sadly, it's of no use to us,' Henry concluded, thumping the book shut in a cloud of dust. 'Not unless we can find the flintlock that fired it.'

Yet however hard we searched the old brewery and Miss Jardine's private chambers, no flintlock could be located.

Meanwhile, as the days went by, Sir Montagu Gibbons painstakingly stitched together the bodies of Edmund's victims so that each was reassembled like a kind of grisly jigsaw. Luckily many of the parts had been pickled in alcohol. Those parts 'stored' in the well were in rather worse condition. Piece by piece, these poor victims slowly became whole again.

'I'll say this of that fiend, Edmund,' Sir Montagu told me one afternoon. 'For someone with no formal training, his surgical handiwork is extraordinarily good. Shame,' he said, almost wistfully. 'He might have made an excellent surgeon.'

One by one, Malarkey and I meticulously ticked off Edmund's first three victims. But what of poor Grace? None of the body parts that we found seemed to belong to her, so where was her body?

I had one theory. Edmund must have known that no one would come looking for the first three homeless and destitute victims – but Grace was different. The full force of the law had been mobilized to find her. Perhaps he had been more careful about hiding her remains to avoid being caught.

I shuddered to think where he might have concealed her body. Malarkey told me that murder victims were often thrown into the Thames, their bodies never seen again.

It was another bitterly cruel blow for Lord and Lady Davenport. Had we found Grace's body, they could at least have laid her to rest in the family chapel. As it was, Edmund had denied them even this crumb of comfort.

22

The next day I found that Henry had been up since before first light preparing his opening address to the court. I could hear him pacing about practising his delivery in an assortment of fruity, theatrical voices.

If my uncle's Achilles heel was his shambolic approach to money – in fact, to almost everything – public speaking was where he came into his own. He was a natural performer. People would crowd into the public gallery just to hear him holding forth – so much so that there was often a carnival atmosphere to his court sessions. His summings-up were renowned for their scholarly references and witty wordplays – often peppered with obscure Latin quotes. But more than anything, he could be relied on to poke fun at those in high office. This was probably the reason why he had been overlooked as a judge. He was being punished for making fun of his 'betters'.

Meanwhile Percy had been handed the responsibility for giving Edmund's hearse the final once-over. I should say hearse*s*. The hearse we'd found at the brewery was quickly dealt with and returned to its grateful owner, Mr Pilcher.

But this still left the *other* hearse – the one that had been used to kidnap Grace and had got stuck fast in the alleyway in Jack Ketch's Warren. So far we had found no evidence that placed Grace inside it. Both Edmund and Miss Jardine were still vehemently insisting that they had taken no part whatsoever in her abduction – a ploy, my uncle suspected, to lessen their sentence.

He was hoping there might be some evidence that we had overlooked: anything that could prove beyond doubt that Grace had been inside the hearse. Keen to pass the time before the trial began, I decided to help Percy give it one final examination. Two sets of eyes would be better than one.

The bell jars full of pickled body parts had been stored at Sir Montagu Gibbons's anatomy school while their contents were pieced together. The hearse, however, was being stored in a local warehouse.

With the slight thaw came a new menace. Instead of being frozen solid, the mud in the streets had become a sloshy swamp. Crossing the road was treacherous, even though several enterprising shopkeepers had laid planks of wood down as makeshift walkways. As I tiptoed across one of them, Percy leaped onto the other end, catapulting me several feet in the air. Yet again, I found myself ankle-deep in a mire of sewage.

Once we reached the warehouse we spent nearly an hour crawling about on our hands and knees trying to find a clue – even a hair or piece of fluff – that could link Grace to the hearse.

There was nothing. The more we searched, the more we failed to turn up anything.

As the hours began to drift past, a thought started to nag away at me. Thinking back, I hadn't *actually* seen Grace in the hearse; she had been inside the coffin . . . or so I had been told. But if the defence attorney asked me under oath if I had seen Grace inside the hearse, what would I say? I couldn't lie. I was hopeless at it.

As I continued my search, I heard Percy tapping desperately on the window: he had managed to get himself wedged in the doorway of the hearse. Given that his incessant chatter was now muffled behind the glass, I was sorely tempted to leave him. But he complained that the dust was playing havoc with his sinuses, so I was forced to drag him out by his breeches.

As Percy began to dust himself down, he burst into a series of whinnying sneezes. In total I counted twenty-two. When he finally stopped, I was about to suggest we head home when a new thought occurred to me. During my painstaking examination of the hearse, I had never seen a single bullet hole – though I distinctly remembered Gabriel firing a volley of pellets from his blunderbuss. Some of them must surely have embedded themselves in the woodwork – and yet there was not a single blemish. Miraculously, every one of those tiny lead balls had completely missed its target.

As I pondered on this, I noticed Percy staring cross-eyed at a tiny silver object in the palm of his hand.

'M-Master Thomas,' he stammered. 'I do believe I may have found something.' I clambered across the foot-plate and carefully plucked the object from his hand. 'I found it hidden behind one of the drapes.'

It was a silver button. Holding it up to the light, I made out its intricate engraving: a miniature rearing stallion.

Ten minutes later I threw open the door to number 4 Bow Street and rushed up the stairs to tell Henry. Percy huffed his way up behind me. If my hunch was right, the button he had found belonged to Grace. After all, we had been told by both Miss Jardine and the housemaid that she was a keen horse-rider. The button could have dropped off her coat when she was bundled into the coffin.

If it did belong to her, we had found the vital last clue that would place her inside the hearse. But when I burst into the study, I found only Esther shooing out Titian, Henry's fat ginger moggy.

'If you're looking for my father, he left five minutes ago.'

Percy appeared behind me, crimson with exertion. 'I'll go after him,' he panted, turning wearily to head back down.

'Wait,' I called. For once I was determined to get my facts straight first. I had made too many rash mistakes already. 'We have to speak to Lord Davenport first. We need to know for sure that the button was Grace's.'

Twenty minutes later, all three of us were standing in Lord Davenport's library again. We had just managed to catch him before he left for the trial. His carriage was standing outside, the horses chafing at their bits and snorting great clouds of steamy breath.

His lordship's eyes narrowed inscrutably as he traced the button's tiny stallion with his thumb.

'I can tell you one thing with complete certainty,' he announced after a moment. 'It is not Grace's.'

My shoulders sank in dismay. 'Are you sure?'

He studied me severely. 'I think I would know a button off my own daughter's coat.' He tossed it back to me. It arced through the air, glinting in the sunlight that shone through the French windows. 'I can tell you which regiment it came from, if that's any use.'

'Which *regiment* . . . ?'

'It bears the insignia of the Royal Dragoons. My old stableman, Claybourn, fought for them.'

'The old man you fired?' Esther asked.

'Precisely.'

'Your maid said that Lady Grace was very close to him,' I ventured cautiously.

Davenport's face clouded with irritation. 'She should not have been speaking to you about private matters. Nonetheless, it's true. For some reason she was fond of the old reptile. But I fail to see what that has to do with anything.'

'Is it possible that the button was some kind of present from him to her?'

'You'll have to ask him yourself – if he's still alive. The maid will tell you where he lives. She seems to have told you everything else.' He adjusted the collars of his coat. 'But don't be surprised if he slams the door in your face. I threw him out on the street when he nearly broke my daughter's back. Now, if you'll excuse me, I have an execution to go to . . .' He paused to correct himself. 'My mistake – a *trial*.'

23

Lord Davenport's old stableman lived to the south of the city in a notorious slum called Jacob's Island. In reality, it wasn't an island at all; it only felt like it because at high tide the river filled every street and alleyway. The only way to pass from one reeking passageway to the next was via a network of rickety gantries and bridges. These were so rotten that one wrong step could see your foot burst straight through into the slime below.

There was not a straight or perpendicular line to be seen anywhere. Everything was crooked and leaning against its neighbour for support, like drunks falling over in the street. Broken-down privies clung to the backs of houses, the excrement emptying straight into the river. The narrow ditches beneath were solid with filth.

One benefit of the freezing weather was that the fumes were moderately bearable. Normally, Percy informed me, wrinkling his nose in disgust, the waterways bubbled with sulphurous gases. Now the putrefying carcasses of animals and fish jutted up through the ice, making it look like a graveyard. But with the start of the thaw, how much longer before the whole area reverted to a stinking swamp?

All along the backs of the houses, pigs rubbed shoulders with rats, snuffling through piles of cinders and rotting vegetation. Just above, gaunt children, their skin white as parchment, dangled buckets to scoop up drinking water through holes that had been bored in the ice.

Percy, Esther and I approached across the frozen expanse of the Thames, which had iced over at low tide. As a result, much more of the so-called island was visible above the water line. It looked like some toothless old crone who had hoisted up her skirts to reveal her knobbly knees.

At its tip, a series of rotten jetties formed a makeshift dock. I saw the masts of a cargo ship – perhaps one of Lord Davenport's, back from a trading voyage to China laden with opium, I thought. A vast spider's web of ropes tethered her to the jetty. Not that the ship was going any-where. Like the vessels I'd seen during my chase across the river, she was now embedded in the ice at a precarious angle, looking like the ribcage of a giant whale.

As we passed underneath the bow, a huge groan made

the ice shudder. The tremor sent a crack zigzagging across the surface.

Percy went pale. 'We need to get off the river,' he cried. 'The ice is starting to break up.'

Another low grumble emanated from somewhere beneath us, as if an enormous beast was waking from hibernation. Percy waddled along as fast as his legs would carry him (which wasn't very fast), following us clumsily onto the jetty. From here we set off into the gloom of the warren beyond.

The dwelling we sought lay amongst warehouses devoted to the tannery trade. Here the stench of boiling carcasses made my eyes water, just as they had when I first crossed London Bridge nearly two weeks before. Half submerged under the ice were the large wooden doors where the wagons wheeled in the pelts of the dead cattle.

As we crossed one of the footbridges, I caught sight of a small girl watching us mutely from the far bank. She was wearing a torn apron over ragged clothes; her bare feet were filthy and covered in weeping sores. In her hand she clutched a piece of string that was tied round the neck of a duck. It was pecking hopefully at a pile of ash and manure. I couldn't work out if the girl's expression was one of complete bewilderment at the sight of our shoes, or a warning of what might lie ahead.

'Maybe this wasn't such a good idea,' Percy muttered. His voice was squeaky, making him sound as though he'd swallowed a penny whistle.

'We're almost there,' Esther reassured him. 'If the maid's directions were correct, the stableman's door is the last on the right.'

I noticed Percy's hand reach into his coat pocket and clasp the butt of his flintlock.

'Is that entirely necessary?' I asked. 'He's an old man.'

'Besides,' Esther added, 'we're only asking him if he gave the button to her.'

'All the same,' Percy insisted, 'after what happened at the old brewery, I'm taking no chances.' He gripped the pistol even tighter and we pressed on.

As we approached the house, we saw that the windows were blocked up with old newspaper and rags to keep out the cold.

I swallowed hard and knocked on the door. When there was no response, I tried a second time. Again, nothing.

'You go down below,' I told Percy. 'See if there's another way in.'

'By *myself*?'

Esther scowled at him and he set off, grumbling that he wasn't paid enough to put himself in this sort of danger twice in one week.

I turned to examine the door again. 'There is one other way to get in.'

'How?' Esther asked.

I drove my metal fist clean through the rotten door frame. The lock exploded, sending splinters of wood flying like shrapnel.

'Subtle,' she remarked drily.

I stepped cautiously through the door, now hanging off its hinges. It took several seconds for my eyes to adjust to the gloom, but when they did I saw that the room was tiny and sparsely furnished. There was a simple cot bed in one corner, the blankets neatly tucked in. Clearly the old stableman hadn't forgotten his military training. Nearby stood an old stove.

Esther put her hand to it, then withdrew it sharply. 'It's still hot. He can't have gone far.'

On the table next to it were two pewter bowls, the remains of some soup sitting in a pot beside them.

Looking around, I saw that the room was like a museum, every surface covered in cavalry memorabilia. Nailed to the walls were sketches of horse-drawn canons and a ceremonial harness; a highly polished helmet and a tricorne hat with a bullet hole through one of its tips; a bugle and a sword in its scabbard.

Shifting a few papers, I came across a small gun chest made of polished walnut. It was empty, but the felt

padding inside followed an instantly recognizable out-
line: surely it had housed a flintlock pistol. As I wondered
where the pistol might have got to, Esther hissed from
across the room, 'Thomas . . .'

I turned to see her pulling a long black coat down off
a high shelf. Each sleeve bore a row of silver buttons.
Suddenly an image of the Undertaker pointing his pistol
at me jolted through my head like an electric current.

'It's the same type of coat the Undertaker wore!' I
gasped.

'Are you sure?'

I was certain of it. Then something else occurred to
me. Was it possible that the missing flintlock pistol was
the one the Undertaker had used to shoot the cabbie?

'You don't think . . .' Esther began, reading my mind.
Then she seemed to dismiss the idea. 'No, it doesn't make
any sense.'

'You think the old man was the Undertaker, not
Edmund?' I said. It was absurd, and yet . . .

'We *know* that Edmund was the kidnapper,' Esther
insisted. 'We found the bodies . . . the skull mask.'

'We found the bodies of the first *three* victims,' I
replied, my mind still trying to make sense of everything.
'But what if Edmund was telling the truth when he said
he never took Grace?'

'Then how come we found her handkerchief in the

well? Anyway, why on earth would Lord Davenport's old stableman kidnap her?' But Esther was frowning, and I could tell that we were thinking the same thing. 'Unless he was seeking revenge on his lordship for firing him.'

The idea seemed so far-fetched, and yet the coat looked identical to the one the Undertaker had worn.

There was only one way to be sure. I opened my palm and held the button next to the ones on the coat to see if it matched.

'Well?' Esther asked impatiently.

'They look the same,' I muttered. All that remained was to see if there was one missing . . .

Esther slowly unrolled the sleeve, but every button seemed to be in place.

Suddenly a shadow fell across us and I spun round. Standing in the doorway was a frail old man hunched over a walking stick. He was tiny, less than five feet tall, crooked and gaunt, with wisps of white hair trailing over the collar of his overcoat. The skin on his face was so lined, it looked like someone had crumpled it up like a piece of old paper.

In one fluid motion he drew a thin, razor-sharp rapier out of the walking stick.

'What business do you have here?' he asked suspiciously.

I cleared my throat, hoping that my voice didn't betray my nerves.

'My name is Thomas Fielding, sir. We've come from Bow Street on a matter concerning Lady Grace Davenport.'

As I spoke, I noticed something peculiar about the old man's eyes. Though they were looking towards us, they were glazed over and milky. I'd seen the same thing back home in a donkey with cataracts.

The old man was entirely blind.

'You have no right barging in here,' he said gruffly. 'Now, be off with you.'

He flicked the tip of his sword, expertly removing a button from my coat. It dropped to the floor with a tinkle and rolled under the bed. He may have been blind but the old man was clearly still dangerous.

'Mr Claybourn,' Esther appealed to him. 'We're only here to ask you a few questions.'

'Well, maybe I don't care for your questions,' he croaked. 'And don't play no funny tricks neither. I may have lost my sight but I could still cut you in two.'

During all this I had forgotten about Percy. Suddenly I saw him shuffling past one of the broken panes of glass. In the blink of an eye, the blade of Claybourn's sword flashed through the air, arcing full circle till the tip was delicately pricking Percy's belly.

'This large pudding will be the cavalry, will it?' the old man asked mockingly.

'Begging your pardon, sir,' Percy bleated.

But as Claybourn held his sword to Percy's gut, something caught my eye and made my blood run cold: his overcoat was identical to the other coat – except for one vital difference . . .

It was missing one of its silver buttons.

'Mr Claybourn,' I said, anger building inside me. 'Did you kidnap Lord Davenport's daughter?'

For a moment he seemed to falter. 'What would put a fanciful notion like that into your head?' he blustered.

'The button that's missing from your coat – we found it inside the hearse that was used to kidnap her.'

The old man started to speak, then sighed and lowered his sword. Percy gasped with relief.

'Did you abduct Grace to punish Lord Davenport for sacking you?' Esther asked. The old man's milky eyes welled with tears as he hung his head in shame. 'Did you kill her?'

He slowly shook his head. 'No,' he said softly. 'I swear to you on my honour as a soldier that I didn't harm a hair on that sweet girl's head.'

'Then why did we find your coat button in the Undertaker's hearse?'

Before Claybourn could answer, I heard a muffled noise behind me. It had come from the other side of a rickety door.

'Is someone else here?' I asked, my mind starting to whirr.

'That'll be the rats,' Claybourn insisted, but I could see that he was panicking. I looked at the bowls on the table, the pot of half-finished gruel beside them.

'Who else were you cooking for?' I asked suspiciously. 'The rats?'

For once the old man was stumped for an answer, but as I took a step towards the door to try the handle, he suddenly raised his sword again. 'Don't make me use this, young man, I beg you.'

However, in the blink of an eye, Esther had taken a step between us so that his sword was pointing directly at her. 'Then you'll have to go through me,' she told him defiantly.

Claybourn hesitated, the sword trembling in his hand. Then he lowered it and slumped into the chair. Esther quickly took his sword and threw it to Percy, who nearly dropped it in his panic.

I turned to the door handle, only for Percy to hiss, 'Thomas, wait.' He held out his flintlock. 'Take this.'

But I shook my head. Even if I'd known how to use it, I couldn't grip the handle with my clumsy iron claw.

I tried the door, to find it unlocked. Behind it was a tiny airless chamber – more like a store cupboard – and a set of crooked stairs leading down to the frozen river below. On the floor lay an old mattress covered in blankets. Next to it were some bits of stale bread and a candle stub on a saucer. Someone had clearly been hiding out here, possibly for days. But who?

It was only then that I turned to see what was hanging on the back of the door . . .

A white mask in the shape of a crow's skull!

How could this be? Edmund had been wearing the Undertaker's mask when we confronted him in his dissecting room. So why was there another one here? I picked it up and examined it. Esther had followed me; her face was even whiter than the mask. Studying it more closely, I saw that unlike Edmund's mask it was crudely made – almost child-like.

'It's made of papier-mâché,' Esther said, bewildered.

I turned and looked back at the old man, furious. 'Is this yours? Did you make it?' He shook his head gravely. 'Then who did?'

Esther gripped my arm. 'Look . . .' I followed her gaze and saw a silk coat hanging from a hook behind the door. I hadn't even noticed it before. It was expensive and fashionable – the sort of coat a young lady might wear.

All at once I realized who had been sleeping here – who it was the old man had been trying to protect.

Before I could say the words, Percy cried out in shock. 'Thomas!'

I turned and saw that he was pointing down towards the street below. 'It's a gh-ghost,' he stammered.

I raced over and followed the direction of his trembling finger. Two figures were fleeing across the ice towards the open river.

One of them was a man – who it was, I couldn't yet be sure. But the young woman with him – the *ghost* Percy had seen – I recognized instantly.

It was Grace.

24

I leaped down the rotting wooden stairs, Esther hard on my heels. Percy's mouth hung open like a goldfish as he tried to process what was happening. Then he gave up trying and set off after us, clutching Claybourn's sword. In his deluded way, I think he saw himself as a dragoon guard charging into battle.

Before long I was skidding to a halt on the ice near the cargo ship that was moored to the old jetty. I looked around frantically, but Grace and whoever she was with had disappeared.

All around the ship huge cracks had appeared in the ice. The hull, still tilted slightly to one side, started to shift and groan, trying to right itself. The trouble was, it was still moored to the wooden jetty, and the ropes were now straining. Something had to give: either the ropes – or, more alarmingly, the jetty. A large crowd had now gathered and was desperately trying to untie the ship before it was too late.

'Tom, wait!' Esther called as she rushed to catch up with me. 'I don't understand. How can Grace still be alive?'

'I don't know. But I think she's been hiding here, maybe ever since she went missing.' As I looked around, Percy joined us, puffing like a grampus.

'So the old man *did* kidnap her?' he gasped, finally getting his breath back.

I shook my head. 'If anything, I think he was trying to protect her.'

'But who was that with her?' Esther asked, more confused than ever.

'That's what I'm trying to find out.'

Suddenly Percy pointed one of his stubby fingers. 'There!'

I turned and caught a glimpse of Grace and her companion hiding behind a stack of barrels beneath the jetty. Seeing me, they leaped up and began sprinting across the river. There was now no mystery about the identity of the other figure: it was Gabriel, Davenport's footman. Grace was clutching his hand.

My mind reeling, I set off after them again.

Gabriel was athletic and quick, but Grace was handicapped by her fashionable shoes and couldn't run fast. I was within twenty yards of them when she stopped abruptly and turned to face me. I recognized her delicate features from the painting above her father's mantelpiece – though now she looked exhausted by the days and nights she'd spent in hiding.

As I ran towards her, she took a pistol from her coat and aimed it straight at me. It was a flintlock – almost certainly the one that belonged in the gun case I'd found.

'Walk away – or, so help me God, I'll use this,' she said, her arm trembling.

'Grace, no . . .' Gabriel implored her. 'It's too late.'

'No, it isn't,' she cried. 'I'm not going back. Not after everything we've been through. Can't you see? They'll hang us.'

'*Hang you?*' I repeated, confused. 'But why? You're the victim.'

Grace shook her head grimly. 'Who do you think was driving the hearse you were chasing that night? Who fired the shot at you?'

My mind raced to try to make sense of what she was saying. Then, slowly, the pieces began to fall into place.

'That's right,' she continued. 'It was me.' Her eyes suddenly filled with tears of remorse. 'It was supposed to be a warning shot. I never meant to hurt him.'

'Hurt *who?*'

'The cabbie. He just came out of nowhere.' She blinked away her tears, wiping her cheeks.

By now Esther had caught up; she could barely comprehend what she was hearing. 'It was *you* driving the hearse? But how is that possible? You were inside.'

'No,' I said, the truth dawning. 'I only had Gabriel's word for that.' I turned to confront him. 'You knew that it was Grace pretending to be the Undertaker. That's why there were no bullet holes in the hearse. You must have loaded the blunderbuss with paper wadding so you couldn't harm her.'

'That's why I found all those tiny pieces of blue paper frozen into the ice,' Esther gasped. 'They came out of the gun you fired.'

Gabriel looked down, ashamed. 'All we wanted was to get away from here.'

'But *why?*' Esther asked. 'What is it you're running away from?'

'Don't you see?' Grace cried, spitting the words out in disbelief. 'My father, of course. Have you any idea what he'll do if he finds out?'

'Finds out *what?*'

'She's lying,' Gabriel suddenly blurted. 'It was all my idea – Grace had nothing to do with it.'

'*What?* She looked mystified.

'I'm the one you're after. I forced her into this.'

'No, Gabriel!' Grace rested her hand tenderly on his chest. 'I know you're trying to protect me, but they need to know the truth.' She turned and looked at me sorrowfully. 'We both did it.'

Suddenly I realized what she was talking about. I remembered how her father had said how devoted Gabriel was; how Grace had held Gabriel's hand as they ran away.

Of course. Gabriel wasn't devoted to *Lord Davenport* – he was devoted to *Grace*.

'You're in love,' I muttered.

Percy bounded up, interrupting the stunned silence. 'Who's in love?' he wheezed, looking around, confused. 'You and Esther?!'

'Shut up, you goose-head!' Esther scolded him.

'This whole thing . . . the kidnap . . .' I said to Grace. 'It was all an elaborate hoax. You made it look as though you'd been kidnapped by the Undertaker so you and Gabriel could run away together.'

'Wait . . . You and *Gabriel* . . . ?' Esther said, astounded.

'Is that so hard to believe?' Grace said, raising an eyebrow accusingly. 'Or is it only your father who can fall in love with a slave?'

Esther looked chastened. 'I'm sorry. I just had no idea.'

'No one did,' Gabriel said. 'Have you any idea how hard that was – hiding it all this time?'

'But if you told your father how you felt . . .' Esther persisted, turning to Grace.

She let out a mocking laugh. 'You really don't know my father at all. He hates everyone, but most of all he hates people like Gabriel and you; people he thinks are beneath him because of the colour of their skin.' She took Gabriel's hand and clasped it tightly. 'I knew my father would sooner have me dead than let us be together. So what better than to make him think I was?'

By now the rusty cogs in Percy's brain were beginning to turn. 'So you never were kidnapped? You set the whole thing up so people would *think* you were dead?'

'I'd found out the truth about that witch Jardine,' Grace hissed. 'That her son was behind the kid-nappings.'

'How?' Esther asked.

'It was a few months after my riding accident. I'd accompanied my father to the anatomy school. Sir Montagu wanted to give me a final check-up and show off his students to my father. While Papa was being shown around his grisly dissecting theatre, I wandered downstairs. It was then that I saw that evil creature Edmund whispering to Miss Jardine. It didn't take long to get Mama to admit that Jardine and Edmund were mother and son. Mama wanted to help fallen women like her to get a fresh start in life. She even helped secure Edmund his job delivering to Sir Montagu's anatomy school.' Here she paused, trying to control her voice. 'Papa always told my mother how gullible she was. Now he's been proved right.'

'What about all the bottles we found in your bureau?' I asked.

'As soon as Miss Jardine suspected that I was on to her, she started slipping a draught of laudanum into my hot milk,' Grace explained. 'She obviously thought that if my mind was addled by drugs, I wouldn't reveal what I knew. But I'd seen where she hid the bottles and managed to fill most of them with water. Then I slipped them back into the bureau so she never knew.'

At this point Gabriel took up the story. 'I started to follow Miss Jardine late at night – to find out what she was up to. One night I followed her to the old brewery. That was when I discovered what they were *really* doing—' He broke off.

'That he was kidnapping homeless people off the street to cut them up?' I asked.

Gabriel nodded. 'I found that room – where he did that to those poor people. All those jars full of . . .' His voice trailed off.

'But why keep that to yourselves?' Esther asked,

sounding cross now. 'You should have told someone – my father for one! What if Edmund had abducted someone else?'

'As soon as we'd fled the country I was going to write an anonymous letter to your father unmasking Edmund and my governess.'

'You should have said something the moment you found out!' Esther said reproachfully.

'What choice did I have? People had to think I'd been killed so they wouldn't come looking for me,' Grace insisted. 'How else could a rich lord's daughter run away with her black sweetheart? Besides, Miss Jardine was obviously lining me up to be Edmund's next victim. I wasn't going to wait around to be one of his *specimens*!'

'So the handkerchief . . .' I said. 'The one we found down the well . . .'

'That was my idea,' Gabriel said. 'I sneaked back one night and put it there. That way people wouldn't wonder why there was no body.'

'What about the hearse?' Esther asked, beginning to make sense of it all.

'Claybourn borrowed it from one of his old soldier friends who'd gone into the business,' Grace explained. 'The plan was that, after we'd faked my kidnap, I'd ride back here and hide it underneath his lodgings.' Here she turned to me, her voice angry. 'Except you had to chase me into that infernal alleyway.'

'Pissing Alley,' I sighed, remembering it all too well.

'Thanks to you, it got stuck fast. It was all I could do to scramble off before you turned up.'

'So, the skull mask . . . ?'

'We knew what the Undertaker looked like, thanks to the newspaper reports. It wasn't hard to make one of our own.'

'So how did you escape?' I asked, astonished. 'Did you hide in the tavern? The Fortune of War?'

Grace shook her head. 'I dived into one of those stinking doss houses and switched my clothes. The occupants were too stupefied by gin to bat an eye. Then, when that brute of a constable clubbed you senseless, I seized my chance to slip away. They were all too busy arresting you to notice a young woman disappearing into the night.'

I stared at her, speechless. I had to concede that her plan had been daring.

However, during her story, Percy had begun nervously glancing over his shoulder. 'I hate to interrupt, but I think it would be a good idea to take this discussion somewhere else. Only, that ship is making some very scary noises . . .'

'My father can talk to yours – explain everything,'

Esther tried to reassure Grace. 'He doesn't have to know that Gabriel had anything to do with this.'

'No,' Gabriel said adamantly. 'I won't have her telling any more lies to protect me.'

'Please . . .' Grace's eyes were wet with tears. 'Can't you just let us go?'

'There's no point,' Gabriel told her sadly. 'Don't you see? Even if they did, where *could* we go? Your father will be looking everywhere for us.'

Grace began to cry hopelessly. I took a step towards her, gently reaching for her pistol. 'Gabriel's right. Let me take the gun . . .' I'd hoped my words would be comforting, but they had the opposite effect.

She suddenly raised the pistol, her hand trembling. 'I told you. I can't go back there. You don't know what an animal my father is. He hates *everyone*.'

'Not you,' I said softly, trying to keep her calm. 'He's been out of his mind with worry.'

'Only because I'm one of his possessions! Believe me, if it came down to me or the precious money he makes from selling that opium, I know which he'd pick.' Using both hands, Grace cocked the hammer of the flintlock, but instead of aiming it at me, she suddenly pointed it at her own chest. Tears were streaming down her face.

'Grace, no . . .' Gabriel cried in horror.

'I don't want to go back to him,' she sobbed. 'I don't want to live without you. I *won't*!'

Suddenly a huge *boom* shook the ice and sent Grace's pistol spinning out of her grasp.

'The ship!' Percy gasped, staring wide-eyed across the ice. I turned in time to see the last of the mooring ropes snap and snake through the air. With an almighty groan the ship righted herself, pulling away an entire section of the jetty.

That wasn't all. The jetty was fixed to the back of a rickety wooden tavern. As the ship yanked the jetty from its moorings, there was a huge splintering sound and the entire back of the tavern sheered clean off, spilling drunken customers onto the ice below.

As the ship lurched back into the water, a giant wave burst up through the surface, sending huge shards of ice into the air. They arced through the sky, falling like meteors around us.

'Run!' I shouted, grabbing Esther. We had to try and reach the other shore. Meanwhile Gabriel was making a desperate dash for Grace, but a vast block of ice crashed down beside him.

'Look!' Percy cried, pointing at Grace's feet. 'It's breaking up!'

Grace looked helplessly at the crack spreading around her. The ice finally gave way and she was plunged into the freezing water.

'*Grace!*' Gabriel cried in horror, tearing off his tunic.

'No!' I shouted, trying to stop him, but he had already dived into the inky, swirling water.

Percy was staring down, trying to see any sign of the pair under the ice. 'What should we do?'

Suddenly Gabriel reappeared, gasping for air. 'It's too dark under there! I can't see her!'

'Look!' Percy shouted, pointing to a shape moving beneath the ice.

Grace was looking up at us, ghost-like, her eyes staring helplessly from where she was trapped.

'Break it!' Esther cried.

Gabriel had clambered out of the water, and together, he, Esther and Percy began kicking and jumping on the ice, but it was too strong.

'Move!' I shouted, shoving them aside. I knelt on the ice, less than a foot from Grace's panic-stricken face, and punched down with my iron fist. Then, with every ounce of my strength, I began pounding.

It was like striking marble. With each blow, my iron hand became more dented and contorted. But still I persisted, hammering frantically.

'Hurry!' Gabriel begged.

Slowly the ice began to crack, and then, as my fist broke apart under the onslaught, it gave way. As I fell back, exhausted, blood seeping from the mangled wreck of my left hand, Gabriel and Percy dragged Grace's body out of the water.

'Please!' Gabriel wept, rubbing her hand. 'Breathe!'

Esther put the heels of both hands squarely in the centre of Grace's chest and pushed down with all her might . . .

25

'Will she survive?' Henry asked anxiously as Sir Montagu gently closed the door to Esther's bedroom.

'Fortunately the young lady has a strong spirit,' the physician assured him.

As soon as Grace had spluttered back to life on the ice, Percy had hurried off to raise the alarm. Henry – accompanied by Welch – had come straight from the Old Bailey. He looked almost as white as Grace when he saw that she was only just alive. He immediately ordered that she should be rushed back to Bow Street. Welch was dispatched to fetch Lord and Lady Davenport, while Percy went to find Sir Montagu Gibbons.

Waiting outside Esther's room, I clutched the throbbing stump of my left hand. Sir Montagu had carefully removed the iron casing and dressed the cuts underneath. Without its iron cladding, my arm felt strangely light

292

and exposed. Meanwhile Gabriel was being held down in the kitchen, where he was warming himself by the fire.

'I owe you an apology, Sir Montagu,' I mumbled to the esteemed surgeon.

He frowned at me. 'My dear boy, I think it's fair to say that Lady Grace has had us all deceived. Let us say no more of this unfortunate matter.'

Suddenly we were interrupted by a commotion downstairs.

'The boy is my property, damn you! I have a right to see him.' Lord Davenport's voice rang out, cold as steel, from the hallway.

'Astley,' came his wife's imploring voice. 'Gabriel can be dealt with later. All that matters is that Grace is alive!'

I followed my uncle as he hurried downstairs to find Welch trying to keep Lord Davenport at bay. Lady Davenport was at his side, trying to reason with her husband. She looked very different now. Her colour had returned and her face was full of relief.

'Gabriel is in our custody, your lordship. I cannot let you see him,' Welch persisted, standing his ground.

'*Fielding!*' Davenport roared, his eyes blazing furiously. 'I want that boy to pay for this!' The veins in his temples throbbed as he spat the words.

'Once I have questioned the lad, I will make my decision on what punishment is fitting,' Henry said, trying to placate him. 'But you should know that from what Grace has told us, the instigator of this sorry enterprise was not Gabriel; it was your own daughter.'

'*Poppycock!* I want him to swing for this, you hear me? Now see to it that my daughter is transferred out of this' – he looked around disdainfully – '*cesspit* to my carriage and taken home immediately. I will not have her staying here another minute.' With that, he swept his cloak around him and stalked out of the house.

Meanwhile Lady Davenport had no intention of leaving.

'Please,' she said to my uncle. 'May I see my daughter?'

'Of course.' He nodded to Sir Montagu, who stepped forward and led her upstairs.

I followed Grace's mother at a discreet distance. As the physician opened the door to Esther's room, Lady Davenport gave a cry of relief: her daughter was sitting propped up in bed.

'I'm so sorry, Mama,' Grace wept, stricken to see the anguish she had caused.

'Oh, my precious darling!' Lady Davenport rushed over to embrace her.

Thinking it best to give them some privacy, Sir Montagu and I stepped back onto the landing and Esther gently closed the door, leaving mother and daughter sobbing in each other's arms.

* * *

A little later that evening, after Lady Davenport had finally prised herself from Grace's side and left, a mournful-looking Gabriel was brought up from the cells to be questioned.

Judging by his expression, he had resigned himself to his fate. I'd tried to reassure him that my uncle was a most lenient man – far *too* lenient, if Welch was to be believed – but my words made little impression.

'I know you mean well, sir,' he told me sorrowfully, 'but, you see, I *want* to be punished.'

'What?' I asked, thrown.

'When I worked for Lord Davenport, I could see Grace every day. She was all I lived for. For her I would have suffered any indignity my master inflicted on me. But now . . .' He stared down at the manacles around his feet, lost in despair. 'Now I will never see her again. His lordship will make sure of it.' He looked up at me defiantly. 'So let your uncle do what he will to me. It will be nothing to what I already feel.'

I tried to convince him that there might still be hope. Yet, in truth, I could see that his situation was desperate. Lord Davenport was a cruel and vindictive man. He would stop at nothing to exact his revenge.

26

'Please,' Grace begged. 'You have to help us. My father will not rest until Gabriel is hanged.'

It was a little later that evening, and Henry had come to hear Grace's version of events. Percy was taking notes with his quill as I hovered by the door with Esther.

Grace clasped my uncle's hands. 'I implore you – do anything with me. Transport me – hang me, if you must – but spare his life.'

Henry stroked her hand reassuringly. 'My dear, if Gabriel has done nothing wrong, then the law will find him innocent.'

She shook her head bitterly. 'You think the *law* will stop my father? Once he has set his mind to a thing, *nothing* will stop him.' Her face hardened. 'Fine. If you will not help me, then know this. At the very first opportunity I will run away again. And I will keep running away, because I will never allow myself to be under the same roof as that *monster* again.'

Later that night, as Grace lay sobbing in her room, Esther and I were locked in a furious argument with Henry in his study.

'My mother has given me more than enough money for a return trip to Virginia,' I insisted. 'Maybe even two. Why not let Grace and Gabriel use it to run away?'

'This is *preposterous*!' Henry exploded. 'You're suggesting I allow Lord Davenport's daughter to get away with shooting that poor cabbie in the head?'

'That was a tragic accident!' Esther protested. 'The gun went off by mistake. She never meant to hurt him. She hates herself for what she's done.'

'Besides,' I added, 'isn't letting her leave the country exactly like transporting her?'

The thought obviously hadn't occurred to my uncle.

'Even if what you say is true,' he remonstrated, 'I can't let her simply elope with . . . with . . .'

'With whom, *Papa*?' Esther asked pointedly. 'Her *slave*? The way you did!'

For a moment her father was lost for words. 'What about her poor mother?' he finally blustered, trying a new tack. 'She has already lost her daughter once. You want her to go through it all over again?'

'If she loves Grace, as I think she does, she will understand.'

'As soon as they land in Virginia, Grace can send word to Lady Davenport that she is safe,' I insisted. 'My mother will see to it that no harm comes to them. They can stay with her as long as they need to.'

'What makes you think they would fare any better in *Virginia*?' Henry retorted.

'If they don't, they can sail to the West Indies,' Esther argued. 'You yourself have often spoken of communities there in which different races may marry freely.'

Henry started to speak, then stopped and prodded the fire furiously. Suddenly he realized that he was using the end of his walking cane instead of the poker and was forced to smother the flames.

Esther went over and took his arm.

'Oh no you don't,' he protested, trying to shoo her away. 'Don't try and get round me with affection. I know you far too well for that!'

'Please, Papa,' she said. 'All these years you have told me how much you loved my mother; how you would have done anything to keep her alive.'

Henry was avoiding her eye, his head turned firmly away. But she gently took his stubbly chin in her hand, and made him meet her gaze.

'This is your chance,' she told him softly. 'Please. Let

Grace and Gabriel have the life together that you and Mother never could.'

Henry stared at her, his eyes filmed with tears, then his shoulders slumped in defeat.

Just before dawn the following morning I and my three companions, all wrapped in scarves and cloaks against the bitter cold, tumbled out of a carriage that had pulled up by the dockside in Portsmouth. Out across the Solent, I could see a few pinpricks of light from windows on the Isle of Wight. Behind me, the sky had split open just above the horizon and dawn was peeking through the drizzle. Moored next to us was a vast sailing ship bound for Virginia; her crew were uncoiling the ropes as the rigging moaned in the wind. I recognized the gnarled old ticket inspector checking tickets on the gangplank.

Suddenly one of my companions took my hand. Her head was carefully covered by the hood of her cloak.

'I can never thank you enough. Either of you,' Grace said, turning gratefully to Esther.

'I hope you find happiness together,' Esther told her. 'Just promise me – no more fake kidnappings.'

'I promise.' Grace allowed herself the ghost of a smile.

'Thank you – for everything,' Gabriel said, holding out his hand to shake Esther's.

She pushed it aside and hugged him tightly. 'Good luck,' she whispered.

'You will make sure Mama gets my letter?' Grace asked me anxiously.

'You have my word.' I held the envelope she had given me tightly in my hand.

Grace turned towards the gangplank and suddenly hesitated. A few more steps and her life would change irrevocably. I knew all too well how she must be feeling – leaving the security of her home and family behind her, possibly for ever. But for Grace and Gabriel it was far more daunting. Who knew what their future together held?

Steeling herself, she linked her arm through Gabriel's, and they headed up onto the deck without looking back.

As the ship's sails filled with wind and snapped taut, Esther and I stood nudging against each other in the freezing drizzle, watching the ship glide silently out of the harbour.

'*You let him escape?!*' Davenport roared.

Later that day Henry had broken the news that Gabriel had fled the country – and that, *coincidentally*, his daughter had also run away. Predictably, his lordship had become incandescent with rage. So much so that he broke three of the priceless Chinese ornaments in the library, causing his elderly deerhound to pee all over the Persian rug in fright.

Of course, Henry avoided any suggestion that Grace and Gabriel had eloped *together* – or any mention of where they were bound – but Davenport immediately suspected foul play.

'Be certain of one thing,' he snarled. 'If – or should I say *when* – I discover that you had a hand in this, you won't just be out of a job. I will see to it that the Home Secretary has you publicly flogged and then hanged!'

Henry continued to apologize profusely, insisting (cunningly) that it was due to the Home Secretary's stinginess that the cell wall leading to the cesspit had collapsed and that Gabriel had escaped.

Meanwhile Lady Davenport was struck dumb with shock – though she seemed a little less distraught when I slipped her Grace's letter. In it, she begged her mother for forgiveness and urged her to be happy that she had found true love.

Her mother was grief-stricken, but she quickly hid the letter in her bag before her husband could see it. She was devastated to lose her daughter again, but not so much that she would betray her. Lady Davenport had long since reconciled herself to living with her bully of a husband, but Grace was a different matter. She was determined that her beloved daughter would be free of his cruel tyranny.

* * *

The day of Edmund's execution arrived – a Monday. (This, Henry grimly informed me, was because Mondays were best for business: the day most likely to draw the biggest crowd.) We had made our way to Newgate Prison, where Edmund and his mother were being held.

Miss Jardine had also been found guilty, the jury unanimously agreeing that she had helped source her son's victims – though her execution was scheduled for two days later. Holding the hangings on separate days meant double the business.

For weeks the newspapers had been a frenzy of lurid headlines. As a result, the two-mile route from Newgate to the Tyburn Tree, where they would both draw their last breath, was lined with thousands of spectators. It was like a public holiday, taverns overflowing with drunken revellers and children pushing between people's legs to get the best view. At the site of the execution itself, a huge scaffolding stadium had been erected so that the wealthy could purchase front row seats.

The stench of Newgate permeated every corner of the local streets. The prison governor had selected eleven inmates to scrub the walls clean with a solution of lime and vinegar in an attempt to wash away the foul odour.

Undeterred, I joined my uncle as we entered the small vaulted room where Edmund was preparing to take his last journey. It was little more than a dank storeroom, with a low ceiling and walls streaming with moisture. The communal cells were crammed full of lice-ridden inmates; there the air was thick with the stench of sweat and excrement, but here it was so bitingly cold you could see your breath. The stone floor was smeared with urine-soaked straw, while a thin grey light struggled through the filthy window facing out onto the pavement.

Miss Jardine sat hunched against the far wall, her face pinched and gaunt. Next to her lay the wooden box that would be her son's coffin. After the execution his body – like her own – would be taken back to Sir Montagu Gibbons's anatomy school for dissection . . . *if* the baying crowd didn't get to it first.

She glanced up as we entered. Her eyes desperately searched ours for a flicker of hope: just occasionally the King himself offered a last-minute stay of execution.

'Please,' she asked. 'Is there any word of our appeal?'

My uncle shook his head gravely and for a moment she looked on the verge of collapse, but she recovered herself when the rusty gate on the other side of the cell opened with a groan. The small stooped prison chaplain shuffled in clutching a Bible. Behind him, still manacled, but now dressed in his finest suit, came Edmund, flanked by two gaolers. His skin was pallid and sweaty despite the cold, his lank black hair matted and unkempt.

His mother leaped up and clutched him to her, sobbing. 'My poor sweet boy . . .'

But Edmund barely seemed to hear her. He looked numb, closed in on himself as he tried to shut out the bedlam of the baying crowd.

'Edmund,' the minister muttered softly. He was a tiny, twitchy bird-like creature with a pointed nose and almost no chin. 'There is still time for you to make your peace with God before you meet him. I beseech you, before it is too late, repent of your sins and he will shine his forgiveness on you even now.'

A cruel smile spread across Edmund's face. 'Why?'

The minister frowned. 'My child, for the lives of those poor defenceless wretches you stole.'

'Do you think anyone cares? Do you think *they* care?' Edmund sneered, nodding towards the crowds outside. 'Or Lord Davenport? How many defenceless wretches has he sold into slavery or poisoned with his opium? How many of Gibbons's corpses were truly dead when the grave robbers found them?' His eyes flashed with malice. 'Do not ask me to repent. I have done no more than any of these men. I have used the lives of others to pursue my own ambitions. Yet I do not see Lord Davenport's coffin waiting here beside his mother.'

'Then may God have mercy on your soul,' the minister said with a sigh, before shuffling out of the room.

The guards took hold of Edmund and began to drag him towards the door. His mother threw herself forwards and clung onto him desperately.

'This is my fault,' she sobbed. 'If I had not given you up . . .'

Henry gently pulled her away as her son was led up the stairs to where the cart was waiting. As the door onto the street opened, Edmund winced and turned away from the blinding daylight. Thin and grey as it was, it was the first light he'd seen in over a week.

As soon as they saw him, the crowd roared and began pelting him with rotten cabbages, cow dung and even their own excrement. Edmund staggered up into the back of the cart, which instead of driving off, waited there for several minutes. I wondered if the driver was deliberately stalling to give the crowd extra time. Either way, Edmund refused to cower from the missiles and abuse. He sat there, proud and unbending to the last. Finally the driver flicked the reins and urged the horses on, their hooves trampling through the rotten vegetables and filth.

I refused to follow the procession. No matter how wicked Edmund's actions had been, I didn't wish to see him suffer the same fate as his victims. Sickened, I turned and made my way back towards Bow Street.

27

Through the window of my attic room I could see across the roofs of Covent Garden all the way to the river. It would be dark soon. In the distance, over the usual hubbub of commerce and traffic, I heard the muffled roar of the crowd gathered at the Tyburn Tree.

Suddenly there was an eerie silence and my heart lurched. I knew what was to come. The silence seemed to last an age, but it was probably only a matter of seconds. Then a huge cheer went up.

Edmund would now be dead, or at least twitching on the end of the noose. I should have felt elated – after all, I had played an important part in his capture. Instead I felt only a sense of melancholy. Those jeering, gleeful people who had watched him being 'fetched off' didn't seem so very different from Edmund himself.

I dragged my trunk out from under my bed and

gloomily began to throw my things into it. Somewhere between leaving Newgate Prison and arriving back at Bow Street I had made up my mind to return to Virginia. Watching Grace and Gabriel heading off to stay with my mother had made me long for home again. Perhaps I had needed to leave in order to get over the shock of my father's death, or maybe to atone for my guilt at doing nothing to stop it. But London was not for me – I felt sure of that now.

No sooner had I started to pile my possessions back into my trunk than the door opened and Esther appeared.

'I've got something for you.' She handed me a wooden box and I stared at it, uncertain what to say.

'You got me a present?'

'Don't read too much into it.' She watched me expectantly, then sighed. 'Well, open it then.'

I lifted the lid and immediately froze.

Inside lay my iron hand. Apart from some little dents from when I'd pounded on the ice, it looked like new. Better than new. I took it out and examined it in the light. It had been expertly restored, all the wires replaced with gleaming new ones.

'I don't understand . . .' I began.

'Papa's brother – Uncle John. I told you about him, didn't I?'

'The blind one who does the accounts?'

'That's right. Well, he also mends carriage clocks. It's a hobby of his. Don't ask me how he manages it when he can't see. Anyway, I knew he'd be the perfect person to restore it. Look' – Esther was gabbling in her excitement – 'he's even welded on some extra attachments so you can do more things with it. Percy wanted him to add a clip so that you could attach it to a flintlock, but I managed to persuade him not to—' Seeing my face, she suddenly stopped. I was completely still. 'You don't like it,' she murmured, disappointed.

'No, no, it's not that—'

'I'm such an idiot. I should have asked you first. I just thought—'

'Esther, just for once could you stop talking?'

Her mouth snapped shut mid-sentence. It must have been a novelty for her to be on the receiving end of a tongue-lashing.

'Thank you,' I said, deeply touched. 'It's . . .'

'Perfect?' she suggested.

I smiled and nodded. 'Yes, it's perfect.'

'Good. Then put it on and come downstairs. Papa wants to talk to you about something important.' She was already back to her bossy ways – but no sooner had she spoken than she caught sight of my trunk. She frowned, confused. 'What are you doing?'

I took a deep breath and decided that honesty was the best policy. 'I'm thinking of returning home. As soon as I can.'

For a moment she looked stunned; then her face hardened. 'Were you even going to say goodbye?' She started to walk out, then spun round again. 'I don't ask that you care anything for me. I mean, why would you? But my father . . . You must see how much he's taken to you. Needs you . . . If he keeps drinking and gambling, he'll die in a pauper's grave. But why should you care?' she scoffed bitterly. 'You're right. You should go back. Back to your New World.'

She turned and swept out of the room, leaving the door swinging on its hinges.

I sat there, clutching my new iron hand, stunned. It hadn't occurred to me that Esther would react this way . . . or, for that matter, that Henry might have come to rely on me.

When I entered my uncle's study a little while later, the fire was crackling. His wig was back on its stand, and in its place he was wearing a little silk night cap that looked like it had come from one of his exotic travels. He brought me a glass of port; I was about to remind him that I didn't touch the stuff, but he was one step ahead of me.

'None of your nonsense about not drinking! We must

toast your success, my dear boy. To your good health!'

I forced a smile and raised the glass to my mouth, only to find that the edge was chipped and cracked. I carefully turned it round and let the velvety liquor slip down my throat like honey. Henry allowed himself a contented sigh, then fixed me with a severe stare.

'I know what you're thinking. Today was obscene. All those people baying for blood. Unfortunately you grow used to the sight – and the sound.'

'I don't think I ever want to get used to it,' I muttered. I was about to broach the matter of leaving, but Henry was one step ahead of me again.

'Then you should do something about it.'

'Like what?' I asked, thrown. 'I'm not even fifteen. What could I possibly do?'

'As a junior magistrate, you might be able to exert influence on the politicians. Maybe even become one yourself,' he suggested with an impish glint in his eye.

I gave a snort of laughter, then stopped abruptly. 'You're serious?'

'Why not?'

'I'd need to train in the law for a start.'

'Usually. But there are other ways. If I were to make you my assistant, for instance . . .'

I stared at him, trying to work out if he was jesting. From the way he was studying me, he wasn't.

'I don't understand. Welch is your assistant.'

'Saunders is the high constable for Holborn,' Henry corrected me. 'Not my deputy magistrate. As dogged and incorruptible as he is, it is not a post suited to his many talents. It is, however, one most suited to yours.'

'But my age—'

'I agree, it would be most *unusual*. Indeed, unprecedented. You would certainly cause a stir.' He looked at me quizzically. 'Does that frighten you? Stirring things up? Maybe even making enemies?'

'No,' I blurted, before answering more honestly. 'Yes.'

'Good. It should do. Look around you,' he said, waving a hand towards the piles of manuscripts and discarded wine glasses. 'Esther and my brother are right. I am a liability to myself and to them. Whereas together, you and I have the chance to do something really special. To make history.'

I started to protest and then stopped before the words had formed in my mouth. It was useless. I already knew I couldn't turn my uncle down.

'I have one condition before I agree. In fact, I have three.'

'Demand away, good sir,' Henry said, delighted.

'I want three assistants. Detectives, if you will. To be professionally trained and paid.'

'Absolutely! That bulldog of a Home Secretary has

allocated me a handsome new stipend. You can use it to recruit the very finest men you can find. I'll get Saunders on the case immediately.'

'That won't be necessary. I already know who I want.'

'Capital!' Henry said enthusiastically. 'Do I know them?'

'You should do. One of them is your daughter.'

For a moment he looked at me as if I was a lunatic. '*Esther?*' he spluttered. 'It's completely out of the question.'

'Then it looks as though I will be boarding my ship for Virginia after all.'

'With what? You gave your fare to Gabriel,' my uncle pointed out.

'I have just enough left over to cover my passage as well.'

Henry glared at me, but I was utterly implacable.

'Please, Uncle. You know she's far too clever and far too scary to be some companion to a bored old lady. Do you want her to resent you as much as Grace did *her* father?'

Henry went puce with anger and I thought he was going to explode. Had I pushed it too far, comparing him with Lord Davenport? But finally he sighed and shrugged his shoulders. 'Oh, very well. So long as it doesn't interfere with her studies, mind. Now who are these other two scoundrels?'

'Percy and Malarkey.'

'*Malarkey?*' he cried. 'Good God, man! He's a known felon. Are you trying to make me even more of a laughing stock?'

'Those are my conditions. Take them or leave them.'

Henry harrumphed a bit more before finally sinking into his chair, defeated. He immediately leaped up again as Titian squawked and shot out from under him.

'Yet again I see I am to be bullied in my own home,' he groaned. Then his face crinkled into a smile. 'You shall have your team of detectives, sir. At this rate, we may soon have our very own police force to boot! Now that *would* cause a scandal!'

28

The following night the house shook as a blazing argument ensued. Esther, Percy and I were huddled downstairs listening when the door to my uncle's study was thrown open and Welch stormed down the stairs. Seeing us lurking there, his eyes narrowed balefully before he marched out of the door.

Henry appeared at the top of the stairs looking a little pale.

'I take it he wasn't pleased about our new positions,' Esther observed as Welch's footsteps echoed away down the street.

'He'll come round,' Henry assured us. 'Now – to business. You must be sworn in immediately.' He suddenly paused. 'What about Mr De Vaux? Will he not be joining us?'

'Malarkey?' I said, shrugging. 'I've tried looking for him, but he's vanished as usual.'

'What a shame,' Esther said with a sarcastic smirk. The idea of him joining our ranks thrilled her even less than it did Welch.

I turned and began to make my way towards the courtroom.

'My dear fellow,' Henry exclaimed. 'Where are you going?'

'I assumed you would want to do it in here,' I said, puzzled.

He looked at me as though I was an imbecile. 'This is far too important a ceremony to be conducted in a mere courtroom.'

'Then may I ask where you had in mind?' Percy asked tentatively.

'An occasion of this magnitude calls for somewhere much more venerable.'

'Which is . . . ?' Esther asked.

'Why, the Anacreontic Society, of course. Where else?'

'The *what*?' I asked, bemused.

Esther groaned. 'It's Papa's drinking club.'

'*Singing* club,' Henry corrected her.

Percy's face clouded over. 'Begging your pardon, your honour, but isn't the Anacreontic Society men only?'

'Quite right, lad. But considering Esther's recent endeavours, I'm minded to make an exception tonight.'

He gave her a mischievous wink and snatched up his cane. 'Lead on, young Persimmon!' he cried, as if heading into battle.

The Anacreontic Society, I discovered, met in an ancient tavern not more than a stone's throw from Newgate Prison. Looking across the road, I felt a shiver as I remembered the crowds waiting for Edmund as he was led out to his execution. Now the streets were deserted.

The tavern was full of gentlemen of all ages – and from all professions, by the look of it. But one thing united them. They were all singing raucously while downing tankards of frothing ale and spiced wine.

As I sat down, Percy tapped my arm and nodded towards the corner. Sitting by the fire was a florid-cheeked, paunchy man with several chins and a bulbous nose. He looked like a large toad.

'Who's that?' I asked.

'Don't you know anything? Why, it's Handel, the most famous composer in all London.'

The next thing I knew, the landlord was shoving a large tankard of beer in front of me. Out of politeness, I decided to allow myself the occasional sip; but to my astonishment, I soon discovered I'd polished off the lot!

For two or three hours we sat and sang songs, while Esther did her very best to moderate her father drinking.

In the end she gave up, realizing it was useless. By the early hours of the morning even she was a little tipsy from the hot port she had consumed. By this stage Henry had gone from uproariously drunk to fast asleep to bleary-eyed and maudlin.

'My darling daughter,' he said, slurring as he took Esther's hands fondly in his own. 'Sing for me.'

In the corner, Handel banged his tankard on the table to show his approval.

Henry shushed everyone, thumping his own tankard down on the table as if he was back in the courtroom, until the room fell completely silent.

When Esther began to sing, I was completely unprepared for it. It wasn't so much that her voice was sweet; in fact, it was quite husky, almost boyish. But it had an earthy, honest quality to it, and I found myself strangely moved by her ballad of a lost soul being found. Perhaps it was the influence of the wine and beer, but before she'd finished the first verse the entire room was rapt.

It was a simple song, an old slave hymn her mother used to sing:

'Amazing grace! How sweet the sound
That saved a wretch like me.
I once was lost, but now am found,
Was blind but now I see.'

Henry had taught her the words almost before she'd learned to talk. Now he sat and listened like the others, tears streaming down his cheeks.

Suddenly the tubby landlord tapped me on the shoulder. 'Begging your pardon, but there's a cunning young cove asking for you outside. Goes by the name of Malarkey. Want me to sling him in the gutter?'

'No, no,' I said, rising from my chair. 'He's a friend of mine.'

Judging by the look on his face, the landlord was distinctly unimpressed by the company I kept, but I was already halfway down the corkscrew stairs.

Plunging out into the freezing night air, I saw to my dismay that the street was deserted; all I could hear was Esther's voice.

Suddenly there was a snorting sound behind me. Spinning round, I was startled to find a plump little horse trotting out of the shadows towards me. Not just any horse: he was brown, with a bold white stripe down his nose, and white socks.

Somewhere out of the darkness came a loud wolf-whistle. The horse promptly stopped and lowered itself onto one knee as if it was bowing to me.

'*Archimedes?*' I said, astonished.

'That's the fella,' said a voice I knew at once. Malarkey stepped forward out of a doorway.

'How did you find him?' I was grinning from ear to ear.

Malarkey shrugged nonchalantly. 'Like I said, it's all about knowing the right people. Or maybe the wrong ones. Anyway, I wasn't sure you'd still be here. I heard a little rumour you might be heading back across the water.'

I was about to answer when something suddenly struck me. 'Hold on. How did you hear that?' Before he could reply, I beat him to it. 'Let me guess – it's all about knowing the right people?' Malarkey grinned smugly. 'Well, in that case you'll also have heard that I'm setting up a squad of detectives. You're going to be one of them.'

Malarkey laughed; then stopped when he saw that I wasn't joking. 'You're serious?'

'Why wouldn't I be?'

'No, no, no – it's one thing, me helping you out over them resurrectionists. But if people discovered I was working for your uncle full time . . . Let's just say I like my neck attached to the rest of my body.' He started to walk away.

'You'd get paid,' I called after him. 'Double time for a Sunday. Just think how much gin that would buy you!'

Malarkey stopped and turned back, a glint in his eye. 'Triple time for a Sunday, and every other one off. Plus,

Saunders here has to be on the payroll too. One saucer of milk every morning.' The weasel poked out his nose and squeaked approvingly. 'Oh, and I won't go nowhere where there might be rats.'

'Done. So, do we have a deal?' I extended my iron hand for him to shake.

Malarkey looked at it warily before a smile spread across his face. 'Why not, *Iron Hand*?'

He gripped my fist and shook it vigorously. Up above, Esther finished her song and the tavern erupted into appreciative applause.

It was official: the Bow Street Detectives were well and truly in business!

The real-life Henry Fielding

Henry Fielding really was a famous magistrate and writer who lived at number 4 Bow Street in London in the 1740s. In real life he never worked on a plantation in the Caribbean, but he did marry his maid, Mary, which caused a huge scandal.

Henry didn't mind in the least. In fact, he took great pleasure in mocking the rich and powerful. This led to the Prime Minister, Sir Robert Walpole, shutting down the theatres to stop Henry writing plays that made fun of him. As a result, Henry became very poor – which wasn't helped by the debts he ran up with his drinking and gambling. His solution was to return to his earlier career as a lawyer and become a magistrate.

At this time London had no police force to speak of – just a collection of doddery (but often brave) night watchmen and constables. To many people's surprise,

Henry immediately set about trying to improve things.

Thomas is a fictional character, but Saunders Welch really existed (though there's nothing to suggest that he was nearly as bad-tempered and gruff as I've made him!). Along with his half-brother, John (who really was blind), Henry set about creating a team of hand-picked detectives known as the Bow Street Runners.

For the first time London had a group of trained and paid detectives. Unfortunately one of their first recruits was killed when he was run through by a smuggler's cutlass! In due course, however, these officers became the inspiration for London's first official police force.

Just like my version of the man in *The Demon Undertaker*, the real-life Henry Fielding suffered terribly from gout, an affliction brought on in part by his love of fine foods and wine. There is no evidence that he ever owned a stuffed monkey with scooped-out brains!

GLOSSARY

Beak

This was a common term for a magistrate or judge. You can sometimes still hear it used today. No one's certain where the word came from, but one possibility is that it was named after the beak-shaped mask that judges and doctors wore during the plague as a form of gas mask.

Bow Street

This is a real street in the heart of Covent Garden, but unfortunately the original building where Henry Fielding lived has been knocked down. Before he became a magistrate and moved there, his predecessor (a man called Sir Thomas De Veil) turned the front parlour into a courtroom. When Henry and his half-brother, John, set up the Bow Street Runners, Britain's first detective squad, number 4 Bow Street was their headquarters. The cesspit really did leak through the cell wall!

Cat's Paw gin shop

In Henry's time, gin consumption took on epidemic proportions. One in four houses in Covent Garden sold gin illegally, using increasingly devious means to hide their business, and mixing the spirit with everything from ash to sulphuric acid! The gin shop with the cat's paw that Malarkey visits is based on a real establishment.

Charlies

This was the nickname for night watchmen, possibly named after Charles II, who was King when they first appeared on London's streets. It was their job to keep the peace at night. Their pay was very low, so they were often old and poor, armed with little more than a staff, a lantern and a rattle.

Coffee houses

Modern-day coffee shops have their roots in the popular coffee houses of the seventeenth and eighteenth centuries. London's first coffee house was set up by an ex-slave called Pasqua Rosee in the 1650s. Within years there were thousands of them throughout the city. Intellectuals and tradesmen rubbed shoulders to read newspapers and gossip. When tea became more popular than coffee, many of the coffee houses started to charge for membership, and the first gentlemen's clubs were born.

Cove
This was a popular slang word for a person, like 'guy'.

Ether
This is a clear liquid that can be inhaled to stop you feeling any pain and paralyse you. It was discovered in the 1500s by a German chemist who noticed that it made his chickens fall asleep. It wasn't until 1842 that its full potential was realised, when it was used by surgeons and dentists to perform operations. Who knows, however, whether there were untrained surgeons like Edmund who had secretly discovered its 'magic' powers sooner!

Fleet Ditch
This was once a fast-flowing river that crossed Fleet Street and ran into the Thames. In Henry Fielding's time it became clogged up with dead animals and sewage, and much of it was closed over to create a market. Eventually it became an underground sewer that still exists to this day.

Garrotting
This was a very nasty means of killing someone by strangling them with a wire. It originated in China and became a popular means of execution in eighteenth-century Spain.

Grampus
In the 1740s this was a common name for a killer whale.

Jacob's Island
Like Jack Ketch's Warren, this was a real rookery (shanty town or slum) on the south bank of the Thames. Some claim that Charles Dickens based Fagin's den there in his novel *Oliver Twist*.

Laudanum
Derived from opium, laudanum (a little like modern-day heroin) contained a powerful painkiller called morphine and was seen as a wonder drug that could cure almost anything. Alarmingly, doctors didn't realize how addictive it was at first, so it was available without prescription.

Posset
This was a comforting drink made from hot milk mixed with beer or wine and spices.

Resurrectionists
A popular name for grave robbers who dug up recently buried bodies to sell them to anatomy schools for dissection. These schools would pay a higher price for a fresh corpse, so some resurrectionists resorted to

murdering people rather than waiting for them to die.

Thirty Thieves

The Thirty Thieves is a made-up name, but eighteenth-century London was overrun by criminal gangs or mobs who claimed certain streets as their territory and ran extortion and shop-lifting scams. One of the most notorious and brutal gangs was called the Mohocks, who attacked their victims in the street.

Turpy

Workhouses were originally set up as charities to help the most deprived in society. Here they could receive food, medicine and a bed for the night. But increasingly poverty was seen as something immoral that people brought on themselves through laziness. In many instances workhouses became a sort of prison to punish the poor and sick by setting them to work doing laborious tasks. The inspiration for the Turpy in my story comes from an institution called the London Society for the Suppression of Mendicity – known to poor people simply as *the Dicity*. This was set up to purge the streets of 'immoral' vagrants, employing a number of officers to 'arrest' the poor and take them back to the workhouse. These *Dicity* officers were so despised and feared, they were often set upon in the street.

Tyburn Tree

This was a gallows supported by three wooden legs on the site of modern-day Marble Arch. Criminals were brought by wagon from Newgate Prison and then hanged in front of a crowd of thousands. A spectators' stand was built so that the rich could pay for the best seats.

Acknowledgements

In researching the world of *The Demon Undertaker*, I am indebted to a number of excellent books about the period: Liza Picard's indispensable *Dr Johnson's London;* Lucy Inglis's *Georgian London: Into the Streets;* Jerry White's *London in the 18th Century;* Patrick Pringle's *Hue & Cry;* Emily Cockayne's *Hubbub: Filth, Noise and Stench in England;* Sarah Wise's gripping *The Italian Boy* and *The Blackest Streets;* Penguin's *Dictionary of Historical Slang;* Patrick Dillon's *The Much-Lamented Death of Madam Geneva;* Anthony Babington's *A House in Bow Street;* and *Henry Fielding: A Life* by Martin C. Battestin.

I would also like to thank my wonderful publisher, Annie Eaton, and editor, Kirsten Armstrong, as well as Rebecca Carter, my agent, for their unflagging support and razor-sharp minds! Sue Cook also provided a wealth of ideas and guidance.

BP 11.16

CAMERON McALLISTER

Finally, I would be nowhere without the insightful comments of my other team of editors: Katie, my wife, and my four boys, Fin, Rory, Louis and Jack.